D1301473

Inspired by the history and the current affairs of Wazaristan, Pakistan

A TULIP IN THE DESERT

A TULIP IN THE DESERT

SYED RAZA HAIDER

Library of Congress Control Number:		2014900886
ISBN:	Hardcover	978-1-4931-6505-6
	Softcover	978-1-4931-6504-9
	Ebook	978-1-4931-6506-3

Printed in the United States of America by BookMasters, Inc
Ashland OH
May 2014

Rev. date: 04/22/2014

To order additional copies of this book, contact:
Xlibris LLC
1-888-795-4274
www.Xlibris.com
Orders@Xlibris.com
549160

Contents

To all those voiceless souls who dare to raise their voices

One

I AM AMINA

My story here starts many years ago, when I was a little girl, about nine years old. I lived with my family in a small village in the Northern Waziristan region of Pakistan, very close to the Afghan border. My father, Baba, had two younger brothers. The first one was Noor Chacha (a *chacha* is your father's brother). He had moved to a nearby city, Bannu and lived there with his wife and their three children. The youngest of Baba's brothers—we just called him Chacha—still lived with us at home. Then there was Mamma and my elder brother, Zameer. Baba's mother was known to all as Mather-Khubi, because that was how Baba and his brothers addressed her. She also lived with us.

Our house was large but very basic. It was one of the many houses in a compound enclosed by high walls. Such compounds, called *kots* (pronounced as coats), are common in our region. Most *kots* have a courtyard in the center that is surrounded by the homes of closely related families. In the courtyard, there is usually a communal kitchen with a deep tandoor oven for baking naan breads and several stoves. Ladies from the whole *kot* gather there to cook the meals for their families. A well for water is also nearby. In our *kot*, there were the homes of most of my baba's male cousins and uncles.

Baba and Chacha did some farming, and being city-educated, the two brothers taught at the village school. The school was for boys only. Girls were allowed just until the fourth grade, after which schooling for girls ended altogether. The school was located near the village-center. Our village-center was built around our mosque. Two separate madrassas— one for boys and one for girls were on the two opposite sides of the mosque. Children went there to learn the Holy Koran and other religious books. The only store in the village was also nearby. There, we bought our food and other necessities. If the village store didn't have something, we would have to wait till Baba could go to the city.

The village affairs were governed by a council of elders, called the *jirga*, which met regularly in the mosque. They resolved conflicts, made laws, and kept order in the village. The imam of the mosque was a powerful man who told the villagers right from wrong. Our village followed centuries old norms of living. While the rest of country was slowly but surely adopting some of ways of the changing world, our village proudly guarded traditions. Women were kept inside the four walls. They were only allowed to go out fully veiled and accompanied by a male relative. Men made all the decisions for the entire family.

Growing up in those circumstances, I developed a forbidden passion. My story here is about my struggles, during which I found some unlikely allies as well as some unforeseen opposition. My story moves from one struggle to the next. Sometimes I fought against the injustices imposed by the society. And at other times, I struggled against the prejudices of my own mother and the grandmother. The political situation and the raging wars claimed their victims. My life rocked with the ups and the downs. Downs outweighed ups most of the time. I achieved unimaginable victories while I stumbled again and again on the hurdles that my fate placed in my way.

Two

FOURTH YEAR

Since the first sighting of snow on the mountaintops, the only thing we could do was to talk about our plans to play in the snow. Be it on our walks to school or playing on the playground, we tried to outdo one another with our sliding plans for the first snow fall on our valley floor. Sohail couldn't contain his excitement when he talked about how the sheet of metal that he had found on the roadside would glide like the wind. Sohail also made sure that we all knew whom he was going to share his ride with. His choice changed daily, but he never included me. He didn't want to share his ride with me or, for that matter, with any other girl. And Zia, who screamed when he talked as he thought that otherwise no one would notice the sound coming from his small body. He boasted about how slick the water bowls from his sheep barn would slide on snow. His family had many of those bowls for their herd of sheep, and he promised to bring several to share. He even included me in his plans. Zia swore that he used them the previous year and that he was the fastest slider on every slope. I happily showed off my new jacket, which felt very slippery, and I believed that if I tied it around my waist tight, I too could slide on the snow. My brother, Zameer, showed off his jacket, which was very similar to mine, but in black color. Baba bought those for us when he went to the city. Like me, Zameer was also confident that his jacket would let him fly down the hills on snow.

At the window, Zameer was speechless. After some stammering he shouted, "Amina! Amina! It is snowing. It's ankle high. Let's go."

"Eat your breakfast first," commanded Mamma.

We inhaled our bread and butter and were about to dash toward the door when we heard, "Zameer, put this sweater under your jacket and take this cap to cover your head.

"Amina, don't forget to take your shawl. Girls your age should not go out in public without covering their heads with a shawl."

Mamma's list of demands was not ending, and we just wanted to run.

Other children were already on the hillside. Sohail was sliding down on his sheet of tin. Being the shell of a car door, it had several holes, and Sohail had put ropes through them to use as handles. He and his friends were taking turns sliding down the slope. And yes, Zia's water bowl seemed like it was the slickest thing on the slope but only for those who could hold on to the rim tight enough. Both Zameer and I wrapped our new jackets around our waists and tried to slide down the first hill we could get to. Our jackets proved to be a total flop when it came to sliding. After a few failed attempts, we quickly found ourselves standing next to Zia, admiring loudly how the water bowls from his barn were sliding faster than Sohail's rusty old car door. After taking several turns himself, Zia allowed us to use his water bowls. We were thrilled. Not wasting another minute, we ran to the top of the nearest hill and slid down as quickly as we could. Other children pushed one another or just fell on the fresh snow.

Out of nowhere, I was hit by a snowball the size of my face right in my eyes, completely blinding me. Quickly, I wiped my eyes and saw Zameer, his arm cocked back, ready to launch another. I dodged the next one, and then I was all revenge. I formed an icy ball and shot straight at him, followed by a couple more. All three hit him hard. He should have known better. My aim is spot-on and my throws hurt, be it a snowball or any other ball. Zameer was down, but the boys on his team were still attacking me.

"You can run, you can hide, but I am going to get you no matter what you do," I warned the boys.

"Sadia, Azra, Rahela, let's make a girls team and attack the boys." I yelled at the girls around me.

Our hands and feet were freezing, but no one was complaining.

As Zameer and I walked up a hill, I whispered, "Let us pray that Mamma stays busy."

"Amen," he replied.

The thought must have been a bad omen.

"Amina . . . Zameer . . ."

"Is that Mamma?" I asked, wondering if he heard her too.

We pretended not to hear any sound at all. I was sliding down the steepest hill, followed dangerously close by Zameer. We were just trying to get a few more slides in.

"Amina . . . Zameer . . ."

The sound got louder each time. The softness of the voice was unmistakably that of Mamma's. Very few women have such soft voices. I knew very well that first, she would scold me for playing with boys and then she would command us to get home right away.

"Why can't you play with other girls? Why must you mix with boys?" she would scold me. "Girls at your age should not play with boys," she might also add, I guessed.

As she appeared, I turned in her direction and innocently greeted her, "Salaam, Mamma. What do you want us for?" knowing well what her reply was going to be.

Both Zameer and I pleaded with her to leave us for a little while longer, but she ignored us. Surprisingly, she didn't tell me off for playing with the boys. She looked preoccupied. There was a mysterious expression on her face as she tightened her chador around her head.

"Let's go home. I promise that you won't be sorry," she told us with a twinkle in her eyes radiating through her long dark eyelashes.

Zameer and I were suspicious about her intentions, but we had to give in. On the way, we barraged her with questions and begged her for hints, but she remained tight-lipped. All we could do was to walk faster. I, being the shortest of the three, practically ran all the way. As we entered the compound of our *kot*, we saw two of our uncles chopping wood. Nothing seemed too exciting about that. They did that every day to prepare wood for burning in the tandoor and the stoves. In the courtyard, we saw nothing unusual either. Mather-Khubi was sitting in her regular spot, baking naans in the tandoor. Passing by the houses of our uncles, we reached our house door and still saw nothing exciting. As we entered the house with visibly long faces of disappointment, thinking that we have been tricked, we were startled by a loud "Boo!" from behind the door. It was Noor Chacha hiding there. He surprised us when we were not expecting him even in our dreams. Everyone laughed, pointing at our shocked faces. Zameer and I threw our arms around our beloved uncle. Holding on to Noor Chacha's hand, I asked, "When did you come? You missed the sliding." He just laughed with the rest of the family.

As we sat down for lunch, he gave us treats that he always brought for us every time he visited us. This time, it was a bag of fresh oranges and a box of sweets.

Before we could dig in, Mamma stopped us. "Wait till after you eat your meal."

Mather-Khubi looked very happy, which gave Baba and Chacha the courage to tease her a little.

"Brother Noor is her real son. You and I must be her stepsons," said Baba with a little chuckle to Chacha while facing Mather-Khubi.

Chacha gave the biggest nod in agreement just to annoy their mother.

"Don't speak like that, even as a joke," she snapped, pointing her crooked index finger at both of them. "It hurts me, I love all three of my sons equally. It is just that Noor has moved so far away, and I miss him every minute of every day." Mather-Khubi scolded Baba and Chacha, while the two brothers kept laughing as they ganged up against her and Noor Chacha.

Every time Noor Chacha came to visit us, Mather-Khubi's smile could be seen from the other end of the courtyard. It was no different that day. All day, she prepared food that Noor Chacha liked to eat, especially the *shaab-degh*. She didn't even complain once about her back hurting. We all liked *shaab-degh*. And who wouldn't? Big chunks of beef and juicy turnips in sweet and spicy sauce—you dip fresh naans over and over into it and eat till you can't sit up straight.

During lunch, the same old topic came up. Mather-Khubi had tears in her eyes.

"What's the matter? Why are you crying Mather-Khubi?" Baba asked, pushing up his dark glasses on his nose.

"I'm fine. It's nothing," she responded, removing a strand of white hair from her face.

Crying even more dramatically, she pleaded with Noor Chacha, "Why have you deserted us? Why are you living in a foreign land, away from your own family? Don't you realize that our lives are miserably incomplete without you? Your children are growing up without knowing your family. Just give up whatever is out there and move back home. Who knows how long I will live? You won't even be near your own mother's deathbed." Her scolding continued while both Baba and Chacha nodded in agreement.

"I miss you all, but I'm not that far away. Look around. So many other families in the village have sent their sons across the oceans to Arabia, Europe, and America. They only come for short visits, at most once a year and often only after several years. Bannu is only a few hours ride by bus from our village," explained Noor Chacha in his defense.

After Mather-Khubi's sobs waned, Noor Chacha continued, "Look, I visit often. Our village lies on the main Pakistan-Afghanistan road through Waziristan with daily bus service. I travel from Bannu to home in less than half a day. There are no jobs here in the village. Farming is very hard work, and still, there is not enough money in it to feed my family. Besides, city life is much better. I work at a squash club. The work is easy and well paid. As a bonus, I play squash and, more importantly, teach it to my son. Who knows? Maybe, one day, he might become a professional."

As usual, Mather-Khubi, Baba, and Chacha were not convinced. Their argument snaked on and on, while Zameer and I stuffed ourselves with hot *shaab-degh* and naan.

After lunch, we walked to the village center. The three brothers— Baba, Chacha, and Noor Chacha—went to the mosque together for the afternoon prayers. On their way, they walked me to the girl's madrassa and Zameer to the boy's madrassa for our Koran-reading lessons. After our lessons and their prayers were over, we walked together to the village store. While Baba bought groceries, the storekeeper gave us a handful of dried mulberries to snack on. The storekeeper was like an uncle to us; he always gave us some snacks while we waited around. That day Baba and his brothers got very excited as they saw fresh sugarcane for sale at the store. After getting his regular items, Baba picked up a stack of sugarcane, enough for every household on the *kot*. Each one of us had to carry some home.

After unloading the sugarcane near the tandoor, my brother and I went door to door, announcing, "Please come out. Join us in the courtyard for some fresh sugarcane. Noor Chacha is here too."

All of our relatives from the whole *kot* slowly gathered around the tandoor. Everyone chewed sugarcane and chatted with Noor Chacha about his life away from the village.

How he could live in a foreign land without any relatives around him was the question that almost everyone asked Noor Chacha.

I took my first stab at the sugarcane. Using all my strength, I dug my teeth into the hard peel and pulled it apart. The sharp edge of the peel did its job. I got a cut in the corner of my mouth and one on my lower lip. It didn't bleed much, but the juice from the cane stung the fresh wounds every time I tried to bite into it. Did I stop chewing sugarcane? No, absolutely not. Who could resist munching on those sweet, juicy treats while absorbing the warm yellow sunshine? Not a moment passed when Zameer got the same cuts on his lips. He didn't give up either. Mamma came to our rescue. She took our sugarcanes and bit off the peels. She handed us the pulps that we chomped off without doing all the hard work involved in peeling.

"Make sure you throw all your peels and pulps in the tandoor. It makes our naans tasty," Mather-Khubi kept on reminding everyone.

Our sugarcane party came to an abrupt end as the sun went down. Everyone dispersed, returning to their houses to escape the cold of the evening.

The winter that year was particularly cold. Evenings were bad, but waking up in the icy dark morning was especially dreadful.

"Come on, get up and don't make me say it again and again!" yelled Baba in his deep voice.

"Zameer, you get up first. Let us not make Baba angry," I whispered.

Baba was kind and funny most of the time, but when he got angry, he got really angry. I escaped his wrath, but Zameer would get occasional beatings from him.

As we dragged our warm bodies out of our comforters into a freezing house, I heard Baba's stern voice for the fourth time, "Chacha and I are leaving. You will have to walk by yourself. That is what you get for not being ready on time."

Baba and Chacha were teachers at the school—in fact, the only teachers the whole school had. They went there early and demanded that everyone arrive ahead of time. They were both very strict about tardiness. Students who came in late were scolded and often spanked.

Girls were allowed only up until fourth grade, while the boys could go there until the tenth grade. It was my last year, so I wanted to enjoy every day, even cold wintery ones, when our breaths would freeze back on to our faces. Although Baba promised to keep teaching me at home, I was sad about my school life ending so soon. I knew that I would miss my friends and all the fun at school. We played all kinds of games together during the breaks. That was my favorite part of the day.

"Let us get Amina out. She doesn't miss her throws, and each time she throws the ball, she hits someone," Sohail told the boys during our *pitho* ball match.

I was very good at *pitho* ball. It is a simple game where the only aim is to catch the ball and hit someone with it, while everyone else tries their best to dodge or run to avoid being hit. Whoever is hit has to sit out of the game.

"I got Zia. He is hit. He is out! He is out!" I screamed with excitement.

His elder brother disputed, "No, he is not hit."

Trying to control my fury, I fought back. "You are lying."

"No, you are the liar!" yelled Zia's brother, bending down to come face-to-face with me.

"Don't try to start a fight with me. I am strong and fast. I can beat up both of you. And remember, if you want a fight, then don't go telling on me," I threatened, knowing well that Zia's brother was, for sure, bigger and stronger than me.

"Here is your ball, we don't want to play." They walked away. Recess was over anyway, and we returned to our classroom.

"I don't even like playing *pitho* ball. I can't wait till the ground dries up a little so we can start playing cricket. Nobody cheats in cricket," I told Zameer. "Can some girls play on your team?" I asked.

"No. Other than you, all the girls are too afraid or too slow. If I pick girls, I lose the match, guaranteed. Don't try to get the girls to play," pleaded Zameer.

"You can also have Baba and Chacha on your team when they come to play with us. They are both tall and strong, and they hit the ball far to score many runs," I suggested to him as if we were picking our teams there and then.

"Baba has told you not to play with boys. Some of the other parents don't approve," reminded Zameer.

To downplay his concern, I explained, "I don't think that Baba was all that serious when he told me that. He just said that in front of those parents to calm them down."

Zameer was in no mood to concede. He went on, "Mamma also scolds you for the same reason. You will have to stop playing with boys sooner or later."

"You just don't want me to play because I am better than you at every sport. Isn't that right?" I threw the last punch. He had no choice but to change the subject.

Out of nowhere, he asked a totally unrelated question, "Why has Chacha build a separate room on the *kot*? Why does he need a room of his own?"

"He is getting married soon. He will live in the new room with his family. See, all of Baba's cousins have built their own houses on our *kot* to settle down with their families," I explained.

Zameer asked, "Will I have to build my own house when I get older and get married?"

"Yes, of course," I replied.

He argued back, "No! I will take over this house. Look at all of our uncles. They are taking care of their elderly parents. In the same way, being the only son, I will have to take care of our baba and mamma when they get old."

"Where will I go?" I asked.

"You will get married, and your husband will take you away to his family's *kot* or maybe even to some other village," he explained.

I wasn't ready to accept that fate. "No, I will never leave this house and my mamma and baba."

To end the argument, this time, I was the one who changed the subject. "The cricket match must be on the TV now. Let us go to Chacha's room to watch it."

After years of waiting, we got electricity in our village. Chacha had brought in a TV from the city. Children and grown-ups from the whole *kot*, and even from the neighboring *kots*, gathered in his room to watch news and shows. There were cartoons, children's programs, Islamic lessons, drama series, movies, and news. Most importantly, they showed cricket matches.

The match between Pakistan and India was on. All the uncles, aunties, cousins, some grandparents, and even some neighbors were gathered in Chacha's room to watch it on his TV.

Suddenly, one of my aunties, who was otherwise known to be fairly reserved, screamed, "How could he drop that catch? He should be removed from the team!"

"Good ball!" shouted Chacha, admiring the next ball.

Commentary filled the room. "Run faster! Stop the ball! Don't let it cross the boundary. Oh no! Not a sixer at this stage, they should change the bowlers. These bowlers are useless. They are giving too many runs to the Indians."

Suddenly, there was a communal sigh of relief, the kind you hear when someone reaches a shady tree after walking a long distance in hot, baking sun. As if the Pakistani team had heard our pleas, the bowler was changed. The new bowler slowed down the Indian's run rate a little. A pin-drop silence fell on the room; we watched every single ball as if it could change the fate of the match. Miraculously, two Indian players got out within one over, and then the remaining two in the next. Pakistani team won the match. Chacha's room was shaking. Uncles were jumping, some were slapping hands. Others were hugging one another; the aunties were singing, and the children were screaming and wrestling—plain and simple.

One of the uncles announced, "Everybody, wait here. I am going to buy some sweets for everyone here just because I am so happy."

Another uncle added, "I have some pomegranates. I will bring those for all of us to share."

Soon, there was a victory party in Chacha's room with a lot of goodies. After eating more than our share of sweets and fruits, we ventured out to the courtyard.

"I am Imran." I took the first pick quickly.

"Okay then, I am Javaid." My brother Zameer quickly claimed the second-best choice of the famous cricket star's names.

"I am Rammez," announced one of my cousins.

"I take Waseem," called another.

"That is not fair—I wanted to be Imran," whined Riaz. "I didn't know that we were picking names. You have taken all the good names even before I could join in. And how could Amina be Imran? First, she is a girl. And second, she is short and scrawny, while Imran is tall and wide. It doesn't make sense," he complained about me.

"It is too late to change. Besides, like Imran, I am the best cricket player here," I taunted him to make him angrier.

Our courtyard cricket was in full swing, but the match had to be cut short because the sun went down. We returned to Chacha's house where Baba and Chacha were watching a squash match on TV.

"Look at their squash court, it even has a roof, and the walls are made of glass," Baba told Chacha with glitter of astonishment radiating through his graying beard, bushy eyebrows, and dark sunglasses.

Chacha replied with similar excitement, "I know, I know, but I don't complain, we have our own home court that we have made with our bare hands. We were lucky that the walls of our *kot* were high enough and the space wide enough. Although our court is not the right size, we have four walls where we can play squash. No one else that I know—has a private squash court in their backyard."

Facing us, Chacha explained the basics of squash to all the children in his room, "Squash is a very fast and tiring, but extremely exciting, sport. Two players stand facing the front wall in a rectangular room that is thirty-two feet long and twenty-one feet wide. The front wall and the back wall are shorter than the two side walls. The aim is to hit the ball with your racket at the front wall, making it as difficult as you can for your opponent to hit back. Each shot must reach the front wall. If the ball touches the floor more than once before you hit it back, you lose the point. Similarly, there are red lines on all four walls, and if your shot hits outside the red lines, then you also lose a point. Whoever gets to eleven points first wins the game. A match is five games, and to win the match, you must win three. Players use drops, to make their opponents run to the front of the court, or a lob, to push them all the way to the back wall. They hit boasts, smashes, or rails to make their opponent run to all four corners of the court. Pretty soon, you get exhausted. You start making mistakes and loosing points."

Our court at the *kot* looked nothing like the ones on TV, but the brothers still played hard. There was no roof, so the ball used to bounce out all the time. It was the children's job to fetch balls back for them. Zameer and I also tried to play. Baba wanted to train Zameer. He even brought him a squash racket and a pair of running shoes. I just had to use someone else's racket and my house slippers.

Baba would scold me every time he caught me playing squash. "Amina, I have told you many times don't use my racket. You will hit it on the wall and break it, and squash rackets are very expensive."

Baba's scolding was mild compared to Mamma's. She yelled and shouted at me very angrily each time she caught me playing squash or any other sport, "People will think low of you and also of me for not teaching you manners."

She wanted to teach me how to cook dinner and keep our house and the *kot* clean. She showed me how to pull water from the well and wash clothes. Pulling water used to be fun, even though the pail would get awfully heavy, but washing clothes was a boring chore.

Three

UNDERNEATH THE SUNDALEE

Baba, Mamma, Chacha, and Mather-Khubi returned after meeting with a family to see their daughter for our Chacha. They had done it many times before, but that day they sounded quite serious. They were talking about a wedding date.

Mather-Khubi sounded happy as she said, "Their daughter will make a good wife for my son. She is beautiful and yet simple."

Baba pushed his sunglasses up his nose and turned his face toward Chacha. Expecting to hear an opinion, he said, "They are a decent family. We would be honored to have them as our relatives."

"Is she another one of those shorties that you all find for me?" Chacha inquired with a chuckle facing Mamma.

Showing the height of the girl with her hand, Mamma responded, "No! She is no shorty—she is about my height—possibly even a finger width or two taller."

"Thank God for that. I wouldn't want to marry a girl who would have to get on a ladder to come face-to-face with me. And her nose—is it sharp like a samosa or round like a plum?" he asked.

"I told you she is beautiful, so don't ask such rude questions about a daughter of a respectful family. And also don't brag about your height. Bragging displeases Allah," Mather-Khubi scolded Chacha with a smile while all of us laughed.

We wanted the wedding soon because weddings are always fun. All the beautiful clothes and the best food only happened at weddings. I got my prettiest outfit at Noor Chacha's wedding.

"Bring out your outfit that we got you for Noor's wedding. I want to see if it still fits you. You will need a fancy outfit for your chacha's wedding soon," ordered Mamma.

Trying to muster all the arguments against the reuse of an old outfit, I responded, "No, it is too small on me. I should get a new one. I have grown a lot, and besides, it has food stains all over it."

She wasn't convinced. "We can wash off the food stains. Unlike Zameer, you haven't grown all that much in the last few years, and I had intentionally made your outfit pretty loose on you. Try it on for me."

I was left with no choice but to obey. As I walked out after changing, she made me turn around a few times before announcing her decision, "I will have to do some alterations. The outfit is a bit short and tight on you. Leave it out here with me, and I will work on it when I get some time. It is late—time to go to sleep."

"Please, God, don't let her fix this one for me so that I can get a new outfit," I prayed and prayed some more till I fell asleep.

Our school closed down a few weeks earlier than our scheduled winter vacation because of the bitter cold that year.

"Why do children in the rest of the country get long summer vacation and short winter holidays and we get long winter vacation and short summer holidays?" I asked Baba.

"O because we have long and very cold winters, which makes it hard for children to get to school," he replied in his typical teacher-like tone.

Thank God for that, I thought. On cold days, sitting on the school floor was very hard. I remember, some winters, Baba sent us home because the floor got too cold for us to sit on. Up until second grade, we sat cross-legged on the floor and wrote our numbers and letters in the dirt with our fingers. Baba had permanently carved those letters and numbers on the beam of the ceiling, and we simply copied those on the classroom floor. Most children complained about their necks hurting from looking at the ceiling beam. But Baba made us write those lines over and over day after day. From the third grade on, our parents bought us slates to write on.

Children from the whole village walked to and from the school. In summer, it used to be fun, as we would play around on the way. But in winters, it was a different story. I didn't have good shoes. My feet would get wet walking in rain or snow. I would take off my wet shoes and warm up my feet by rubbing them with my hands or wrapping them in my shawl.

Zameer had an extra pair. His shoes were nice and shiny but he had ruined them by wearing them in mud. And I wouldn't let him forget his mistake. Every time he wore those shoes, I would taunt him, "I told you, take good care of these shoes. If I had shoes like these, I would have never worn them to go out. All that mud! You will never be able to clean them up completely." This would make him furious and sad at the same time.

Evenings in winter used to be cozy family time. After all the households would finish cooking their dinner, the ladies would collect the ashes from the stove and tandoor to make *sundalees* for their homes.

Mamma taught me how to make one: "Take this clay pot and carefully fill it up with the ashes from the stove and the tandoor. You have to be very careful, as some of the pieces could still be very hot and burn your hands or, worse, put your clothes on fire," she would warn.

Showing the table in the center of the room and the iron frame under it, she taught me how to place the hot pot on that frame and center it properly. In our *sundalee* room, we had our family carpet on the floor. It was big enough to cover the whole room and it was thick and cushy. At the center of the carpet, there stood a small table. Under the table, we placed the pot of hot ashes on its metal frame. A soft colorful comforter the size of the whole room covered the table like a gigantic tablecloth that hung loose on all four sides. There were enough pillows in the room for everyone. After dinner, we would pray our evening prayers. Then one by one, we would slip under the comforter from all four sides. We would all try to stretch our feet as close to the hot pot as we could bear. Mamma and I always joined in after washing dishes, sweeping the floors, and putting everything away. During those cold winter evenings, *sundalee* always felt heavenly. Within minutes, our feet would warm up and then, soon, the rest of our bodies. We munched on pine nuts while sitting under the comforter around the *sundalee*-table.

One evening, Baba announced, "Finish up and we can play carom board or cards."

My brother and I raced to finish our math homework.

"Done!" he shouted, but I had a long way to go. I tried to finish, but Zameer ended up doing the rest of my homework when Baba wasn't looking.

"I am done now too," I proclaimed, moving my arms and legs deeper underneath the comforter to get warm and comfortable.

I had barely started to warm up when Baba ordered, "Go get my book from the other room."

I dreaded getting out of the *sundalee*. My whole body would cool down in seconds because the house would get very cold in the evenings. "Since you are up, bring me some water as well."

After bringing Baba's book and water, I was about to slide back under the *sundalee's* comforter when Mather-Khubi asked for some water too. I returned with her water when Zameer demanded, "Get my school bag, I have to show Baba something."

"Why don't you get up yourself?" I protested.

"Don't be heartless. He is nice and warm, and you are already out. Why make him get out into the cold when you can do that much for your brother?" lectured Mamma while trying to keep her tone gentle.

"This is not fair. You always make me get out of the *sundalee* but not him," I muttered.

After a few games of carom, we slid down deeper in more of a sleeping posture. Mather-Khubi started the story of our own great-grandfather, the famous Nawaz Khan, who fought bravely to save our village from the British Frangies. After drinking her water and clearing her throat a few times, she narrated, "Your own great-grandfather, the grandfather of your baba, lived in this *kot* many years ago with his clan. He was also the leader of our clan. He was kindhearted and a just leader. The people of the clan loved and respected him. He was very wise and thoughtful. There are many stories about his bravery and kindness. When the British Frangies came into our region, he formed an alliance with other local tribes and stopped the British from taking over our region completely. He showed excellent leadership and made some fair deals with the Frangies. The deal allowed the British to do trade with our people until the foreigners started violating the pacts. War became the only way out. Your great-grandfather gathered a brilliant army from the local tribes and trained with them for nearly a year. The Frangies knew of our preparations so they also brought a huge army from India. They attacked our village in late spring. We were ready for them. We lured them deeper and deeper into our region, as our watchful soldiers hid in the caves and the valleys. Once the Frangies reached deep into our mountains, we attacked. Our attack was fierce and coordinated. The Frangies didn't know the ways around in our valleys and mountains. We then blocked all of their escape routes. The battle raged for weeks. Finally, our brave soldiers and their fearless leader, your great-grandfather, Nawaz Khan, finished off the whole Frangie army. We spared one white man and allowed him to go back to India to describe their defeat to the Frangie leaders. After that day, the Frangies never dared look in our direction with an evil intention."

Zameer and I would bombard Mather-Khubi with dozens of question about the battle. She would answer our questions with a pride in her voice. We had heard this story many times, but every time, it sounded equally exciting. Each time, Mather-Khubi added a few new details about the battle. Often, my brother and I, along with other children, played the roles of Nawaz Khan and Frangies. Zameer used to make me play Frangie, and he always played Nawaz Khan. I hated playing Frangie.

I was happy for the winter holidays but was very sad too, knowing that it was my final winter break. "Will you let me go to school next year?" I quietly asked Baba while squeezing between him and the arm of his chair.

"You should stay home and help Mamma in house chores. You are too old to go to school with boys," he replied folding his newspaper down.

"All the girls your age will be staying home learning to cook and clean for their family. None of your friends will be there next year," he said, holding my hands and looking at them just to avoid my gaze. I knew that he felt bad about my sadness over ending my schooling. From his tone, I guessed that he didn't mean what he said about me staying home to do house chores. *Maybe I can change Baba's mind*; I entertained my wishful thought staring at his bushy eyebrows above his dark sunglasses. He wore those glasses at all times except during sleeping.

"But yesterday in the *sundalee*, you told me that you wouldn't mind if I went to school for another year," I reminded him.

"If I let you in the fifth grade, you would be the only girl in that class," he responded, running his fingers through his graying curly hair.

Fixing her stares at me, Mamma said sternly, "I have told you many times not to talk about more schooling for yourself. This is how things are, and that's how they should be."

As always, her stare sent shivers down my spine. I couldn't stop wondering how she could use those beautiful round green eyes as weapons.

Mather-Khubi couldn't let this pass, so she jumped in, "Don't burden your baba by asking the same thing again and again."

"Why are you against schools for girls? In the rest of the country, girls go to school till they are all grown up and even when they have become mothers. Why are we so different?" I asked, raising my voice in anger.

Mamma calmly argued, "It is wrong for girls to go to school. The whole family suffers if girls don't learn to cook and clean the house and take care of their husbands and children."

I had heard this over and over from all my elders.

"I promise, if I go to school, I will still learn every chore you teach me, and I will be good at doing those," I assured Mamma.

"If girls go to school, it dishonors the family. They learn bad habits and get bad ideas from all those books," Mather-Khubi said, trying to console me.

"Everything they teach at school is for men. Girls don't need to read or write or do calculations, they have their fathers, and then later on their husbands, to do all that for them."

I knew that my arguments had no chance against my mother or my grandmother, but I was sure that I could get a change of heart in my Baba.

I will get a few more girls on my side, and we will convince our babas to let us do the fifth grade at our school. I came up with a plan.

I pleaded with every girl in my grade, "Ask your baba to let you go to school for another year."

They all told me, one after another, "Our parents don't want to even hear about us going to school after the fourth grade."

One of the girls reminded me, "Remember, last year, how your baba put the question of more schooling for girls to the *jirga* and how they rejected his request?"

I knew that she was right, but I was not giving up.

Four

THE WEDDING

After a torturous wait, Chacha's wedding day was in sight. Mamma updated my outfit nicely. She washed the stains off and added more material to make the dress larger for me. She sewed alternating rows of beads and sequins in front and hundreds of shiny stars and crescents around the neck, along the lower border and on the edge of the sleeves. I kept looking at my dress and imagining how beautiful I would look in it, but Mamma had strictly forbidden me from trying it on.

In preparation for Chacha's wedding, Baba hired two workers to repair our house inside and out. After finishing repairs in the walls and doors, they whitewashed our whole house, as well as Chacha's room. The whitewash had a pungent odor, but the house looked fresh and new. It was then time to decorate the house and the *kot*. Noor Chacha and his family arrived for the wedding from Bannu. Daily that week, aunties from all over the *kot* gathered at our house. They sewed and embroidered their own and their children's clothes. They spent most of their time making and decorating the dresses for the bride's dowry. All day long, we danced, sang songs, ate special snacks, and drank tea. There were fried cookies, popcorn, roasted peanuts, pine nuts, and nougats for everyone. And yes, we also did a lot of work. We cut thousands of colorful paper triangles and glued them up on strings to make hundreds of yards of streamers for the entire house and the *kot*. Mather-Khubi made pot after pot of glue from flour and water, and we used it all up.

The tedious job of hanging those streamers was given to the tallest boys of the clan. They had to climb a ladder to reach the top of pillars on both sides of the *kot* gate and up on the high walls surrounding the *kot*. They climbed the courtyard tree to wrap the streamers, the sparkly decorations and the strings of beads around it.

Just two days before the wedding, a carpet weaver delivered the carpet that Mather-Khubi and Baba had ordered for Chacha's household. Everyone wanted to unroll it to see it, but Mather-Khubi wouldn't allow that.

She declared, "I want all the men, women, and the children of the clan to be present; only then I will unveil this carpet. Unveiling of the son's wedding carpet is a monumental event in a clan's history, and it deserves utmost respect."

In preparation for the unrolling of the carpet, Mamma swept the floor and moved all the furniture out of the way. We waited until evening when our entire clan could gather by Chacha's room. Mather-Khubi asked Baba to recite some *suras* from the Holy Koran to bless the carpet and all those present for the occasion. Special prayers were said to bless Chacha's future household. Mather-Khubi cut the strings and unrolled the carpet. The history of our whole family was on it. Scenes of the wars that our ancestors had fought were woven around the border. Images of the war that our own great-grandfather fought against the British Frangie were illustrated by downed British flags and high-flying Islamic flags with their crescents and stars. The Russian war that our grandfather and my baba fought and won was depicted by downed Russian flags and high-flying Islamic flags. The carpet was big, thick, and very colorful. Generations of our family stood around the carpet to show respect.

"Most families give one such carpet to each of their sons on the occasion of their wedding. This is how the story of their family is passed on from one generation to the next," she told us with a proud smile.

Turning toward Chacha, she advised, "Take care of this carpet more than your life and pass it on to your eldest son."

With the carpet-unrolling ceremony over, our family rushed to finish Chacha's room. Mamma had been yelling at us for days to decorate that room first, and by then, she was in real panic.

She scolded, "I have been warning you all to work on this room, and now the wedding is tomorrow. How are we ever going to get this done? There is a lot of work, and this room is the most important place in the whole *kot*."

She started wiping the furniture and placing them on top of the carpet. I grabbed a cloth and cleaned whatever was within my reach. Other aunties and cousins joined in. Chacha had bought some new furniture in preparation for his wedding. He had a bed, few chairs, and a table for his famous TV. He received a new bed, more chairs, and new bedding as gift from the close family members. In the weeks before, our aunties stitched two new comforters with a beautiful mosaic patchwork pattern. Together, they had also crocheted two lovely white bed covers and decorated them with lace. The beds were neatly made with the newly crocheted bedcovers. Streamers, chains of glass discs, and countless crescents and stars in gold and silver covered every surface of chacha's room. The decorating took all night. We all stayed up, and no one felt the least bit tired. The singing, dancing, snacking, and the decorating went on till morning.

Mamma forced us to go to sleep after the adults did their morning prayers. "You children must get a few hours of sleep. Otherwise, you will all be overtired and will not be able to enjoy the celebrations," she insisted.

After a few short hours of sleep, we had to get up. None of the adults got any sleep at all. By the time we got up, Mamma had boiled several pots of water for everyone in the family to take bath. The men were already dressed up and busy making the travel arrangements. The aunties had gone to their homes to get ready.

Mamma woke me up, "Your bath water is ready. Go take a quick bath and start getting ready. It will take you many hours, and we don't have that much time."

After my bath, Mamma dried my hair thoroughly with two towels. She didn't want my wet hair to touch my new outfit. I was finally allowed to put on my dress. As I walked out after changing, Mamma's pride and smile could be seen from the other end of the courtyard. I couldn't stop looking into any mirror that I happened to pass by. Never ever in my whole life I had worn anything so special. Mamma then fixed my hair. She used a little oil to make it glossy, and then she braided it tightly. She added a colorful braid extender that had many rattling ornaments. Anytime I walked or shook my head, the bells and the ornaments on my braid rattled musically. Noor Chacha's wife and Mamma made similar braids for each other. They too used braid extenders with jewels and ornaments. With my hair done and my ornate outfit, I received many compliments about how beautiful I looked. Mamma, Mather-Khubi, and most of the aunties couldn't stop calling me a doll. Even Baba addressed me as his doll that day. Mamma and Noor Chacha's wife also got dressed up in clothes with gold and silver embroidery on them. They wore jewelry around their necks, wrists, ankles, and in their hair. Most of our aunties and girl cousins wore similar clothing and jewelry.

Men also dressed up for the occasion. They wore either new or freshly washed *shalwar* and *kameez* suits. These suits are worn by both men and women. A *shalwar* is like a baggy pair of pants, narrow at the bottom but very wide, with a lot of gather around the waist. A *kameez* is a long shirt that reaches past the knees. These are also baggy and feel very comfortable, especially in hot summer days. Men's suits are very simple with choice of color limited to gray, white, cream, or light blue. Women's suits are also simple for everyday use, but for special occasions, like religious festivals or weddings, they are extremely colorful and embroidered on every spot that is visible. Baba and Noor Chacha wore dark gray *shalwar kameez* that were made especially for the occasion. Baba had his hair cut. He got his beard trimmed and stained brown with henna.

The *barat* procession was ready. Our uncles, aunties, and close cousins joined the procession heading to the bride's village to bring back Chacha's new bride. We rode in horse-drawn carriages. Chacha rode a horse by himself. He looked very handsome wearing his brand new white *shalwar kameez*, black weskit, shiny black shoes, and a beige shawl wrapped around his shoulders. A new gun hung across his chest. His curly hair and well-trimmed beard appeared glossy. The kohl around his eyes gave them a distinguished dark look.

On his head he wore a *sehra* made up of a golden crown fitting his head like a cap. Dozens of superbly decorated strands were attached to the crown that partially hid his face. Some strands were golden, others were silver, some were made up of fresh flowers and others were made up of five and ten rupee notes. Beads, glass discs, stars and crescents and other sparkling ornaments were generously used to decorate the strands of his *sehra*.

Mamma and Noor Chacha's wife carried the dowry for the bride's family. There were many new outfits for the bride herself in different colors with beautiful embroidery. The yellow outfit decorated with thousands of tiny little glass discs was my favorite. Mather-Khubi gave gold and silver jewels, some with precious stones that she had been saving for years for her third son's bride. Mamma gave away several pieces of her own jewelry as gift while Chacha added some new ones that he had bought for his bride. Throughout the procession, Baba and the uncles danced and played music, which was interrupted only by celebratory gunshots. Upon reaching the bride's village, the uncles shot their guns into the air to announce the arrival of the procession. A lavish lunch awaited us. A row of whole lambs, their bellies stuffed with savory rice and baked in deep tandoor, was served. The host insisted again and again that we eat to our hearts' content. The gunshots continued during lunch and only subsided when the *nikah* rituals were recited by the imam.

The bride looked just like a doll that every girls plays with as a child. She wore an extremely heavily embroidered bright green outfit. Every inch of the outfit was decorated with beads, stars, crescents and other sparkling adornments. On her face she had a *sehra* also just like that of Chacha's but thousand time more bejeweled. Her hands and feet had intricate designs made from henna. Her eyes were closed most of the time but the mascara outlined her eye lids and her lips appeared shiny bright red. Throughout the ceremony, she sat with her head down, surrounded by her sisters and other relatives.

As we got ready to leave, she bid a very emotional farewell to her baba, mamma, sisters, brothers, and other relatives. All of them had tears in their eyes. She herself cried out loud as did her mamma and her sisters. I couldn't hold my tears just looking at them. We rushed back and barely made it home just after the sunset. Mamma and other ladies walked the bride to Chacha's room. Being our chacha's wife, we started addressing her Chachee. We joked and teased her. She just smiled. She had become a part of our family, and a new home got added to our *kot*.

Two days later, Chacha arranged the *walima* lunch that is offered by the groom's side to welcome the bride's family. The main course was lamb pilaf accompanied with mildly spiced yogurt *raita* sauce. Halva, garnished with almonds, pistachios, and saffron, and layered with silver-paper was served, along with other sweets as dessert. Tea and cold sweetened milk were available as drinks. Many from the bride's immediate family and close relatives attended the lunch. We all got ready in our best clothing. I got another excuse to put on my new outfit. The guests, however, came in rather simple clothes. On their way home, they took our new chachee with them. A few days later, Chacha went to bring her back. Upon the bride's return, life for all of us returned back to routine.

Five

IT ALL BEGAN

Baba and Chacha cleaned up their squash court and started playing regularly. As usual, I fetched the ball for them when it bounced out of the court. They trained Zameer every day. I watched closely when they taught him how to hold the racket, hit straight shots, or lob and drop the ball in the front of the court. It didn't look hard. I couldn't understand why Zameer had so much trouble. Every time they left him alone to practice by himself, I joined him. We did drills together. I used to be afraid, though, because I had to use Baba's racket, and he had warned me to never touch his racket. Being fearful of Baba's anger, I paid more attention to protecting Baba's racket than to the oncoming ball.

Khaleh and her children came to visit us. This was Mamma's sister and her family. Mamma was joyous about having her over. Her daughter, Rahela, was a little younger than me, but we got along quite well. We could talk and play together for hours. Rahela and I stood by to fetch the ball as Baba drilled with Zameer. While waiting for our turn to pick up the ball, we played rocks and ball on the rooftop. It is an easy game. You just toss the ball and try to pick as many rocks as possible before catching the ball back.

"Zameer, you practice this shot that I have just shown you while I go to the village center to meet someone," Baba instructed before leaving.

I couldn't miss the chance. I grabbed Baba's racket and started playing with Zameer while my heart pounded with fear. I didn't want to be seen playing squash by either Baba or Mamma.

"Rahela, are you watching the road? Make sure you signal me in advance when you see Baba returning," I kept on reminding her again and again.

I had my doubts, so I kept looking at her after every few shots. Each time I looked up, I caught her playing the rocks and ball instead of watching for Baba.

While concentrating on Rahela, I completely ignored the back door of the court. As I got lost in the rhythm of the game, I didn't even hear Mamma opening the door. Upon my next turn back, I suddenly saw Mamma standing, arms folded, on the door of the court. She was furious. As usual, the stare of her deep green eyes sent shivers down my spine, but the worst awaited me.

She grabbed me by my hair and landed a series of slaps on my face and head. Pulling my hair hard, she yelled into my face, "I have warned you many times not to play this sport, but you don't listen. You deserve a good beating. This sport is for boys, and God forbid if anyone else sees you playing it will disgrace the whole family. Our good name, which our forefathers have made with their precious blood, will be ruined."

She dragged me back into the house and pushed me in front of a tall stack of dishes. "Finish these dishes, and I have a list of housework for you after that!" she shouted.

How can anyone with such calm and innocent-looking face be so vicious and nasty? How can a woman with such average build become so strong? I asked myself about Mamma. *Why did Allah make squash and other fun sports for boys and washing dishes for girls? Why didn't he make me a boy?* The thoughts popped up once again in my head.

The stack of dishes and the pots and pans were just too high for me. Wiping my tears off and tying my hair back, I began washing one item after another while my mind wandered off.

The cricket match between India and Pakistan has reached its deciding stages. As the captain, I'm under a lot of pressure. Their captain, Sunnil has already scored two centuries, and we are not getting anyone out. Our fielding is in disarray. Everyone knows that India is going to win. I have a plan in mind. I start bowling myself. But Sunnil is too settled in. The fast bowlers are not scaring him. I put an amazing swing on the first three balls. I get two of their players out. My team is alive again. In my next over, I bowl to Sunnil. He knows my bowling very well, but he misjudges the swing on my third ball. He's caught in the slip—a stunning catch indeed. Sunnil's departure is what we have been trying to get for the last two days. We have won the match. No one can believe it. The whole world chants "Imran! Imran!" I wave back at them in thanks.

I was snapped out by mamma's yelling, "What are you doing? In all this time, you haven't even finished half of the dishes. You are sitting here waving your hands when you should have been rinsing the dishes. Go and sweep the floor, I will finish up the rest myself."

For the next few weeks, I didn't dare go even in the direction of the squash court. I didn't even go on the rooftop to pick the balls for Baba and Chacha. But I couldn't stop playing imaginary squash when I was alone. I played my shots in the air without the ball or the racket. I made all the movements with my hand, or sometimes I used a stick, a spatula, or a broom. I even admired my own imaginary shots and applauded myself, the way people applaud a good shot during a match on TV. My determination to give up squash was not to last very long. Knowing well the consequences of being caught again, I succumbed to the temptations of the squash court. I sneaked in to practice alone, hoping that I won't get caught. Every time I entered the court, my mind would be focused on the back door, watching for the slightest movement, instead of concentrating on the ball. Luckily, nobody paid much attention to the court those days since they thought it was just filled with puddles. They didn't know that I had cleaned it up and had been playing by myself.

Six

FIGHT FOR THE FIFTH YEAR

Our winter vacation ended, and we went back to school. Those were the last few months of school for me. I was not alone it was the same for all the girls in my grade. My friend, Azra—we call her Billo, a nickname given to girls with blue eyes—was not only extremely beautiful but she was also an excellent student. Baba used to make her do the schoolwork of two grades higher. He used to say she was the smartest student he ever had in his school. She wanted to become a teacher or a doctor and not just end up at home with only a fourth-grade education.

"Ask your baba to go to the *jirga* and tell them to change the rules," I told her.

"My baba has asked the *jirga* several times, and each time, they have told him that they will not consider allowing any girl's schooling beyond fourth grade," Azra replied.

"The same happened to my baba when he went to the *jirga*. You know what? Maybe our babas are not telling the *jirga* how much we want to go to school. We should tell the *jirga* ourselves," I blurted.

Azra looked at me with a strange expression. Her lit-up face was saying, "What a brilliant idea!" But her dropped jaw was telling me, "You must be completely out of your mind to even consider talking to the *jirga*."

"That is it. We must ask our babas to arrange for us to plead to the *jirga* ourselves," I concluded.

"It is not going to happen. It can't happen," refuted Azra.

But my mind was made up. I insisted, "We have to try our best. That is our only chance."

After staring at the sky for a moment, Azra's bright blue eyes twinkled even brighter as she announced, "Let's stop eating and go on a hunger strike. Our health worries our parents the most."

"They get scared when we don't eat our meals properly, especially in winter," I added enthusiastically.

Even before I could finish my sentence, she reasoned, "They worry because we have no doctor anywhere near our village. They have to take us to Bannu, which is a long way away, and the roads are very bad during winter."

Remembering what I did the previous year, I said, "Using a hunger strike, last year I got the clothes that I wanted for the Eid day instead of another outfit that Mamma wanted me to have."

"Yes! You are right. My parents have given into my demands every time I have stopped eating," Azra concluded, agreeing with me.

"But I get so hungry and my stomach starts growling by the end of the day," I hesitated.

She consoled, "Don't worry, normally, by the second day they give in."

We started planning immediately. We asked other girls to join in. Despite our best effort, we were only able to get two more. Azra convinced both Sanna and Sadia too. We agreed that all four of us would stop eating starting Friday morning. It was already Wednesday, and we only had two days left. I was worried. I knew how hard it would be for me not to eat anything all day. For the next two days, I ate more than my share. I wanted to build up reserves to tide me over during my hunger strike.

It was Friday. Everyone was at home. As we sat together for breakfast, I announced, "I am not going to eat anything."

"Are you not well? Is your stomach hurting?" Mamma asked me, touching my forehead.

"I feel all right. I am going on a hunger strike. I will not eat till you get us a hearing at the *jirga*," I announced facing Baba and Baba only.

"Hearing at the *jirga* for what?" snapped Mamma.

"We want to tell the *jirga* ourselves how badly we want to continue going to school," I replied, once again facing Baba only. "Four of us are together in this."

Baba looked at my face to figure out if I had lost my mind completely or only partially.

"Who wants a meeting with the *jirga*?" he inquired sarcastically. "Do you mean that you and three other girls want to argue in front of the *jirga*?" he asked, as if giving me a chance to rethink my statement and come back to my senses.

"We want to stand face-to-face in front of each member of the *jirga* and them ourselves why we want to go to school," I reiterated.

"No female has ever spoken at a *jirga* meeting in our village. This is completely out of the question," he replied, adjusting his sunglasses and stroking his beard. "Besides, *jirga* has repeatedly rejected the idea of school for girls, and that is no secret," he reminded me.

"Please go and talk to Azra's baba and the fathers of the other two girls who are with me on this," I begged, wrapping my arms around his neck. I didn't want to cry, but tears just rolled down my cheeks uncontrollably. Maybe it was because I was hungry and I was eyeing all that yummy Friday breakfast that I was going to miss.

"All right! All right! I will talk to your friends' babas after the Friday prayers. Now you should eat your breakfast," he told me, gently patting my back.

"I will not eat any food until *jirga* agrees to listen to our plea," I said, not looking toward Mamma because I knew that her stare would shatter my determination.

Baba was gone all evening. As usual, he didn't tell us where he was going nor for how long. I didn't know if he had gone to talk to the other fathers or was just out doing his own things. Mamma and Mather-Khubi kept on asking me to eat something all day, but I was determined to not touch food until Baba came home with some news. It was already dark, and Baba was not back. The rest of us were all sitting in our *sundalee*. Mamma and Mather-Khubi finally stopped asking me to eat.

"Amina, get me some water, I don't know why I have been so thirsty all evening," demanded Mamma.

I was dreading this command all evening. I knew that, sooner or later, I would have to leave the warmth of the *sundalee*. I dragged myself out of the comforter and went to the kitchen to get Mamma her water. I felt tired and weak from hunger, so I walked slowly toward the water pitcher. While pouring water into a glass, I noticed a plate with a naan right behind the pitcher. Very quietly, I lifted the naan, and to my utter surprise, I found a kebab and some roasted tomatoes under the naan.

That's what they had for dinner, I remembered.

Looking at the plate, I wondered, *That is certainly some leftover from dinner and somebody must have forgotten to put their plate away.*

The food looked too scrumptious for me to pass up, and besides, there was no one around to see me eat. With that thought in mind, I ate the food bite by bite, being very cautious not to be seen or heard by anyone. Both the naan and the kebab had gotten cold and a little stiff, but that was the best kebab that I have ever had. I was so hungry that it didn't take me very long at all to eat every last morsel of food on the plate. I quietly rinsed the plate and carefully laid it on the stack of washed-up dishes without making a single sound.

"What is taking you so long? Are you gone to get water from the well? By the time you will bring water for me, I will die of thirst." That's what I had been expecting to hear from Mamma. But to my surprise, Mamma was waiting patiently. I obediently handed over her water and slid back under the comforter.

Mather-Khubi had started telling us the famous story of Syed Ahmed Shaheed, and we were all listening to it as if we had never heard it before: "Once, there lived a learned gentleman by the name of Syed Ahmed in Delhi. He had spent all his life in learning and teaching. He even traveled to Baghdad and Medina to acquire knowledge. In Delhi, he ran a school where thousands of students from all over the world came to study. Those students spent their entire lives learning. As the British Frangies became more and more bold, they started interfering in his school affairs. Syed Ahmed tried his best to reason with them, but they wanted his school closed. Syed Ahmed had no choice but to declare jihad against the Frangies. He and his army fought against the Frangies for years. They had to escape the comforts of city life and find refuge in the mountains near our village. Many locals joined him in his struggles. The Frangies didn't give up on him. They followed him into the mountains. Syed Ahmed fought the last battle of his life at the bank of the river Kabul. The battle lasted many days. One night, as he swam to cross the fast-flowing river, the Frangies encircled him and his troops. They shot every single one of his soldiers. As for Syed Ahmed himself, they wanted to arrest him alive, but he didn't surrender. He died fighting bravely on the bank of the river. After his death, he became to be known as Syed Ahmed Shaheed. *Shaheed* is a title given to someone who dies fighting in the service of Allah. His grave is on the bank of river Kabul, and thousands of people visit his grave each year. Ask your baba to take you there—it is not very far from here."

I had full intention to wait for Baba to come home, but the warmth of the *sundalee*, the food in my belly, the and sweet sound of Mather-Khubi's story were too much. I must have drifted into a deep sleep by the end of her story. In the morning, when I opened my eyes, I saw Baba. He was getting ready to go out again.

"What did the *jirga* say?" I asked him without even greeting everyone with a good-morning salaam.

"I have met the fathers of all the other girls, and there is some good news. Sanna's grandfather—who is called Babaji—is a member of the *jirga*. He is a highly learned and respected member, and being the oldest person, everyone in the *jirga* listens to him," my baba told me after pulling me down to sit next to him. "All the babas will go and see the *jirga* members and ask them to grant a hearing to you girls. I am still not sure if the *jirga* will agree to our request, but that is all I could do," he told me, holding my hand apologetically.

I was not sure what was good in that news, but I was happy, nonetheless.

"Now you must eat," he insisted. I didn't resist. I could see that he had done his best. Knowing that Sanna's grandfather was in the *jirga* somehow gave me the confidence that we might get a hearing after all.

In the morning, I arrived at school earlier than normal. Sanna was already there, and soon, Azra and Sadia also arrived.

I announced with a shriek, "I am so happy that now we can tell the *jirga* why we need to go to school."

Sadia pointed out the obvious, "Do you have any idea how scary it would be to stand in front of those men and speak up loud and clear?" She added, looking worried, "How are we so sure that they will even agree to the hearing? We haven't yet heard of the *jirgas'* decision. Maybe they will turn down our babas' appeal. After all, no woman has ever spoken in front of our village *jirga* ever before."

"Oh, you be quiet," all three of us shunned her, knowing well that she was right on both accounts.

All day long, we talked about different ideas that might convince the *jirga* to open up the rest of the schools to girls.

"I will be home later. I have to go meet with the members of the *jirga* separately. You walk home with other children of the *kot*," Baba instructed at the end of the school day.

Just before dinnertime, Baba returned. After eating dinner, he crawled into the *sundalee* to drink his tea.

"I went to meet each member of the *jirga*. Babaji is fully with us, and he wants the *jirga* to hear what you all want to say about the school. But the other two are against hearing about the girls' school issue from anyone, especially from the girls," he blurted out in one breath.

"What about the remaining two members? There are five." I asked.

"The other two members were not at home, I will have to try to find them tomorrow," he replied.

We didn't know how the other two would react till Baba had seen them. Baba tried to meet them the next day after school. Again, they were not available.

Baba might give up. He can't go looking for them every day, I worried.

That evening, Zameer added to my fears, telling me that the imam of the mosque was the one who was utterly against the idea of girls' schooling and that his voice was pretty strong in the *jirga*. I fell asleep fighting sobs.

At school, the four of us wouldn't go out to play. We couldn't pay attention to our lessons. Baba caught us talking to one another during lessons many times.

Our goal was to coach Sanna to get her grandfather, the Babaji, fully on our side. "Remember, always try to bring him his dinner plates, water, and tea, so he doesn't have to get up for anything," I coached her.

Azra added, "Get him warm water for his *wozu* before his prayers. Pour the water for him so that he can easily wash his hands and face for wozu in comfort. Also, find his shoes when he gets out of the *sundalee*, roll up his prayer mat after he finishes his prayers, and most importantly, say salaam to him at every opportunity you get."

How could Sadia be left out? Sounding as nervous as ever, she said, "And yes, always agree with him if he tells you something, and never ever act irritated if he asks you to leave the *sundalee* to bring him anything— no matter how warm and cozy you have become."

Every day Sanna would report to us about how she took good care of her grandbaba and how happy he had been with her. Until one day, unable to control her giggle, she reported, "When my mamma was scolding me yesterday, Babaji came out and told Mamma off. He then took me away from her to another room." We were now sure that Sanna's grandbaba was fully on our side. And we needed him there.

Like every day that week, Baba left again to find and meet the members of *jirga*, and we had to walk home from the school without him. My stomach growled with hunger. We always felt so hungry after school. Maybe it was the long walk home or such a long time since breakfast. After lunch and helping Mamma with some house chores, I sneaked out with Baba's squash racket hidden under my shawl. Once alone in the court, I bounced the ball against the wall. The ball was not bouncy at all. It had to be warmed up by hitting it hard against the front wall a few dozen times. Since the walls of the court were so cold, I had to smash the ball harder and harder. After hundreds of hard strokes, the ball finally warmed up and started to bounce decently well. Suddenly, I caught myself thinking about the *jirga* and what I was going to say there if I ever got my chance. I was really angry at Imam Sahib and the other person who was refusing to even hear us out. I realized that the angrier I was getting at the *jirga*, the harder I was hitting the balls.

"Imam Sahib, why are you against school for girls? What have we done to deserve this? What is our crime that you want to punish us by making us sit at home and wash dishes and sweep floors? Why do the boys get to have fun playing cricket, football, and pitho ball with their friends? Why can't the girls of the village also learn to read and write? Look at the other parts of the country. Women are going to schools and studying at universities. Then they go to cities and even to other countries to study more. They don't spend their lives doing kitchen chores only. They play sports and compete in matches and tournaments. Are they all wrong? Maybe you are."

The squash ball was now hot and very bouncy. The echoes of my shots somewhat rhymed with the questions I tossed at the imaginary Imam Sahib whose picture I could vividly see on the front wall of the court. I heard footsteps coming toward the court. Out of breath, I tried to hold still.

Is it Baba? He will catch me using his racket. Or worse, it could be Mamma. If she catches me playing squash, this time, for sure, she is going to give me a memorable beating. Her stern warning—that next time, she would break my bones—rang in my ears. I tried to hide myself, but there is no place to hide in a squash court. With my heart pounding, I peered through the cracks in the back door and was relieved to see it was only Zameer. Still behind the door, I hoped he would not see or hear me.

Apparently, he already had. Opening the court door, he asked me bluntly, "Who were you talking to? It sounded like you were quarreling with someone."

"I beg you, please don't tell anyone that I was playing squash using Baba's racket," I pleaded.

With a big smirk on his face, he responded, "All right, but remember now you owe me a favor."

"Do you want to play?" I asked him.

Before turning back, he replied, "No, I have lots of homework, and so do you. You better get back to start your homework before Baba returns."

I returned to drilling my shots, hitting the ball a few more times, but by then, it had cooled down too much and was hard to control. I needed to warm it up again, but the fear of getting caught by Mamma had taken my enthusiasm away. Giving up and quietly sneaking back into the house, I put Baba's racket exactly where it was before and made my way to the *sundalee*. Mamma was still busy elsewhere in the house. Only Zameer and Mather-Khubi were there. I sat with them and started my homework.

It was late into the evening when Baba walked in the door. Mamma served him his dinner, and then he joined us in the *sundalee* with his cup of tea in his hand.

"You are very late. Was there a special event at the mosque?" Mamma asked, slipping into the *sundalee*.

Addressing Mamma and Mather-Khubi, he replied, "Yes, there were some mujahedeen visiting our mosque. They told us how the war in Afghanistan is getting harder. More people from our village are joining them. Many of our neighbors have been martyred. We will have to support their families now." Even I could feel the deep sorrow in his voice.

Do you have any news from the jirga? I thought while refraining from interfering in their somber conversation.

Although I sat obediently, without uttering a single word, Baba must have read the question in my eyes. "Listen, Amina, after I've run around to find them for nearly a month, Azra's and Sanna's babas and I met with every member of *jirga*, but three of them oppose girls' school and don't want to discuss it any further, especially not with children."

I was surprised that our babas had fought so hard on our behalf. I thought that they would have given up sooner. "So what are you going to do? We can't give up just like that," I said with my voice cracking and my eyes tearing up uncontrollably.

"I don't know what else we can do," he replied, sounding very irritated. I didn't know if he was angry at me for my stubbornness or at the members of *jirga* for theirs. Blowing on his cup of tea to cool it down, Baba continued, "Our very last hope lies with Sanna's babaji. He wants to talk to the members of the *jirga* again to change their minds."

I wanted to fall asleep with his last sentence in my mind. Once again, Mather-Khubi was telling some story, but I didn't hear a single word.

A few days passed with no news. Every time I asked Baba about it, he would have the same response, "Babaji has not yet been able to talk with the *jirga* members. He will try again tomorrow." That left me hoping that it might happen the next day or the day after. One evening, as Baba walked home, I ran out to meet him in the courtyard. Mamma served him his meal and the tea. As he ate, Baba fed me a few bites, while Mamma gave me dirty looks. She didn't like it when we ate from his plate after we had already eaten our share. Baba smiled on. After dinner, he picked up his tea, and holding my hand, he walked to the *sundalee*. We slipped under the comforter. His feet were icy cold. I started rubbing them to warm them up.

He stopped me. "Don't worry about my feet, my daughter. The pot under the *sundalee* is still warm. I am deep enough under the comforter that my feet are nearly touching the pot. They are warming up already. You get back to your homework right away. "Sanna's babaji and I met with the members of the *jirga* again, and we had a very long talk with them. Babaji argued very strongly to change their minds—"

"Are they convinced?" I interrupted. With a chuckle, he nodded yes. Mamma and Mather-Khubi were not amused. I jumped and wrapped my arms around him.

Mamma chided, "This is wrong. You are pushing your baba into doing things that no one has done before."

Mather-Khubi scolded Baba, "The way you listen to every wish of your daughter—if you had listened to your own mother that way, you could have secured yourself a place in heaven. What is this world coming to? Now fathers are obeying their daughters and that too for wrong reasons, like schooling for girls. What, all our forefathers were fools that they didn't let girls go to school?"

"Mather-Khubi, listen, girls' education is not such a bad thing after all. I will be happy to teach girls past the fourth grade if the *jirga* agrees," Baba explained apologetically while still smiling at me from behind his beard and sunglasses.

In my excitement, I even forgot to ask Baba the date of the meeting. In the morning, I ran up to the school, as I wanted to be the first to tell my friends the good news. No surprise—they had already found out. Azra told me the *jirga* meeting was on the coming Friday.

None of us knew what we were going to say. I panicked then began to summarize my key points: "I will tell them very clearly that I have so much fun at school and don't want this to end. I want to keep playing cricket, *pitho* ball, and football with other kids. I will also tell them how good I am at all these sports and how the boys fight with one another to have me on their teams."

Next, Azra shared her ideas, "I want to learn about other places, other worlds, and what else is out there, outside this village of ours. I want to read about medicines and the stars. I will also say that I want to know how other people live in the world, how they eat, drink, how they make their homes, what kind of animals and farms they have, what kind of clothes they wear, how many different kinds of animals there are in the world, and—"

I interrupted Azra from going on and on, "Sanna, do you know what you are going to tell the *jirga*?"

"Yes, I will tell them I want to stay in school so I can learn to read and write about whatever I can get my hands on. I want to read all those big books with tiny letters that my grandfather has in his cupboard," she answered passionately.

"And, Sadia, what about you? Do you know what you will tell the *jirga*?" I was curious.

"I will tell them that I like school more than any place else. At home, my life is very tough. I must work with my baba and mamma on our farm. School is the only break I get from carrying heavy loads of corn, thrashing, cleaning and grinding it, and working in the fields. I also get a break from seeing my baba beat Mamma." She paused, her voice trembling. "School is the only time they can't beat me. I will tell the *jirga* that I don't mind getting a beating now and then, I know all children get those, but I get several daily. Some are so bad that they leave ugly bruises." She stopped abruptly, turning her face away.

It was the longest week of my life. At school, all four of us rehearsed our speeches at every opportunity. Other children knew about it but couldn't be bothered to get involved. Boys didn't care anyway, and the girls? Well, except for the four of us, the others had either accepted their fate or didn't want to join our fight. Our speeches didn't sound at all like the ones we had thought of in the beginning. The girls talked me out of speaking about how much fun I had at school playing all the boy sports. We knew the *jirga* would frown on that argument. Baba also coached us into saying things that he thought might please the *jirga*. At the end, my speech was also about how I wished to learn about the world and read big books. We felt sure our speeches would convince the *jirga* to accept our argument. During our walk home from school, Baba was with us. I told him what each one of us was going to say. He listened quietly. Except for a couple of deep sighs he didn't say a word. I didn't know what to make of it.

I wondered, *Does he know something I don't know? Is he not fully with me on this?* I knew Mamma and Mather-Khubi were still against me. They didn't want me to challenge the system that had worked in our village forever.

It was a warm afternoon, and I was yearning to play squash, but I realized that the outfit which I had picked out for our *jirga* meeting needed washing. I didn't want to wear my plain gray *kameez* that I wore to school every day, so I chose the one with rose prints on it. It was my prettiest outfit other than the one that Mamma remade for me at chacha's wedding. I knew that that one would be totally out of question. I was allowed to wear the rose-printed *kameez* on special occasions, like when guests came. I decided to wash it though. I pulled a pail of water from the well. I had to be quick as the sun was setting and I was afraid that my clothes won't dry after sunset. Also, the well water is warmer when you pull it out, but if you leave it out for a while, it gets freezing cold, and then it hurts your hands to wash clothes with it. I wanted to make my outfit clean and beautiful. I double-soaped my *kameez, shalwar*, and chador then rinsed them thoroughly before hanging them to dry.

While I was on my tiptoe trying to reach the clothes-line, Mamma came by. She asked me sternly, "What have you washed these clothes for?"

"I want to wear these at the *jirga* meeting," I answered respectfully.

"No, you must not wear this *kameez* in public. Don't you realize it has gotten tight and too revealing? You should not go out dressed like this in front of other men," she scolded.

I insisted that the *kameez* was fine, but her decision was final. I was left with no choice but to accept my fate and be prepared to wear my plain and boring gray *kameez*. I decided to wash it though. *Even if it is not as pretty as the one with rose prints, at least, it will look fresh and clean*, I thought, consoling myself.

By sundown, my *shalwar* and chador were dry but the *kameez* was not, and I was panicking. I had seen Mamma hanging clothes near the stove area sometimes. So I did the same. I checked it every few minutes to see if it was drying. I prayed hard to Allah to make my *kameez* dry fast. I even blew on its cuffs every time I came near it. My heart pounded with happiness when, by night fall, the *kameez* had completely dried. I thanked Allah several times while neatly folding my outfit and gently placing it under my pillow to smooth out the wrinkles.

Seven

VICTORY AT THE PULPIT

It was finally Friday. We were all home. Baba and Zameer went out to buy fruits, vegetables, and meats. Mamma and I did our extra Friday cleaning. Mather-Khubi sat out in the sun where other women of the *kot* were. After finishing the cleanup, Mamma also joined them in the courtyard. I saw my chance. I sneaked out to the squash court, with Baba's squash racket and a ball. As soon as I started hitting the ball against the front wall, a mysterious calm came over me. I began daydreaming about my next few years at the school. That put a smile on my face, but right then the fear of getting caught with Baba's squash racket in my hand engulfed me.

My luck has been holding, and no one has come looking for me. I don't want to push it, especially not on the most important day of my life. If Mamma catches me, she might even stop me from going to the jirga meeting this afternoon. With that thought in my mind, I left the court and returned the racket and ball to their place without anyone noticing me.

After coming home from the market, Baba and Zameer got ready for the weekly *jummah* prayers. Mamma and I put the groceries away, and she made a quick lunch. Baba and Zameer were ready in their fresh *shalwar* and *kameez*. We ate naan with *chappal* kebab garnished with onions, mint, cilantro, and fresh tomatoes for lunch.

"Get to the mosque right after the *jummah* prayers. The *jirga* is going to start their meeting right away," Baba instructed just before leaving.

"Sweep the floor before getting ready," Mamma ordered sternly just as soon as the men left for the mosque.

I obeyed immediately without showing any sign of resentment. I didn't want any trouble that day. I picked up the broom and started sweeping from one corner of the house heading to the other corner.

I am playing the most important match of my life. My opponent is very strong, but I am playing extremely good shots. I am making him run from one corner to another. Roars of applause arise from the crowd at every single one of my shots. It has become a long five-set match. I am leading in the final game, only two points away from my victory. I hit an ace for the serve, and now I am playing the match point. I hit my winning shot, a beautiful corner drop in the front of the court. It is all over. All the TV cameras are facing me. I have won the match. People are running toward me. Children are asking for my autograph, and reporters are taking my picture. They are lining up to ask me questions, and in response, I am thanking almighty Allah *for my good fortune and my parents for their steadfast support.*

Just then the broom scraped across my toes, and I realized that I needed to finish sweeping before Mamma came scolding me again.

I took out my *shalwar, kameez,* and chador from under my pillow and inspected them one last time. I felt so proud of my outfit, not a single wrinkle and there were sharp creases formed by the weight and the warmth of the pillow. My outfit looked almost brand new—crisp and creased, as if it had just come straight from the tailor's shop. Even to my own eyes, it didn't look like the same boring *shalwar kameez* that I wore to school every day. I got to the mosque while prayers were still going on. I respectfully waited outside, my heart pounding with fear. Azra arrived first, followed by Sanna. When the prayers ended, the *jirga* members slowly moved toward one side of the mosque as the rest of the people left. I felt completely choked up seeing all five members of the *jirga* together. What calmed me a little was the sight of Sanna's grandfather, Babaji.

As the members talked and laughed with one another, a sense of relief came over me. Just then I realized, *They are normal people who talk and laugh like we all do.*

Baba signaled to us to come in, although Sadia had not arrived yet, the three of us slowly walked in.

"Make sure your shoes are stacked carefully out of the way so no one trips over them," Sanna whispered.

"Is all of my hair completely covered under my chador?" I asked Sanna while carefully tucking in a couple of strands of her hair that were peeping out of her chador. Still there was no sign of Sadia. Azra too adjusted her chador. We walked barefoot and sat cross-legged on the floor at the spot that Baba pointed out to us.

Imam Sahib started the proceedings by reciting a sura from the Holy Koran. After that, Babaji announced the purpose of our meeting,

"Today's meeting is very special. The topic under discussion is that of school for girls. We have four young girls here who want to continue going to school even after they complete fourth grade this year. We should listen to them with compassion."

Just then Sadia walked into the mosque. Oh my god—some of her hair is showing. I signaled to her by touching my own chador. Thank God, she read my signal and pulled her chador to cover her head properly. She came and sat right behind me. I so badly wanted to know why she was late, but I stayed still.

"Dear daughters, now let us hear what your reasons are for continuing your schooling," Babaji invited us in a compassionate tone.

Azra spoke first. She read her speech perfectly, not a single stumble. Then it was my turn. After saying salaam to everyone, I wanted to start the speech that I had so carefully memorized, but I couldn't remember the start. While every pair of eyes was fixed on my face, I stood there without uttering a single word—desperately trying to remember the first sentence but completely unable to move my mouth.

"Going to school makes us happy . . . ," murmured Sanna and Azra in one voice.

"Going to school makes us happy children. Learning new things make us better humans. We can go on to become teachers and doctors. We need both in our villages. In other parts of our own country, girls go to school till they are grown-up. They become teachers, doctors, and even prime ministers. They become famous players in hockey, tennis, cricket, and squash. We in the village should also be allowed to do what the girls in the rest of the country do." I delivered my speech.

Next, it was Sanna, and she also delivered a convincing speech. "I wish to learn to read all those books that my babaji has. I want to be able to read about all the famous Muslims from our history. I want to read all the rules and commands that Allah has sent for us." Babaji smiled proudly as she mentioned his books.

Finally, it was Sadia's turn. She stood up. "Salaam," she said without looking at anyone present. Her gaze remained fixed on the floor. "Bismillah-ir-rahman-nir-raheem," she uttered very respectfully. I realized that none of us started our speeches with the name of Allah, except for her. I felt very proud and happy that she remembered the blessed words, which we all forgot. But then she was quiet, still gazing down. No words came out of her mouth. The silence was very unsettling. Every second felt like a day.

"She forgot the starting line," I whispered to Azra.

"I want to go to school . . . ," we hinted the start of her lines. She did not catch our hints. We repeated her lines but, again, no response.

"Dear daughter Sadia, don't be afraid. We have come to hear your reasons, go on and tell us why you want to go to school," Babaji reassured her kindly. "Do you want to drink some water first?" he inquired. She nodded her head slightly to say no.

"Then you should sit down. Perhaps we can continue without her speech," Imam Sahib suggested. Other members seemed to agree with Imam Sahib, but Babaji insisted on giving her more time.

I frantically looked at her face, silently begging, *Come on, Sadia, come on. Deliver your speech. You can do it. Just start, and then you will be fine.* I could see her eyes flooding with tears.

One more time, Imam Sahib addressed her, "Daughter Sadia, if you don't have anything to say, you don't have to say something. Just sit down and let the meeting continue."

Even before Imam Sahib finished his sentence, Sadia let out a big cry, wailing uncontrollably. We all tried our best to calm her down without success.

In a faint voice, we heard her say, "If I am pulled out of the school, I will die . . . I will die . . . I will die . . . ," although other than us girls, no one could have heard her. Sadia sat down sobbing, with her face hidden between her knees. My heart was sinking with panic, *Sadia's speech is the strongest and the jirga didn't get to hear her arguments.*

The *jirga* started debating the topic. Babaji went first. "The girls have made it clear that they have noble intentions. They wish to continue learning. Our holy Prophet of Islam has commanded that Muslims should do everything in their power to acquire knowledge. They should even go to China to learn. Remember these instructions are for men as well as women. We should allow these girls and even other girls from the village to continue their school."

All the *jirga*-members nodded in agreement. "Indeed, the instructions for acquiring knowledge are for women as well. However, according to sharia, once a girl becomes adult, which happens around ten years of age, she must not interact with men who are not her relatives. Interactions between unrelated adult men and women, is *haram*, even in a school's setting," replied Imam Sahib. All the members agreed with Imam Sahib's reply also.

"Yes, the girls do turn adult at ten, but the boys in their class are still children since they don't become adult until the age of fourteen or fifteen. So the girls can interact with boys as long as the boys are still children," rebutted Babaji.

Everyone looked convinced and impressed by his argument, even Imam Sahib nodded in agreement before raising his next objection, "What about the boys in the older classes?"

Babaji was quiet now as all ears were directed toward him.

Baba stood up at this point, and after running his fingers through his curly hair and pushing up his sunglasses, he said, "I should be able to make the necessary arrangements to keep these girls separated from the older boys. The boys of the upper levels can be moved to the other side of the school."

Now Imam Sahib was quiet as all the members of the *jirga* looked at him, waiting for his verdict. "If the teachers assure us of a complete separation of older boys and girls, then this may be acceptable," declared Imam Sahib after a long silence.

I was about to scream with joy when Imam Sahib continued, "But the teacher is an adult man, and he is not allowed to interact with the girls that are not his daughter, sister, mother, or his wife."

We looked at Babaji for a rebuttal, but he was quiet. The members of the *jirga* talked and argued as we sat very obediently cross-legged on the floor of the mosque. The evening prayers were fast approaching.

Babaji announced the final decision, "Amina can stay because the teachers are her father and uncle, and none of the boys in her class are over fourteen. Daughters Azra and Sanna and any other girl who is still nine years old, and therefore still not an adult, can also be allowed to stay for one more year. The rest of the girls, who have crossed the age of ten, will have to leave the school."

I immediately looked at Sadia, who was still sobbing with her face hidden between her knees.

Babaji was not finished yet. "Is there any issue with an all-girls school with no boys around?"

After a brief thought, Imam Sahib responded, "No, I can't see any issue with a girls' school, except for the problem of the teacher? A man cannot be allowed to teach young women."

"What if we can find a female teacher for the girls' school?" A member of the *jirga* suggested.

After some back-and-forth debating, the *jirga* accepted the proposal. We were especially happy about their decision. Sadia lifted her face, her eyes were still puffy but her tears had dried up. Even she left the mosque with a hopeful smile on her faces. A school for girls only with a lady teacher—we didn't expect such a victory.

Eight

HOOKED

Baba and Chacha started playing squash more frequently. Zameer's training was getting intense. He always complained that he didn't have good shoes. On his next visit to Noor Chacha in Bannu, Baba took Zameer along to buy him a new pair. Noor Chacha was an accomplished squash player. In Bannu, he played at those fancy courts. He used to teach Baba and Chacha at our homemade court. Ever since I was little, I had seen squash being taught.

Baba and Zameer were gone, and the house was quiet without them. There was a lot of work at the orchard. All the trees needed to be watered regularly, and the ground around them had to be plowed and fertilized. The shipment of fertilizer arrived right after Baba and Zameer left. Our uncles and cousins helped us with the spreading of the fertilizer. Plowing around hundreds of trees by hand is a backbreaking job. The ground gets very hard during winter. In between all the plowing and digging, I would sneak out and hit some squash shots. Baba had taken his racket with him to play with Noor Chacha. But Zameer couldn't be bothered to take his, and I knew where he kept it. I played happily without any fear—all by myself—because Mamma was busy in the house and the orchard. I practiced all the shots that Baba had told Zameer to practice. I was learning to play accurate low-drop shots, just above the line, and my lobs were steady and high into the back of the court. Perfecting a shot was such a thrill to me. Baba returned after a few days and immediately got busy at the orchard. Zameer couldn't stop showing off his shoes—real squash shoes.

"You know, even Baba and Chacha don't have real squash shoes," Zameer boasted.

To my surprise, they brought two new squash rackets. Not completely new though, they were Noor Chacha's used rackets.

"Can you give one of these rackets to me?" I asked Baba.

"What do you need a squash racket for?" He brushed my question aside. "You don't play squash, and you shouldn't play squash. It is a man's sport. It is a hard and tiring. Girls are not strong enough to play it. Look at yourself, you are so small and frail, you won't even be able to land your serve in the opposite end of the court," he said sternly, most likely staring at me from behind his sunglasses.

"I will show you that girls play squash, I have seen it on TV myself," I argued back.

"Those are girls from different countries. They are not like us. Our girls can't dress up in those squash shorts and undershirts. How can they play in baggy *shalwar* and *kameez*, and how will they wrap their chador around their heads?" he asked me sarcastically, scratching his beard.

I didn't know the answer. He was right about the clothing. I tripped in my baggy *shalwar* quite often. The chador was not a big problem because I could neatly tie it around my waist. It even helped me to keep my loose *kameez* tied together. I myself wondered often, *how these girls dare come on TV—dressed in such skimpy clothing while thousands of men watch them. Don't they feel any shame in showing so much of their skin in public?*

Baba, Chacha, and Zameer took advantage of longer days and played squash daily. I just sat on the rooftop day after day and watched them. I would get my younger cousins to do the running and ball picking. The harder I tried to think about baking naan or grilling kebabs, or about cleaning the house and washing clothes, the more I found myself playing imaginary squash or cricket matches. For weeks, I would even avoid going anywhere near the squash court or the cricket field, but it never took me long to give into my temptations.

One day Baba was teaching Zameer the drops and drive in both forehand and backhand. I knew those shots well and could do them better than Zameer. "You practice your drops and lobs alone. I have to go somewhere," Baba instructed as he left the court.

I grabbed Baba's racket and started playing against Zameer. He was wearing his new squash shoes, while I was playing in my house slippers. Every time I had to sprint to the ball, my feet would slip a little in my loose slippers. Despite my handicap, I would get to the ball to smash it back. I always knew where he was going to hit his next shot.

Barely an hour passed when Zameer came up with one of his lame excuses. "My shoes are still stiff, and they are hurting my feet, so I have to stop."

"Come on, you have real squash shoes that even Baba and Chacha don't have. How can they hurt you?" I pestered him.

Over the last few months, Zameer had lost against me in every match that we had played together. He didn't like to lose. Losing to a girl, and that too to his own little sister, was especially hard for him to accept. Each time he lost, he would come up with one excuse or another. It was inevitable that I would surpass him in squash. It was a chore that he had to do because of Baba's and Chacha's pressure. For me, it had become an obsession.

One evening, Zameer and I were playing a squash match. He was on the brink of losing badly to me when a younger cousin of ours screamed from the rooftop, "The baby has arrived!"

Zameer looked relieved that he got out of another defeat by me, but he was completely baffled by the news. He had no clue about any baby. I knew well what baby my cousin was screaming about. I ran to Chacha's house. A baby girl had been born there. I was the happiest of all.

"You have always wanted a sister, and now you have got one," Chacha told me, putting my newborn baby cousin into my lap.

"Will you be able to take care of her?" he asked me with a proud smile.

"Yes, Chacha, you don't need to worry about that. My biggest wish has come true, and you will see what a good big sister I will be to her," I replied enthusiastically.

I just wanted to keep the baby girl with me all the time. I was so possessive over her that even Chachee used to get annoyed sometimes. I just wanted to do everything for her. Not surprisingly, no matter how hard she would be crying, she would calm down as soon as I held her. God forbid, if Zameer ever came near her, her screams would pierce all the walls of our house. We all wondered how she could sense his presence around her and why she cried so hard.

She was several months old, and the whole family was trying to find a name for her. We all came up with lots of name, but someone or another objected. Chacha and Chachee wanted the honor of naming the baby to go to Mather-Khubi. But her choices were all so funny-sounding. As soon as she would propose a name, I would come up with a rhyming word that the kids in her school would be able to tease her with. The name would be immediately dropped.

"Zeena—how about we name her Zeena?" Mather-Khubi suggested.

I objected, "All her life, she will be teased Zeena Mena, and *mena* means quail. Would you want people to tease her by calling her a quail?"

Mather-Khubi dropped the name, just like all the others that she had rejected because of my objections. I kept on coming up with name after name for her—I wanted the best name in the whole world for her.

"Siama sounds just right for her," I told Mather-Khubi one afternoon while she was baking naans at the tandoor.

"That sounds very good. We will call her Siama and see how everyone feels about it," she said with excitement.

"Let me take Siama," I asked Chachee before the dinner.

Sounding surprised and happy, Chachee asked, "Siama! That sounds just right for her. Who has come up with this name?"

"Amina has suggested this to me, and I like it. I think we should name her Siama," Mather-Khubi said.

"As long as you approve, I am happy with the name Siama," Chachee told Mather-Khubi, handing over the baby to me.

I felt extremely delighted and proud that I gave the name to my favorite person. I would carry the baby around the whole *kot* and would find some excuse or another to tell everyone that I gave the baby her name. Some people didn't believe me at first because names are given by the parents or the grandparents, not by some child of the family. For months, whenever someone addressed Siama in front of me, I would make sure to tell them that I named the baby.

As always, Noor Chacha surprised us. He came to visit us for a week, mainly to see baby Siama. I knew that there would be a lot of squash. They played before breakfast, after breakfast, before lunch, and after lunch, then into the evening. Of course, I was on the roof watching their matches. One evening, as Baba and Noor Chacha were playing a hard match, I started rooting for Noor Chacha. He didn't need my cheering. If anyone, it was Baba who was clearly in need of some moral support because he was struggling. In the low light of the evening and with his sunglasses on, Baba was having difficulty seeing the ball. He lost match after match.

Without realizing it, I started yelling during their rallies, "Drop, come on, drop," "Lob cross court," "Play a boast."

Every time I would tell Noor Chacha what to do, he would look up at me.

I better shut up before one of them comes yelling at me, I warned myself.

Suddenly, they stopped. I knew that I was in big trouble.

"Come on down into the court," commanded Noor Chacha seriously.

"I am sorry. I will not disturb you again," I apologized.

"No, I want you to come down into the court," he insisted.

As I entered the court, he took the racket from Baba and handing it over to me he said, "Now play. Show me all those shots that you were screaming about from the rooftop."

"I have never played with anyone, other than practice with Zameer a few times," I told him.

I looked at Baba; he only looked amused. He knew that Noor Chacha was having some fun with me. I was not sure what Noor Chacha wanted, but I obeyed.

After playing for only a few minutes, Noor Chacha stopped. I was mentally prepared to get a harsh scolding from Baba for disturbing them, but instead, Noor Chacha ordered, "Zameer, bring your shoes here."

Zameer, who wouldn't let me lay even a finger on his shoes, did so immediately—no one ever said no to Noor Chacha. I knew very well that it would be the first and the last time I could ever touch those shoes. I quickly put them on. They were a little loose. Baba got me some cotton buds to stuff into the shoes. The shoes were still loose, but I didn't complain. I couldn't believe how fast I could run on the court with those shoes. Noor Chacha and I played several games together. I was getting tired, but I didn't want anyone to notice, especially Baba. I wanted to prove to him that I wasn't as frail as he thought. Zameer wanted to play, but Noor Chacha didn't finish with me until it was dark and we were called in for dinner.

"Amina, you should play squash seriously," blurted Noor Chacha in front of everyone at the dinner.

Baba smiled, while both Mamma and Mather-Khubi simply ignored him altogether. As far as I was concerned, this announcement embarrassed me in front of the whole family, but he didn't seem to notice.

"Drill with her every day. She has top-notch squash talent—I know a talent when I see one. I am surrounded by new and old squash players every single day, all day long," he declared, facing Baba.

Noor Chacha liked to use the English terms like "top-notch" at any chance he got. I guessed that the people in the city spoke differently from us. After a minute or two of silence, he continued, "Train with her for a few months, and then I want to have her play at my club in Bannu. We will see how she handles some of the good players there, and who knows, the club might want her to play for them."

Mamma had been sitting silently through all his talk, but at this point, she jumped in, "Have you completely lost your mind Noor? Are you asking our girl to go out of our home, out of our village, and play a man's sport in a foreign town in front of hundreds of strangers?"

She barely finished her sentence when Mather-Khubi took over. "Living away from home has made you lose all respect for our traditions. That is why we want you to move back home. You can forget about your ridiculous scheme. Our daughter is not going anywhere until she gets married." Mather-Khubi stopped to take a breath.

Noor Chacha went on, "You all don't know where the rest of the world is heading. Women are going to colleges, they are flying airplanes, they are fighting wars, they are becoming presidents and prime ministers, and—"

Mather-Khubi interrupted, "Keep your speech to yourself. Don't you know that a girl from a respectable family only leaves her home twice? The first one is when she is taken from her father's home to her husband's house and the second time is when she is moved from her husband's house to her grave?"

Mamma stormed out of the room toward the courtyard and I followed her. "Don't you worry, Mamma, I am not going anywhere," I told her, wrapping my arms around her.

As I looked back toward the room, I saw Noor Chacha and Baba arguing intensely. I couldn't hear them, but I was sure it was about me and my squash.

Noor Chacha left for Bannu, and we got back to our routine life. Baba only drilled with Zameer, and I continued playing either alone or occasionally against Zameer, making sure that no one else would catch me playing. Every time I played with him, I begged him not to tell anyone. Other than trying to keep it a secret, my biggest problems were my feet. I only had my house slippers or my school shoes, and neither was right for playing squash. In my slippers, my feet slipped on every sprint, while my school shoes were so hard that I would get blisters every single time. I would wait a couple of days for my blisters to heal, during which time I had to play again in my house slippers. I practiced shots that Noor Chacha had showed me, and I got better by the day. Whenever my feet hurt, I would think of the time when I played wearing Zameer's shoes. His shoes were loose on me, but I felt like I was running on a soft cushy comforter and all the twists and turns during the game were so effortless.

"Can I please borrow your squash shoes to play again?" I begged Zameer. "You can take anything that I have—anything at all that belongs to me," I offered in return.

"No. I don't want you to use my shoes ever. You will break them. I know," he replied, not even looking straight at me.

As we got into the next game, I heard someone coming toward the courts. *Oh my god, is it Baba or, Mamma?*

My heart pounded as I hid in the corner. The door creaked open, and Baba's face appeared. To my utter surprise, he shut the door and left without saying a word to us. I didn't understand why he didn't scold me for playing squash and using his racket but I couldn't be happier.

It was one of those regular school days, and we had just returned from school. "Amina, after finishing your meal, come to the squash court," Baba casually told me before heading that way. "Yes, Baba, I will be there—you go ahead," I responded obediently.

As promised, I finished my lunch and got to the court. I was about to climb the stairs to get to the rooftop when I heard Baba yelling from inside the court. "Don't go up there, come into the court instead. Completely baffled, I walked into the court. Hit some shots with me, and here is your own racket," he told me, handing over one of the used-rackets that he had brought back from Bannu.

He gently lobbed a few balls at me and noticed my returns. In no time, our back-and-forth shots created a beautiful rhythm. But suddenly, he stopped. That's it? He just wanted to tease me a little to have some fun, I suspected.

"Go get Zameer's squash shoes," he ordered.

Looking at Zameer's furrowed face added five years to my life. *I will see how he gets out of letting me use his shoes now*, I thought.

"Hand me your shoes," I said, unable to hide my thrill.

He obeyed quickly while looking deep inside my eyes as if telling me, "Make no mistake. I will get even with you for this."

I started to put them on, but Baba stopped me. He knew that they were too loose on me. He remembered stuffing cotton in them the last time I used them while playing with Noor Chacha.

"Go bring me a pencil and sheet of paper," he ordered Zameer.

What could be that for? I wondered.

"Put your foot on the paper," he said, and then he traced around my foot. "I will go and see if the store has any shoes in your size," he told me before leaving.

He returned empty-handed. The village store didn't have any runners at all. Next day at school, he asked around if anyone had runners in my size. After school, he went to look at some shoes using the trace of my foot to match the size. One family had a pair that their son had outgrown. Baba bought those for me. Those shoes were also a bit loose on me, but they fit me well after Baba stuffed some cotton in them. We played all evening, and I am sure that I played my best squash that evening.

"I will keep my new shoes and the racket by my side when I go to sleep," I announced. I did exactly that. Several times during the night, I woke up to check if those shoes and the racket were real and not just a dream of mine.

Baba started including me, along with Zameer, in the training. Chacha also helped. Baba and Chacha practiced squash with me for a couple of hours each day. I didn't know what changed Baba's mind. I guessed it had to be Noor Chacha. I noticed big improvements in my shots. Within a few days, I learned all new ways to play drops, drives, lobs, and smashes. Baba and Chacha helped me with my speed and accuracy. They didn't show as much excitement and enthusiasm about my game as they did about Zameer's, but I didn't complain. I was in shock that I could play openly. Defeating Zameer was easier than I expected, but with Baba and Chacha as opponents, I still struggled. I was not able to win against them, though I did make them run around the court a lot.

Nine

BABA'S DEFEAT

The *jirga* asked Baba and Imam Sahib to take charge of the girls' school project. They didn't try to find a woman teacher from our own village since it was known to all that not a single woman in the whole village could read or write, let alone teach others. They started by asking around in the neighboring villages for a female teacher. The result was the same. Most of the women in the whole region couldn't read or write. They found a few capable ladies who could potentially teach girls, but they were either not willing or were not allowed to leave their *kots* and villages. Our only hope rested on the chance of finding a lady teacher from the city of Bannu.

Baba asked Noor Chacha to look for a lady teacher. In Bannu, there were many women qualified as teachers, but we didn't think anyone would want to leave the city and move to our village.

"We'll never find a lady teacher to come to live in our village," Sadia glumly reminded us every day.

"No, no, Baba will find someone to come from Bannu. There are thousands of good teachers there," I kept reassuring her while not feeling all that sure myself.

Many months had passed since the *jirga*'s decision. Winter had made way for spring, and even spring was heading into summer with no progress in our search. We were losing hope and getting on with our routine lives.

Woodpeckers and sparrows were everywhere. In the orchard, their pecking and chirping created its own music, but we had to watch out for them. They are good for the trees, as they eat most of the insects, but at the same time, they can ruin a tree. You get less fruit from a badly pecked tree. As spring neared its end and summer made its way in, our work at the orchard got harder. We would go straight there from the school.

There was a lot to be done, and every pair of hands was badly needed. We didn't play much cricket or football those days. Instead, we pruned and watered the trees, treated the infested ones, and erected support for those that were too weak to stand by themselves. Worst of all, we had to do the backbreaking job of pulling out weeds. Evenings were getting longer, but most of the days, we worked until dark. We thought that we had it particularly bad, but other children would challenge us.

Sadia argued to prove that her life was harder, "You are lucky! The work at orchards is so short and easy. Try working in a cornfield. You plow the land and sow the seeds. Then you have to check the seedlings for insects and pests many times a day. It doesn't end there. You also have to do the backbreaking job of pulling out the weeds and chase away wild animals. The work there is never finished."

How could Zia ever let anyone else have the last word? To top everyone off, he would scream in his screeching voice, "Your complaints make no sense. The work at an orchard or a cornfield is easy and clean. Try dragging a stubborn sheep back to its barn in the evening. After that, go into the barn to clean it. The stench there would make you gag."

Some evenings when we were all done with the farm-work and got home early enough, we would all go to Chacha's house to watch some TV. Many children didn't finish their homework. All of them had the same excuse that after working with their parents, they got too tired to stay up late to do their lessons. Baba scolded them for not completing their homework, but nothing would change. Some days, even Zameer and I didn't finish. We would get back from the orchard late, and then after dinner, we would just fall asleep.

Baba practiced squash with my brother and me. We would get up early in the morning to play a little before getting ready for school. Some evenings, if we could get home before dark, we also practiced together. Chacha joined us most of the time. I loved my training. No matter how tired or sleepy I felt, I still ran to the court. Often, whether he wanted to go or not, I would drag Baba with me.

Chacha and I decided to play an early morning match—just a quick best-of-three games. I won the first game, and then he struggled in the second one. I made him run to the four corners until he started making mistake after mistake. I played my best squash, and points fell one after another into my account. With a precise lob into the back corner of the court, I won my very first match against him.

"You played so well. Your lobs were just at the right angle and pace," he told me, patting me on my shoulders.

Right after that, my next goal was to defeat Baba at squash. I started by winning more and more points, and then I progressed to winning games—one out of five or one out of three games. Then one evening, Baba and I began a match. He started off strong and won the first game, followed by the second, but then he slowed down. I still think he got tired. He was recovering from a bad cold that we all had. I won the next three games, thereby the match.

"I have defeated my baba!" I screamed after my winning shot.

That evening is permanently etched into my memory. I had won against Baba and Chacha, and by then, my brother had already stopped playing me. He had been losing against me for months and didn't want any further humiliation. He would always make excuses that left me to play against Baba or Chacha.

Noor Chacha came to visit us again. As he opened his bags, Zameer and I waited nearby for our treats of fruits and sweets that he always brought for us from the city. He pulled out a bag of oranges and gave it to Zameer.

Nothing for me today? I stared at his face, wondering.

"I am sorry! I forgot to bring the sweets that you like. You should ask Zameer to share his oranges with you," he consoled me—reading the disappointment on my face.

"Zameer sharing anything with me—that never happens," I told him in a whiny voice.

He replied, "Amina, close your eyes and, honestly, no peeking. Then put both your hands out. This is sweet, but don't eat it," he told me, putting something in my hands.

"It is a squash racket!" I screamed even before I opened my eyes. I trembled with excitement, while everyone else looked amused.

"For me?" I asked—just to confirm.

"Yes, it is your own squash racket," he replied with a twinkle in his eyes.

"My very own squash racket?" I repeated my question just to hear him say yes again. I quickly unzipped the racket cover. But there was no racket in here. I was about to cry with disappointment.

"Oh no! They forgot to put a racket in here. They gave me an empty cover only. I am so angry at the store," he told me looking very upset. I was in tears. I couldn't believe my bad luck. Why me? Why did the store cheat him for my racket? He then opened his bag and pulled out a beautiful new racket. "You are so gullible. Here you go! I can't torture you any longer," he said while everyone laughed themselves silly. My sorrow turned into jubilation in no time.

"There is still daylight left. Please come play squash with me," I begged of him.

He looked at Baba. Although there was much work left in the orchard, Baba didn't ask me to work with him. I ran and quickly fetched my runners.

"These shoes are so fast, I can cover the whole court in seconds," I told him proudly while showing off my running speed in the courtyard.

Noor Chacha and I played several games. He was thrilled to see me play. I didn't win, but I gave him some good games.

"Fantastic play," he said, again using English words which I didn't understand, but reading his facial expression, I guessed what he meant.

"I want you to come to Bannu and play at my club. I will get you a squash coach," he dropped another one of his bombshell.

Walking a yard ahead of me to find Baba, he told me, "I know! I know! I will have to talk to your baba first. But he has to accept."

At dinner, while the whole family was sitting down to eat, my heart was thumping with panic. Knowing Noor Chacha I feared, *He will not wait for a good opportunity but will blurt out whatever is on his mind. If he brings up my going to Bannu to play squash at a time when everyone is tired and preoccupied with the work at the orchard, it will not go well. Mamma is sure to reject the idea outright.*

Sure enough, even before taking his first bite, he spilled out all that was on his mind in one breath. "Send Amina to Bannu, and I will get her into my squash club. We have some good coaches there, and she will learn top-notch squash in no time. Pass me those naans. The food looks delicious, and I am very hungry."

Everyone had frozen in their spots, staring at him, while he casually mixed his food on his plate.

I cringed, *He is sure to get a no if he asks like this.*

"These days, there is a lot of work at the orchard, and we can't come to Bannu, even if we wanted to," replied Baba, breaking a long uncomfortable silence. "Besides, it is not right for her to play squash seriously. Our circumstances will not permit her to become a squash player. You know it as well as I do," added Baba.

Mamma and Mather-Khubi didn't take him seriously enough to even respond.

"I see," he responded casually while continuing to chomp away his food.

After finishing his bite and drinking a big gulp of water, he continued, "Well, the main reason for my visit is to tell you that a lady teacher in Bannu wants to come and visit the village and meet with people involved in the girls' school project. She may come any day."

I was thrilled by the news and couldn't wait to tell Sadia and all the rest of the girls in my class. At school, I made the announcement at the first opportunity I got.

"We are getting a lady teacher for our school. Noor Chacha has found one," I said loudly so that everyone could hear.

"Hmm . . . I'll believe it when I see her," replied Sadia in her typical negative tone.

In the meantime, the workers had been building some rooms on a small plot behind the mosque. It was a much smaller school than the boys' school. That made sense though. In our village there were more boys who attended school, while most girls would never have their family's permission to go further than the fourth year.

Ten

RAY OF HOPE

With the hard work at the orchard draining every ounce of energy, no one felt in the mood for squash those days. After school, we would head straight to the orchard. Mamma would bring our food there, and we would eat sitting under the cool shade of mulberry trees. On a very hot day, the deep shade and sweet smell of fruits are among the best pleasures one can experience. Most days, our parents dozed off for a brief nap under the trees, while we ran around playing hide-and-seek. Sometimes I sneaked out to the squash court to practice my shots. Playing squash, even on my own, under the baking afternoon sun used to test the limits of my endurance. Every few minutes, I would seek a shade, any shade—to take a minute or two break.

The apricots were ripening up fast. We picked, cleaned, and packed them in baskets to send those to the city. We also dried much of our ripe apricots and mulberries by spreading them on big sheets under the sun. A truck driver took our fruit twice a week. Dried apricots and mulberries sold very well. Baba packed up large baskets of the freshest fruits and personally delivered them to the poor people of the village. He said that doing so would bring blessings to our orchards. Zameer and I delivered bags of fresh fruits to our neighbors as gifts.

The fruit picking was coming to an end, and so was the school year. The girls of my class were not sure what our future held for us, and some even wondered if they would set foot in a school ever again. Sadia was devastated. She was not looking forward to the vacation anyway. Staying at home, working in the field all day long, and getting beatings from her baba were all that she could foresee in her home life. The little break that she got by coming to school was being taken away from her. I felt very sad for her.

We had just started our summer vacations when, one day, there was a big commotion in the village center. A little boy came running to our house to fetch Baba. He was wanted at the village store. Baba changed and left as fast as he could. Zameer and I tagged along. A lady teacher had come with her husband to see the school and meet with the people involved. After a long wait, Imam Sahib showed up. Food and tea were served to the guests. Baba asked her about her teaching experience. Imam Sahib asked her many religious questions while they toured the school.

"How many girls will be at the school?" she asked.

Baba, Babaji, and Imam Sahib looked at one another as they didn't know what to tell her. No one knew how many parents would allow their girls to go to the school.

She told everyone present there, "I am very passionate about teaching girls. It is my life's mission to teach as many girls as possible. For that, I am ready to go through almost any hardship."

Laying out her only condition for accepting the position, she said, "I also want to teach the women of the village, and I want some women helpers for the school."

"This is not possible. Our women don't go outside the house to work under any circumstance," replied Imam Sahib.

"We should put this to *jirga* before rejecting it on our own," Babaji intervened.

Several members of the *jirga* were gathered in a hurry. After a quick consultation, they rejected her demand. "We cannot allow our women to go out of their homes to work," announced Babaji on behalf of the *jirga*. "You have to understand that we don't want our women to be involved in activities for which they have to leave their houses. If women are gone all day, who would cook and clean and, most importantly, look after small children?" he explained apologetically to her.

As she sat quietly, looking down at the floor, my heart raced. The idea of a girls' school was dying right in front of my eyes.

"I understand. I will do it all alone," she broke the painful silence. As I was about to scream with joy, she went on, "One more thing though . . ."

"Now what?" I murmured a bit too loudly, trying to control my impatience.

"My husband wants to buy a small parcel of land to set up a small leather factory," she explained, pointing toward her husband. "He has to earn a living too," she justified.

After a brief discussion, Babaji again announced the communal decision, "The *jirga* has no objection to that. You are free to buy any land that you need. We will all use our influence to help you in this venture of yours."

With that, the *jirga* meeting ended, and everyone left feeling satisfied. I was thrilled. I couldn't wait to tell Sadia that she had been wrong all along, and we were going to have our school after all.

Over the next several months, her husband approached many people in the village to buy the land for his factory, but no one was willing to sell one to him. Most people were utterly opposed to selling their land under any circumstance. Furthermore, there was a very strong opposition to the idea of having a leather factory in the village. People feared that the factory would make our air and water dirty, which in turn would affect the quality of grains, vegetables, and fruit produced in and around the village. I was so desperate for my school that I didn't care about our food, air, or water. I just prayed every day for the success of our future teacher's plans. Finally, after much searching, a family reluctantly offered to sell a part of their land to the teacher's husband for his leather factory. Over the years they had tried and tried again to cultivate on that land without success. We were thrilled by the news. Everything would work out now, we thought. But things didn't work out so easily in our village. The two parties couldn't agree on a price. Negotiation after negotiation, mediated by Babaji, went on for several weeks. Our hopes would rise and fall each day like a fast-flying bird.

In summers, we slept in the courtyard under the open sky. After sundown, the ground was sprayed with water to cool it down. Then a row of beds were laid out, one for each member of the family. The fragrance that arose from the hot ground after the water spray is amongst one of my most treasured memories. So is the image of the sky loaded with twinkling star that looked like a beautifully embroidered dress of a bride.

I lay on my bed gazing at the twinkle of those stars, remembering what Mather-Khubi had repeatedly told us, *"Each person's life story is written on one star, but no one, except Allah, knows which star belongs to which person."* I lay there wondering what star held my secrets and if there was any squash or more schooling written for me on my star. It was a beautiful evening. After a very hot day, the temperature cooled down, with a pleasant breeze possibly coming straight from the heavens. My bed was right next to that of Mather-Khubi's, while Zameer's bed was on our right, Mamma's on our left, and Baba's bed was the last on the other side toward the squash court.

Mather-Khubi started telling us a story. She started the story of Nawaz Khan, but I objected, "Please tell us the story of Razia Sultan tonight. You haven't told that story in weeks now." Zameer objected, but that night, Mather-Khubi told us the story that I wanted to hear.

"Once, many centuries ago, the kingdom of Delhi was ruled by a very kind and just king named Altamash. He ruled his subjects fairly. He was also very brave and fought many wars to defend and expand his kingdom. At home, he groomed his son to take his place after him, but the son died before the father. He also had a beautiful daughter named Razia and a younger son. After his eldest son died, the king started grooming Razia to rule his kingdom after him. The nobles didn't accept his decision. When the king died, Razia became the next king. She forbade people to call her by the title sultana because it meant the wife of a sultan or a queen only. She demanded to be called Razia Sultan because she was the ruler herself and not merely the wife of the ruler. She followed in her father's footsteps and ruled fairly and wisely. She made many alliances. She even married the ruler of a neighboring kingdom to form an alliance with them. But her enemies didn't spare her. The nobles didn't give up their resistance. They conspired against her and imposed many wars on her. Razia led every war that her army fought. She was a very brave warrior herself. The nobles formed an alliance with her younger brother and attacked her again. Their armies were much stronger than that of Razia Sultan's. She fought fiercely, but at the end, her army was defeated, and she was killed. Her bravery in the battlefield is legendary. Even after her death, the enemy soldiers dared not come near her body. They used a long stick to check if she was completely dead. So ends the story of the most famous Muslim woman king of India."

As Mather-Khubi finished her story, Baba walked in. He settled in his freshly made bed and started talking to Mamma.

I interrupted, "Any news about the land deal for our teacher's husband?"

With a deep sigh, he replied, "We are not going to get the teacher after all. The teacher's husband tried his best, but his best was not good enough for the landowner."

The sadness and the disappointment of losing our battle for a girls' school was devastating for me. I couldn't imagine and did not want to imagine how poor Sadia was going to take the news. I certainly didn't want to be the one delivering it to her. I fell asleep fighting my sobs.

Eleven

THE BANNU CLUB

The sun had already set, but we were still working in the orchard. Baba was digging around the tree right next to me. That's when he told me the good news.

"This Friday, I will take you and Mather-Khubi to Bannu and leave you two there until school reopens."

Such good news in the midst of all that gloom was what I needed to cheer up. I started counting hours and minutes to our travel day. It felt like forever, but finally, Friday's sun rose. We got ready and went to the bus stop well ahead of time, but the bus was a few hours late. The ride turned out to be beautiful. By the time we got near Bannu, the sun was setting between two mountains. Noor Chacha's house was not far from the bus station. We arrived at his house just after dark with empty stomachs because we didn't eat anything all day. After washing up, we enjoyed a delicious dinner that Noor Chacha's wife had prepared for us.

"Can we still go and play squash tonight, or is it too late for today?" I asked him, hoping that he might find a way to take me to his club.

"I can't tell you how I wish you had arrived before sundown. I reserved a court for us, but now, unfortunately, it is too late." He sounded clearly disappointed but said reassuringly, "We must all go to sleep early tonight. I will take you there tomorrow before the club opens to the rest of the people."

We left well before sunrise. Noor Chacha wanted to play before regular hours of the club. He was not allowed to take any court that regular members might use. At the club, he handed me a set of used sweatpants, sweatshirt, and a pair of squash shoes in my size. I had never imagined wearing an outfit like that in my entire life. I had not even seen a girl wearing such strange clothes in real life. I looked at Baba with those clothes in my hand. He nodded. This was the reassurance I needed.

I changed into them. The sweat suit fit me well, but I felt extremely awkward walking around in those clothes. It seemed like every single eye was gazing at my body. Getting in that squash court and hitting the ball was a relief for me. My mind was focused on my game instead of my outfit. After I played for an hour, it was Zameer's turn, followed by Baba's. Even after playing against me and my brother, Noor Chacha was not tired. He won easily against Baba.

"We have to finish up. Members will start coming in soon, and I have to go around, making sure that all the equipment is in its place before that. Quickly, gather your belongings and don't leave anything lying around," he instructed before going around to inspect each court.

As people started arriving, he greeted them and introduced us to them. Most of them seemed to know of me. He had been bragging about my game to them for months. I spent every possible minute at the club, drilling alone or with Noor Chacha, playing with him or with Baba, or just sitting around watching other people's games. I happily helped Noor Chacha with whatever I could.

He approached every player at the club. "Can you please play a few games with my niece? She is a skilled player and will give you a decent game."

Only three of them obliged him. The rest couldn't be bothered to play against a young girl from a village in Waziristan. My trip could not have been timed better though. There was a two-day interclub tournament. Players from the whole region were competing. I watched match after match. I quickly became a fan of the girls from the world-famous Peshawar Club. Simin and Sonya were their top players, and then Asma and Nadia were their B team players. I did not miss a single match of theirs. Their game was so fast and intense that I failed to even appreciate it completely.

"Do you think I could get my picture with them?" I murmured to Noor Chacha while watching one of their matches. I knew that he didn't have a camera because cameras are very expensive, and only the rich own one.

After a brief pause, he told me with a smile, "I can borrow a camera from one of the members here. But you will have to ask the girls for the picture." I was very excited and looked for my chance.

After each game, I would squeeze through the crowd, getting near them, but every time, they darted away, leaving me behind. Finally, I made it to the front before their match ended. Shaking Nadia's hands just at the right moment, when she was leaving the court, I asked, "Can I have a picture with you, please?"

"Okay, let us wait until others get here too," Asma replied for Nadia.

Noor Chacha got the camera all set. Simin and Sonya were heading our way. Asma signaled to them to come faster for the picture. In response, Simin yelled back some words in English from the far end of the court which I couldn't understand. Before I could ask them for an explanation, Asma and Nadia took off without saying a word to me. I couldn't hide my teary eyes.

The week flew by, and we returned home. The school reopened. I made history. For the first time ever, girls sat alongside the boys in the fifth grade of our village school. Although we were only three girls, among thirty boys, I still felt proud and very happy. We knew it was a temporary arrangement while we waited for a lady teacher to come and start the all-girls school as approved by the *jirga*. We considered ourselves as the luckiest girls in the village and held high hopes that, sooner or later, a lady teacher would be found.

My life went back to my old routine. And no one could have been happier than I was to be able to have my routine back. It was a miracle that had happened. School in the mornings, housework in the afternoons, and homework in the evenings, with some playtime in between, I only dreamt about having that routine. At school, I still played cricket, football, and *pitho* ball, but my heart was completely into squash. Although after having played at a court in Bannu, our homemade court felt terrible.

I did not miss any opportunity to play squash with Zameer, Baba, or Chacha. Mamma and Mather-Khubi were still bitterly against my playing squash. Mamma's anger flared when she saw me wearing those sweatpants and the sweatshirt. She worried that someone in the village might see me wearing those strange men's clothing, and our good name would be ruined. She was also worried that other women would taunt her for my boyish behavior. I was extra cautious to avoid being seen in those clothes.

Playing squash became my full-time obsession. "I daydream about playing squash and people watching my game on TV," I told Baba.

"Dreams with open eyes bring bad luck," he responded.

One bitterly cold morning, as I walked toward the school, I heard Sanna yelling my name from behind me. I stopped to let her catch up with me.

"My cousin from the city is coming to visit us," she told me, practically out of breath.

"Oh, that is so fun. I love when my cousins come to visit. Did you finish all your homework?" I asked casually.

"No, you don't understand. My cousin might live with us," she yelled, staring into my eyes.

"That is nice. I feel so sad when my cousins leave," I said, sighing while still walking fast toward the school.

"She might turn out to be the teacher that we have been praying for our girls' school. Why can't you think? Where is your head most of the time?" she scolded.

I abruptly stopped walking and turned around to come face-to-face with her. I asked her angrily, "Why didn't you tell me that in the first place? This is the most important news of our lives. You should have screamed to me the moment you saw me that we are getting a new teacher instead of talking about some cousin's visit."

Sanna chided, explaining to me, "That is what I was trying to tell you if you had only paid attention. Don't you remember her? I have talked about her many times. She is my only cousin who lives in the city, and she has studied many higher grades. She is expected to arrive any day now. We are just waiting for the roads to reopen. Do you know that the road to our village has been closed for weeks due to bad weather?"

"Will you let me meet her as soon as she arrives?" I made Sanna promise me that.

At school, we shared the good news with Azra. We even told the girls from the lower grades about our new teacher. All three of us started waiting desperately for our new teacher.

Sanna told us more about her as the days passed. "Her name is Humma. She has passed sixteen grades. And all she wants to do is to teach girls."

Our winter vacation started with still no sign of our teacher. We were anxious to see her, but her trip was delayed twice because of the road closures. The school reopened after the break, and Sanna's cousin still didn't come. We began to lose hope.

One morning as I entered the schoolhouse, daydreaming about my squash shots, I saw Sanna with her grandbaba accompanied by a petite young lady. I knew right away that the lady had to be her cousin, our new teacher whom we had been waiting for all these months.

"Salaam, Teacher Humma," I addressed her, following some inner instinct of mine. She responded to my salaam warmly.

All through the day, she talked to us and watched us going through our school day. She even sat next to me during one of our lessons. During the breaks, she wanted to know how many other girls might be able to join the new school. Once she heard about Sadia, then all she wanted to do was to talk about her.

"I will start your school this year, no matter what I have to do for that. I will be your teacher," she promised us.

The *jirga* met to discuss the new teacher. All was well, except that Teacher Humma's knowledge of Islam was not satisfactory to Imam Sahib.

"We cannot entrust our children to a teacher with such poor knowledge of our religion," declared Imam Sahib.

"She is going to be a schoolteacher only and not the imam of the mosque," argued Babaji sarcastically.

After an hour of arguments between them, an agreement was reached. Teacher Humma was asked to improve her religious knowledge by attending our madrassa in her free time.

"You will be tested from time to time to make sure that you uphold the values and traditions of Islam," declared Imam Sahib.

Ironically, she not only became our teacher, but at the same time, she became a fellow student at the girls' madrassa.

Twelve

FRUIT OF LABOR

There was no time to waste. School opened. Girls of all ages were asked to show up at the new school immediately. The celebrations started with the recitation of the Koran. Babaji brought some sweets and distributed them among all those present. Right after that, our brand new teacher taught her first lesson to all of us together. At the end of our school day, Teacher Humma asked me about Sadia again.

"What do we need to do in order to get Sadia to join our school?" She wanted to know.

"I will stop by her house on my way home to tell her and, more importantly, to her family that you want her in the school," I assured Teacher Humma.

As promised, I went to Sadia's house. Her mamma was working in the yard. After my salaams, I asked to see Sadia.

"She is not well. She is sleeping inside the house. You can go in and see her," she told me.

"Sadia, it's me, Amina." I tried to wake her up.

As she opened her eyes with deep dark circles around them, I could see the gloom piercing out of them. She looked terrible.

"How are you?" I asked, gently holding her hand.

With a very faint voice, she described her condition. "I have had this fever for several days, and my whole body aches like someone has crushed me with heavy rocks."

"Who is taking care of you?" I asked.

"Mamma has been giving me liquid foods and massaging my body, but that is not helping," she replied. "How is the new school, and how is the new teacher? Is she nice and caring?" she asked me with as much excitement as she could express.

"Teacher Humma—oh! She is the best—she wants you to join the school," I delivered the message.

Trying to hold back her tears without much success, she said in a barely audible voice, "Baba doesn't want me to go to school. I am needed at the farm to work, and besides, he insists that I have done enough learning and don't need any more schooling."

I was surprised to hear that, so I asked her angrily, "What has happened to your baba? He fought with the *jirga* to allow girls into the fifth grade, and now that we have a fifth and upper grades for girls, he is not allowing you to go. That is not fair."

All she did in response to my argument was to stare at my face with tears rolling down from the corners of her eyes. I wiped her tears with my fingertips, patted her shoulders, and said my goodbye.

Several months had passed, but our school had very few students. Babaji and Teacher Humma tried to persuade more parents to send their daughters to the school, and they were having some success. Some parents agreed quickly; others needed a lot of persuasion. Every evening, Teacher Humma and Babaji went from house to house to talk to the fathers of the girls. Sometimes Baba and I went along. One evening, we went to Sadia's house. Her baba was respectful but was not willing to listen to any argument that could change his mind about sending Sadia to school. Every point that they put to him, he rejected outright.

"Who does the accounting for all your farm expenses and income and any other paperwork for you?" inquired Teacher Humma in a very gentle tone.

"There is a learned person who does all kinds of paperwork for me. Anything that involves reading, writing or calculations, I take it to him and pay him to do that for me," he responded matter-of-factly.

"If your daughter could learn to read, write, and add and subtract, then she could do all that for you, and you will save all the money that you pay for these services," suggested Teacher Humma.

The idea seemed to make sense to him because he didn't reject it right away as he had done to all other arguments. "Give me some time to think about it," he asked very humbly.

"Of course," Babaji and Teacher Humma responded before asking our leave and saying our salaams. They looked very encouraged leaving Sadia's house.

"I think that he will let Sadia join the school," Babaji shared his optimism.

Babaji's and Teacher Humma's efforts paid off. Within weeks, many more girls joined our school. Teacher Humma struggled with the girls of different ages and different capabilities. There were girls much older than me, who couldn't read or write at all, and girls like Azra, who were well ahead of all others in all the subjects. Those of us who could read and write well—helped those who had never gone to school. All the children of the village knew how to read Arabic from their Koran lessons, which was a great help. It made learning to read and write Urdu fairly easy.

Spring arrived and the work at the farms and orchards picked up pace. Many of the girls stopped coming to school altogether, and most of us who did come didn't do our homework. We would all be too tired to concentrate during the classes. Teacher Humma was not happy with the situation, but she didn't complain. Then one morning, Sadia walked into the school when we were least expecting her. She was all smiles.

She announced in front of the whole class, "I will do my best and will do whatever I can during school, but I am not allowed to do any schoolwork at home."

Teacher Humma agreed to her condition without any hesitation whatsoever. Sadia's return gave us a cause for jubilation.

"With all the farm work these days, how did your baba allow you to join the school?" I asked her.

"I don't know what changed his mind but remember the strict conditions that he has put on me. I hope that Teacher Humma will not get upset with me," she replied.

"Many students are not doing their homework these days, you shouldn't worry about it. Besides, Teacher Humma agreed when you told her in the class," I reassured her.

Teacher Humma assessed each one of us for our weaknesses and strengths and worked with each student as needed. Final exams were fast approaching. She had added extra hours of teaching each day for the students who needed help. I was lucky to get help at home from Baba and Zameer. Then while at my school, I helped girls from the lower grades. With girls helping girls and Teacher Humma's hard work, the results of our school's first final exams were excellent. Every girl passed her grade and was promoted into the next. With the end of the exams, we started our first summer vacation.

Summer was the busiest season in the village. Zameer and I got busy again in our family's orchard. Other children worked all day long in the fields, in their farms, and in their barns. Teacher Humma left the village to go visit her parents in the city. The summer vacation was relatively short, but in that short time, we yearned for our school.

On the first day of the new school year, Teacher Humma brought in an English book that she purchased in the city for us. She allowed each one of us to touch and look inside the book. The book looked very different from all of our books. The pages were glossy, and the pictures were very colorful compared to ours' dull looking and flimsy books. We were all very excited to learn English. We had heard English on TV, but we didn't understand a word of it. Our first lesson was fun. We had a lot of laughs in the class learning to say the English letters. There was a picture of an apple on the page with the letter "a." Except for Azra, no one knew how to say "apple." We all called it *seeb*, the name by which we had called that fruit all our lives. Teacher Humma also had a good laugh that afternoon. The next day, she brought in a pomegranate to the class.

"What is this fruit?" she asked, raising the pomegranate in her hand.

"Annar," the whole class replied in one voice.

"Just remember that is how you say the first English letter, 'a,'" she told us. "Say 'a' as in *annar*." She made us repeat that many times.

She then showed us a cricket ball and asked us to tell her what that was.

"Ball," I responded before anyone else could.

"So 'b' as in ball." She made us repeat after her several times. "C" as in *kameez*, the shirt that we all wear; "d" as in *dela*, the little rocks that we play "rocks and ball" game with; "e" as in English; "f" as in films that we watch on TV; "g" as in *guur*, the fresh sugar that the village storekeeper gives us as a treat; "h" as in *henna* that we use to decorate our hands on weddings and Eid.

Learning English was very funny. She taught us to say all the English letters by relating them to the words that we knew and not the words and the pictures that were printed in that book. Within weeks, we learned how to say all of the English letters. But this was not to last.

Somehow, Imam Sahib found out about our English classes. He showed up and scolded Teacher Humma in front of all the girls, "Why do you want to teach the language of Frangies and infidels to our innocent daughters?" He demanded an answer from her on the spot. Even before Teacher Humma could get in a word, he announced his verdict. "You must stop this right away if you want the school to remain open!" he yelled as he stormed out of the schoolroom.

Teacher Humma was left with no choice but to promise, "Yes, Imam Sahib. No English in the school."

Thirteen

MY COACH

I couldn't have been happier about our girls' school, but I did sometimes miss my old school. None of the girls played cricket. Zameer would tell me that the boys continued to talk about my cricket, *pitho* ball, and football. I wanted the girls to start playing cricket, but we didn't have a bat and a ball, and none of the parents allowed their girls to play these boys' sports, let alone buy them any equipment. I knew that some of the girls could be quite good at these sports if they were allowed to play.

Since all other sports were out of question for me, I concentrated fully on squash. Noor Chacha was very excited about my game. Anytime he came to visit us, he spent most of his time playing against me. He showed me tricks of the game and practiced those with me. He had learned those tricks by watching the high-level players at his club.

"I have lined up a squash coach for you at my club. You just need to get there," he told me while Baba and I were playing a match.

"How is this going to work? Do we send Amina to Bannu, or do we all move there?" asked Baba, addressing Noor Chacha sarcastically.

"I have used all my resources to make this happen. Getting a coach to teach a little village girl was not easy. Now you need to work out the details and bring her there," snapped Noor Chacha. "Remember this offer is not forever. I can't guarantee that this coach will be able to honor his promise in months or years from now," he warned.

Weeks passed, and there was no talk of our visit to Bannu. "When are we going to Bannu?" I would ask Baba frequently to keep the idea alive in his mind.

He would just brush off my question without giving me a definite answer. I didn't give up either and kept pestering him on daily basis. Finally, he promised, "Once your winter vacations start I will take you and Mather-Khubi to Bannu, provided the roads remain open. You can train there for the whole winter."

After a very long and painful wait, one very early morning, Baba, Mather-Khubi, and I went to the bus stop. To our surprise, the bus was on time.

As soon as I saw the bus, the first thought that ran through my mind was, *We might get to Noor Chacha's in time to be able to play some squash.* I knew that Baba was trying his best to hide his excitement about playing squash with his brother before returning back to the village.

We arrived at Noor Chacha's house even before we were expected. He was still at the club working. Mather-Khubi had a terrible headache from the day's travel, so she went to rest right away. Baba could hardly wait to get to the club, and my feelings were exactly the same. Although Baba was not admitting it, in fact, he wanted to get as much squash as he could in that little time that he was spending in Bannu. As we entered the club, Noor Chacha greeted us. He immediately took us to the training court.

"That is Khurram, your squash teacher. He is teaching a student. We should wait here till he comes out. Then I will introduce him to you," he told us.

"Why don't you and I play a few games in the meantime? Amina could wait here, and once Khurram gets done, she can come and get us." Baba suggested predictably.

Noor Chacha looked at me, glanced at Khurram then at his wristwatch, and, after pausing a moment, agreed to go with Baba to a nearby empty court. I was left standing outside the training court, admiring Khurram. He looked very fit with an athletic, muscular body. His long curly hair was tied back, with a headband around his forehead, and he wore a well-trimmed full beard. His demeanor seemed gentle. I noticed that he was giving his student enough time to talk and ask questions. As for his squash skills, I had never seen such smooth movement of arms and feet in real life. His shots were precise, just above the lines, yet it seemed like he was not putting much effort into them. His student ran all over the court as he paced the balls.

While waiting for him, I started assessing different ways of saying my first greetings to him.

"Salam Mr. Khurram sir. No I don't think I should call him by his name. This is too rude. He is my teacher and you don't address teachers by their name.

Salam, teacher. But he is not a school teacher. He may not like this either. I rejected my second idea as well.

Salam Master Sahib. This sounds good and respectful enough. But then this also sounds very school teacherish." I was still going through my list options, when I noticed that he was getting ready to finish his lesson. I dashed to fetch Noor Chacha and Baba.

Noor Chacha introduced Baba and Khurram first. Then it was my turn. "Khurram, this is Amina, your newest student. And Amina, this is your new squash teacher Khurram." Noor Chacha introduced us.

"Salam Master," I said in a very humble tone.

"Walay Kum As Salaam, Amina." He replied in a mild manner. After our salaams and introductions were over, we started talking about my squash. I was relieved that my addressing him as Master went well. Just then his next student arrived.

"I will test your capabilities in the next few days, and then I will decide how to proceed," he told me as he walked away from us.

Over the next few days, my routine was to come to the club with Noor Chacha in the morning and leave with him at night. All day long, I just lingered around at the club. I happily did whatever he told me to do for him, but most of the time, I watched great squash matches one after another. Whenever Noor Chacha would get a chance, he would play and drill with me too. Other than that, I sat and watched Khurram. The more I saw him, the more I got convinced that he was just right for me. After finishing another one of his sessions, he came to me.

"Get into the court and warm up, I will be right back with you," he instructed. "Yes Master," I responded obediently. He looked a little taken aback at my response but then he just walked away without saying a word.

My heart was beating strangely. I could hear my own heartbeats. This had never happened to me before. He returned and asked me to get into the court with him. He lobbed a ball at me. I returned the shot. After hitting for about five minutes, he caught the ball from one of my shots in his left hand and stopped.

"I will be right back, just keep hitting the ball," he said before leaving.

Noor Chacha watched curiously, and I didn't have a clue either. He returned with a new racket.

"Use this racket instead. This is the right grip size for you. Yours' is an adult-sized racket. Its grip is too big for your hand."

"Thank you, Master," I replied gratefully.

We began again, but now I was missing my favorite shots, my drops were all falling below the line, and my lobs were not even clearing half court. *What is happening to me? Why am I playing like an idiot?* I scolded myself. "Water break please." I requested.

"Amina, do you know what you are doing?" Noor Chacha demanded an explanation.

"I haven't got the foggiest idea of what is happening," I explained, wiping off the drops of tears from my cheeks.

"Don't be nervous. Try to calm down," Noor Chacha told me as if that was up to me at all.

"Let's carry on," Khurram suggested.

As I headed toward the court, not knowing what else to do, Noor Chacha intervened on my behalf. "Can she use her old racket? I know that it has a wrong sized grip, but she is used to it."

Without the slightest hesitation, Khurram agreed, "You may be right. Her racket is wrong for her, but we will have to give her time to get used to the right racket. For now, she may continue using her old one."

His gentle response and his understanding attitude just melted my heart. I stared at his face with admiration, but he didn't seem to notice my gaze. He was too focused on my squash form and footwork. He looked much happier with my performance afterward. Together, we hit shots for a good half hour before we walked out of the court.

There, he commented, mostly facing Noor Chacha while addressing me, "You anticipate well, and you are quick on your feet, but many of your shots are totally wrong. I will teach you how to play those correctly."

"Will it take long Master?" I asked.

"In fact, it will be twice as hard. First, you will have to spend a lot of drill time, trying to unlearn your old shots, and only after that you can learn to play those shots the right way," he explained.

I felt dumb drilling several hours each day. I found it very hard to change my old ways. As he coached me, he must have gotten frustrated, but he didn't show any sign of it. I guessed that he was being just nice to me.

My time in Bannu came to an end, and I returned home. The school had already reopened, and I had missed almost two weeks. Teacher Humma was short with me for missing school. However, I couldn't tell her the reason for my absence. Baba and Mamma had not breathed a word of my squash training to anyone. They had told people that Mather-Khubi and I had gone to spend the holidays with Noor Chacha.

Many new girls had joined our school after the holidays. Teacher Humma had trained some of the top students as her helpers for teaching the lower grades. As expected, Azra was practically her right hand. Sadia was struggling because she had missed more days of school than I had. Her parents kept her from school anytime they needed her to work at home.

I was getting confused about my passion for squash. I wondered, *Even in Bannu, there are only a handful of women players. Nearly all of the players there are men. Mamma and Mather-Khubi don't get tired of telling me how terrible it is that I play this sport. Every woman in the village insists that it is a grave sin that I am committing. If it wasn't wrong, then why wouldn't my parents tell people about it? Maybe I should ask Teacher Humma for advice. But if she finds out that I play this sport, she might also think low of me.*

One day, after school, I showed Teacher Humma some work that girls from the lower grades had completed with my help. "Thank you, Amina. You are a good teacher," she commented with a smile.

Summoning all my courage, I blurted out, "Is there anything wrong if a girl plays a men's sport like squash?"

She was definitely taken aback by my abrupt question. I should have given her a little more background, but it was too late. After a short silence, she said matter-of-factly, "No, there is nothing wrong. Most sports are not exclusively for men or women, especially squash. Both men and women play squash all over the world. Even in Pakistan, there are excellent women squash players. The people in the villages don't know about them. Therefore, they think that squash is only for men." I was thrilled by her response. "Why are you asking? Who plays squash here? Do you play?" she asked, sounding very excited.

In my response, all I could do was to nod yes with a giggle.

"Where do you play? Is there a court here in the village? Where do you get your rackets and balls and shoes? And what do you wear when you play?" She barraged me with all those questions and many more. A very big weight was lifted from my conscience. Not that I had ever felt guilty about my squash—but that was the first time ever, I got an endorsement for my passion from a woman.

Every now and then, I thanked Allah from the deepest core of my heart for granting me all my wishes. I would often reminisce, *What seemed like foolish dreams only a couple of years ago are coming true. I am thrilled about my school. And as for my squash, well it is a miracle happening*

to me in my real life. I can play at home whenever I wish, without any fear
of getting a scolding or a spanking. And now during my school break, I was
able to go to the city to play squash at a nice club. To top it off, I even have a
great coach Khurram. He has changed my shots and style. I play with many of
the good players at the club. I have passed all the women but then there aren't
that many of them. I easily beat all the mid-level men players.

At the same time, my heart would sink with disappointment and
fear. My squash training was not consistent; I trained for a month, and
then there would be break of many months. Khurram had been warning
me that those long breaks were bad for me, but then we had no choice.
Khurram and Noor Chacha both wanted me to move to Bannu and play
regularly at the club, but that couldn't happen. I knew that, and so did
they.

Once again, our school completed its second year with excellent
results. All the girls passed their exams and moved on to the next grades.
Everyone worked hard under difficult circumstances. Azra practically
took over the assistant teacher role. She took in new students and
brought them up to speed before Teacher Humma took them into her
regular class. Many more girls had joined the school. Teacher Humma
continued her Islamic studies at the mosque, and the *jirga* was pleased
with her progress there. Many families in the village still didn't allow their
girls to go to school, but then more and more of them were changing
their minds. There were girls in all grades, from first to eighth. Teacher
Humma was happy with my performance at the school. Everyone
involved with the school, especially the girls, were very happy and
thanked Allah for all His blessings.

Before the start of summer, I desperately started counting down
the days to our summer vacations and with that—my trip to Bannu.
I pestered Baba with my daily question, "What day are we leaving for
Bannu?"

"There is too much work at the orchard these days. None of us can
leave till midsummer anyway." He would repeat his standard response
every time.

He was right though. Work at the orchard was in full swing. We
would get there in the morning and work until nightfall.

One evening, while we were picking apricots for drying, Baba said
abruptly, "As soon as the peak of our harvest is done, I will take you and
Mather-Khubi to Bannu and leave you two with your Noor Chacha. You

can spend the rest of the summer with them, getting your squash training at the club there."

"That is wonderful. Do you know what day we will leave?" I asked, setting down my basket of freshly picked apricots. "Possibly, in a couple of weeks. Oh! Be careful with that basket. Don't let it tip, the fruit could fall and bruise." Baba cautioned as he grabbed my falling basket.

As promised, he took Mather-Khubi and me to Bannu to stay for well over a month. During my stay there I trained with Khurrum several hours a day and played as much squash as I could get. I improved rapidly. I started winning matches against those players who, only a few months earlier, wouldn't even consider me worthy of a single game.

In spite of stretching our stay past the date of my school reopening by a couple of weeks, my time in Bannu was coming to an end. We were getting ready to leave. Baba had arrived to take us back. On my last day in Bannu, I stayed at the club all day. I played matches and drilled with Khurram. In the evening as we were all sitting together watching a fast match, Khurram started joking around with Fareed. Abruptly, he walked to the club store and came back with a racket. He challenged Fareed, "Here is a brand new racket, still in its case. It is the newest model that has just arrived. You play a match with Amina and if you win, I will buy this racket for you, but if she wins you will have to buy it for her."

Fareed agreed without hesitation. He teased Khurram casually though, "If you insist on buying this racket for me so badly then what can I say. I will take it. I just feel bad for you. You will lose all that money to me. You know that Amina has no chance against me if I decide to play seriously. And trust me-to win this racket, I will play seriously. I promise. I have been drooling over this model since it came out."

I was looking at Khurram's face all baffled about what was going on. I pleaded, "Master, please leave me out of this. I know him and you know him. He is in a league above my level. I will lose for sure. Why are you doing this? I will be embarrassed in front of all these people and you will lose all that money. Please don't do this—Master."

"Amina, listen to me. You have lost to him before. Haven't you? So what if you lose again today. What difference would it make to you? I will buy him the racket. You will have nothing to do with that. But just imagine, if you win, you will get a brand new racket and all the players at the club will have a new respect and admiration for you. Don't worry about anything else. Just go and enjoy your match and play your level best. Just give me 110 percent of your effort." Khurram lectured, as he pulled out my racket from my bag and handed it over to me with a reassuring smirk on his face.

"Just let me tell you a quick trick about Fareed. He is very good if you play traditional shots. But he doesn't look back that quickly, so from the back of the court, hit sharp, low boasts to the front corners and he will miss those shots for sure. Other than that, just play your regular shots and you will be all right," he whispered.

"And yes one more thing. If you win today, you will win a new racket, but in return I will ask you for something. Do you promise to grant me my wish?" He paused to hear my response. Without knowing what he might ask for, I said yes to him. He continued, "I will tell you about my wish after you have won the match. Now go in and play your best squash. Please don't make me pay for that racket. I am a poor man and that is a lot of money for me. Besides, it is the newest and the lightest model of racket that I really want you to have." He tempted me with a big grin on his face.

Reluctantly, I went in. Fareed didn't even bother to do a toss. He generously offered me to start. I accepted and hit my first serve which landed perfectly in the back corner. The ball didn't even bounce an inch. He couldn't do a thing with it. An ace for the first serve, I couldn't have asked for a better start. All the spectators applauded warmly. Khurram pried the court door and with a naughty smile on his face he yelled through the crack, "Fareed, are you sure you don't want to withdraw from the bet? I am giving you one last chance to reconsider just because I like you as a friend." Fareed yelled back before shutting the door, "Just get out of the court and let the match continue. That serve was just the beginner's luck—don't make too much of that."

He was so right. I didn't get many more of those lucky serves after that one but I played one amazing shot after another that even surprised me. I used Khurram's trick of back court boast to the max. Every time I found Fareed in the front of the court trying to move back, I would hit that boast. By the time he would turn around to reach the ball, it would be too late for him. He lost dozens of points just by that shot alone. Otherwise, all my other tricks were failing me. My speed and court coverage were my second best ally. I won the first game, then lost the next two in a row, for the fourth game, he seemed a little tired and slow as I had made him run all over the court a thousand times. I won the fourth game. We were even—with two games each.

Fareed couldn't believe how good I was playing. He looked stumped at many of my shots. Not even in his wildest dream did he imagine to play a fifth game against me. I didn't give him any breaks or chances. He was exhausted and seemed completely disheartened. He didn't even fight for points. I won the match. Fareed congratulated me whole heartedly. He took the prize-racket from Khurram and handed it to me. "You deserve much more than this but please accept this as your reward. You have played an outstanding match today." I repeatedly declined to accept the racket but he insisted. Everyone present there convinced me that I had won the racket in a fair contest and therefore I should take it. I thanked everyone for their support. The whole crowd applauded my win and by then pretty much the whole club had gathered there to watch the match.

I was shocked at my victory. I was amazed at Khurram for having so much confidence in me. He really believed in me. He stood there proudly smiling while people were congratulating me. After the crowd dispersed, he walked towards me. Clapping his hands warmly, he said, "Thank you for giving me your 110 percent. Thank you for making me proud. Thank you for raising my respect in the eyes of the whole club. And most importantly, thank you for fully trusting my judgment about you. In response, I just stood there with my head bowed in gratitude. I didn't even know how to thank him for all that he had done to me. I was waiting for him to tell me what he wanted from me after I had won the match. But he was quiet. Then I reminded him, "What was that wish of yours? What did you want from me in return for winning my match with Fareed?"

Sounding a little surprised to hear that reminder coming from me, he replied, "Since you are leaving tomorrow morning, there is no point in telling you my wish this late. You go home now but then try to come back to Bannu as soon as possible. In the meantime do not and I repeat, do not—under any circumstances—neglect your daily squash practice. You are just learning new strokes and if you don't practice them extensively for a few months, you will easily forget them. Long breaks in your training with me are terrible for the progress of your game. Ideally you should be here with me in Bannu so we could train daily and all year around. Since that is not happening—you should come to the club very often and spend as much time as possible here with me."

We said our good byes till my next trip to Bannu. Noor Chacha was done for the day. He was ready to go home and I had no choice but to walk back with him. During my walk, I wondered repeatedly, *what is it that Khurram possibly wants from me?* The question kept bouncing in my head all through the bus ride back to the village the next day.

In October, everyone gathered at Chacha's house to watch TV news. America was bombing Afghanistan. Within days, Afghan refugees started pouring in. Everyone in the village was deeply concerned. People were comparing the American war with the Russian war twenty years earlier. Many Afghan refugees from that war never left our village; now more were coming. Within days, tent cities appeared on the outskirts of our village. Prices of food and other necessities rose. Grazing land was taken over. The water level in our wells sank. The sweet fresh-smelling air of our village was getting replaced by a foul smell of rotting garbage.

"Why are the Afghans delivering the *khudba* speech after the prayers at the mosque?" Baba complained angrily.

"They only talk about the Afghan politics and ask us to go to fight against the Americans over there. We don't get a chance to rebut anything they say," added Chacha.

Sounding very irritated Baba grumbled, "The only other topic that they talk about in those *khudba* speeches is the modesty for women." Shaking his head in disbelief, he continued, "Why do these Afghans insist that women should not be allowed to leave their homes under any circumstance. And where have they come up with this edict that girls should not go to school at all?"

Nodding in agreement, Chacha added, "We are not spared either. We must grow a full beard. Every man must show up at the mosque for all five prayers, and every boy has to attend the madrassa all day long."

That is when Zameer interrupted. "And yes, do you know that we have Afghan Taliban teachers at the madrassa?"

Baba was surprised at Zameer's revelation. He was furious at the Taliban. "That is not fair. How dare they come as refugees and take over our whole society?"

Some of our own boys began to act like the Taliban. Rumors were rife that the Taliban were against the girls' school. They insisted that a girls' schooling was against Islam. Many of the locals joined them. Parents started withdrawing their daughters from our school. Teacher Humma was getting very worried about the new opposition. A *jirga* meeting was called to discuss closing down of our school. People present at the meeting complained about the Taliban influence. Long debates followed even longer debates. Taliban leaders tried to convince families that the school should be closed. They quoted from the religious books, the Koran and the *hadesses*, to prove that sending girls to school was a sin. Even Imam Sahib was on their side. Fortunately, many *jirga* members didn't like the Taliban and were not ready to concede to their demands. Their push to close down the school was narrowly defeated in the final voting.

After failing with the *jirga*, the Taliban resorted to threats. A letter was found in one of the class rooms with a warning of terrible consequences for anyone associated with the school. The letter even frightened Teacher Humma who was otherwise so confident.

Babaji and some other village elders insisted, "We can't afford to surrender to Taliban's threats without a fight. Their influence has grown too much as it is. If we don't stop them here, we will never be able to stop them."

A decision was reached. Two armed guards were posted at the school. They watched the building and the children all day and even at night. They wouldn't let trespasser anywhere near the school building. We all started feeling safer.

Teacher Humma reassured us, "We are all safe now. The guards are very vigilant, and they won't let any harm come to us."

Slowly, the threat to school started fading out of people's minds. The girls were all preparing for the upcoming final exams. My friends and I were studying hard to take the eighth-grade exam. Being the final year of the middle school, those exams could be extra difficult.

Fourteen

CATASTROPHE AFTER CATASTROPHE

It was a Thursday morning in May, and it was turning out to be a very hot day. I came in a little earlier to help Teacher Humma set up the classroom and organize her lessons. The girls were arriving at their normal time—some alone and others in small groups. Suddenly, we heard screaming. We ran to the doorway.

"Acid attack! Acid attack!"

A group of girls had been on their way to school, talking, giggling, and skipping. Two men on a motorcycle rode dangerously close to them. The girls jumped away to avoid being hit and got trapped between the motorcycle and a wall. In a flash, the rider on the back pulled a bottle from his bag and splashed its contents at the girls, and then the men rode off fast. The attacker apparently aimed at the girls' faces.

Neighbors came running out, not knowing what had happened and, even less, what to do. The girls were taken inside our schoolroom. Devastated and crying, Teacher Humma locked us in the room, shutting all the doors and windows. Two seventh graders were horribly burned; others had many acid burns on them.

Baba and Chacha came running; next, Babaji arrived. Since there was no doctor in the village, no one knew what to do. Baba and Chacha picked up some beds from the nearby houses and carried two at a time into the compound of the school. The girls were moved from the ground on to the beds.

"Wash them with a mix of milk and water," Babaji ordered. "We need a doctor as soon as possible."

"There is a military post a few miles away on the main road. I will go ask for help. They can send for some doctors," Chacha said. He borrowed a motorcycle and left immediately.

By early afternoon, a team of female doctors arrived, followed a few hours later by a mob of reporters who took pictures and talked to anyone willing to answer questions. No pictures of the girls were allowed. The doctors treated most of the girls on the spot, but they had to take the two that suffered the worst burns to the nearest hospital. Those two were in severe pain; they were still screaming and crying as they were being taken away.

Many in the village wanted to find the perpetrators to punish them. The provincial police offered to help find the criminals, but the *jirga* rejected their offer. They simply didn't want the police to get involved in our village affairs. Instead, a team of volunteers was set up to find the criminals. Months passed, and nothing happened. The victim's families were demanding a revenge attack on the nearby refugee camp. But most people in the village were opposing indiscriminate revenge killing. They were also arguing that the villagers are not strong enough to fight masses of very well-armed Taliban. Everyone knew that a wider war with Afghan refugees and Taliban was not a sensible option. Some of our own people supported the Afghans, especially those with relatives in Afghanistan or whose relatives were fighting alongside the Taliban against the Americans.

Only one of the badly hurt girls returned home. The burns left her without sight and the rest of her face disfigured with ugly scars. It was impossible to control tears looking at her. The second girl didn't survive. "She was the luckier one," people said.

Much opposition ran throughout the village, but Taliban influence grew. Our small mosque had turned into a big madrassa. Hundreds of Afghans, as well as our own youth, learned the Taliban version of Koran and religion. In addition to our own Imam Sahib, there were many other teachers. They taught our boys to enforce ultra-strict Islam in the community. The young converts policed the streets and imposed their views. On the other hand, opposition to the Taliban was getting weaker by the day, and no one could do anything about it.

As if the acid attack was not enough, within months, a new calamity befell us. We were shaken from our peaceful sleep by a series of bomb blasts. Everyone ran in different directions, not knowing who was hit. Americans had bombed our neighboring *kot*. Nearby villagers rushed there to help. Digging and plowing went on all night. After the daybreak, more people joined in. Even the Taliban from the refugee camp came to help. The wounded were brought into our *kot*, their wounds were washed and bandaged. Since there were no doctors or a hospital in our village, they had to wait all day for help to arrive from the nearby military camp. Some of the badly hurt screamed in pain. The injured children fared the worst, crying terribly. Parents, if surviving, comforted their injured children. Other relatives and neighbors took turns helping out the children who had lost their parents in the bombing.

Many people died that night. Children, who used to play cricket and *pitho* ball or slide on the snow with us, were among the dead. Body after body of all ages was pulled out from the rubble. The villagers came together to make funeral arrangements for the dead. All the bodies were bathed, shrouded, and laid down in a row, and a communal funeral prayer was recited. Before being buried, the dead were laid into their graves with their faces showing for the last time ever. We all walked by to get a last glance. I mostly remember the faces of my shrouded friends. They appeared in my dreams night after night for months.

This second catastrophe shifted our minds away from the calamity of the acid attack. The anger against the Taliban was diverted to taking revenge against the Americans in Afghanistan. The bombing brought the Afghans, the Taliban, and our native villagers together on one platform. Talk of joining the mujahedeen in their war against the Americans, as well as against the Afghan and the Pakistani governments for their support of Americans, was on everyone's lips. The only topic discussed at the mosque was the war, suicide bombing, and terror attacks.

Our own Imam Sahib issued a fatwa that he would repeat week after week during Friday prayers. "Any able-bodied man who doesn't go to fight against the American is committing a sin for which he will burn in the fire of hell for eternity. If you are not able to go to the war, you must help by giving food, clothes, and money toward the war efforts."

To arouse the emotions of the believers, he would conclude his sermon by stating, "Remember, there is no death more honorable than to die a *shaheed*, protecting your homeland. And there is no life more rewarding than to live like a *ghazi*, a soldier fighting in the service of Islam."

The girls' school remained closed. Baba was afraid to let any girls at all back into his own school even in the lower grades. Parents too feared another acid attack. Teacher Humma returned back to her home in the city. Groups of Taliban roamed in the streets of our village, looking for un-Islamic behavior, particularly by girls or women. Any girl walking unaccompanied by a male relative was beaten. Men without beards were also punished. We lived in constant fear. Life in the village had changed completely.

Forced to stay at home, I returned to cooking and cleaning the house. Baba taught me some lessons in the evenings, but it was not the same as going to school. In the midst of the calamity, I found my sanctuary in the squash court. Except for the time I spent at the court, my mind would remain clouded by the faces of my acid-burned schoolmates or of my neighbors' shrouded bodies being lowered into their graves.

Fifteen

GROWING TULIPS IN DESERT

Our best efforts did not keep my squash activities secret anymore. Most people knew that I went to the city to play squash. They talked about how disgraceful it was that I played with men and wore men's clothing. They even added rumors to make their gossip more exciting to them and more hurtful to us. Mamma and Baba were very upset and argued with anyone who brought it up to them, but those people were not willing to accept that a girl from their village behaved in such a shameful manner. Families, including our own close relatives, kept their daughters away from me. No one invited us to their gatherings. On Eid day, when it is obligatory to call on your neighbors and relatives, few came to wish us happy Eid. Baba said that people treated him with disrespect at the mosque.

"Why are people acting this way?" I asked Baba out of frustration.

To calm me down, he explained, "People of our village are under much stress these days. Once things go back to normal, people will return to being kind again. It is the Taliban who are fueling this negativity. After they leave, life will go back to normal, and we will have our village to ourselves. Everything will be fine."

Khaleh, along with her daughter, Rahela, came for a visit. Mamma was happy to see her sister. They enjoyed talking all day and sometimes through the night. One evening, Mamma was cooking our meal at the stoves. Khaleh was with her. Other aunties and Mather-Khubi joined them. Rahela and I were busy playing "rocks and ball" on the ground right next to them. We could overhear most of their conversation about the acid attack, the American bombing, and the life with the Taliban and Afghans. In Khalehs' village too, they had the same plight.

"While some people are sympathetic toward the Taliban's cause, most are troubled by their taking over complete control of our society," concluded Khaleh.

My mind wandered off to other things when Khaleh snapped me out by practically shouting into my face, "Why don't you stop playing the cursed squash? You are bringing terrible hardship on your parents. Do you have no heart or respect for them?" She looked and sounded very scary.

To that, Mather-Khubi added her mantra, which I had already heard thousands of times for years, "You will ruin our good name that our forefathers have earned with their life and blood."

Khaleh interrupted, "Not only will you never get married into a decent family, but you will ruin the chances for my daughter too. Your bad behavior will reflect upon the character of your cousin, Rahela."

Next, Mather-Khubi took over again. "Have you heard the story of your grandfather's brother?" Without waiting for anyone's response, she continued, "Your baba's baba had a younger brother. Well, that makes him your baba's chacha. When he came to age, he left the village to go work in the city just like your Noor Chacha has done. From the city, he went to live in a faraway land. He had to cross seven seas to get there. Everything was completely different there. The people looked different. The food those people ate—we would never be able to swallow a single bite of that, the language—we would not understand a single word. You think British Frangies' language is hard—the language of that land was worse. Their homes were unlike any homes we have ever seen. Your grandfather's brother spent most of his younger years learning the ways of that strange land.

"While there, he fell in love with one type of flowers that are widely cultivated there. Those flowers are called tulips, and they grow in many different colors. We saw pictures of fields of tulips. They are absolutely breathtaking. After becoming a wealthy man, your baba's uncle decided to return home. Upon his return, all he wanted to do was to grow tulips here in Waziristan. The elders, including your grandfather, discouraged him from wasting his life's earning on flowers that are not native to our land, but he was determined. He bought a field that he liked, paying a high price for it. He imported thousands of tulip plants from a nursery and hired dozens of workers to plant those. Within days, all the plants withered away. The plants didn't get enough water. In the summer, our rivers dry up. He tried to use the water from the village wells, but the villagers didn't allow him to take that much water. They worried that the wells might dry up too. He ordered a new crop of plants and had a water-well dug just for the field. The new well was not very rich. There was not enough water in there to supply the whole field. Because the summer that year was excruciatingly hot, his second crop failed. Everyone was telling him to give up, but he didn't listen. Crop after crop died, and he used up all the wealth that he had brought back with him. At the end, he was desperately disappointed. Then one day, he was gone. We never heard from him ever again. He wasted his life on something that was not right for our lands. Obviously, tulips grow very happily in some faraway land, but here in the desert of Waziristan, they simply don't.

"The lesson of this story is that tulips don't bloom in the desert of Waziristan, and neither do squash players, especially girl squash players. You will not succeed in squash, but for sure, you will become a black spot on the family's name." Mather-Khubi drew her lesson for me with a deep sigh.

Another auntie, who was quietly waiting for her turn to bake naans at the tandoor, decided to chime in. "Amina, you are not a child anymore. You must behave more responsibly. You should think about your whole family and the whole tribe and not just yourself. You should give up this evil sport before it destroys your whole family."

Khaleh jumped back into the conversation, "Listen, darling daughter, squash is a sport for rich and powerful army officers and other important men. It is not meant for a poor peasant girl from an unknown village of Waziristan. You are so weak and scrawny that you can barely wash dishes. How will you find energy to play such a tough sport like squash?"

Khaleh's stay with us came to an end. As Khaleh was leaving, both she and Mamma hugged and cried. They did that every time Khaleh left after her visit. Mamma said nothing, but her teary eyes spoke volumes.

"*Khuda hafiz*, may Allah grant you a safe journey back," I told them while exchanging goodbye kisses.

"Remember what I have told you about playing squash. Please promise that you will not go near that cursed squash court ever again," she pleaded.

I nodded to reassure her of my compliance.

Sixteen

MIGRATION INTO THE UNKNOWN

Not long after Khaleh left, Noor Chacha showed up at our house. He was all excited about my squash training with Khurram.

"You all must move to Bannu. Otherwise, Amina's squash talent will die," he repeated his concern.

"Do you think that I will find a teaching job in Bannu?" Baba asked abruptly.

I couldn't believe my ears. *What am I hearing? Is he really considering moving to Bannu?* I asked myself, staring at Baba's body towering over me.

"What will you do with your school job here in the village?" Mamma asked in disbelief.

"Who is going to look after your orchard?" inquired Mather-Khubi.

We all looked at his face for answers. But it was full of questions instead. His gaze from behind his dark sunglasses was fixed at the farthest corner of the room instead of at us.

"That should be no problem. I know so many influential people at the club, and they will get you a job in no time," Noor Chacha replied after a brief thought.

Baba visited Bannu. Both Noor Chacha and Khurram tried hard to connect him to as many of their contacts as they could think of. All the people that Baba met—assured him of their wholehearted cooperation in finding him a job in Bannu.

Upon returning home, Baba announced his decision over lunch, "We are moving to Bannu soon. Life is becoming very difficult here. "My school"—he paused then continued grimacing—"most likely will convert into a madrassa where there will be only religious education. My naan is cold, give me a warmer one from the top of the stack," he told Mamma. "Give me a warm naan, this one is cold and hard, can't your hear me?" He shouted, not even trying to hide his frustration.

Mamma obeyed quickly, as if snapping out of a slumber. His tone signaled to all present that he was not open to discussion. During the whole lunch, all we heard was the chewing of food and gulping of water—not another sound.

"Zameer, come along, it is prayer time, and I want to go to the mosque," he commanded in anger.

Of course, Zameer obeyed without hesitation.

As soon as he stepped out of the door, Mamma wailed, "What is happening? How can we leave our home and migrate to a foreign land? We have no house there. We have no source of income there." Her cries got louder and her questions more numerous as we washed the lunch dishes together. As sad as I was for leaving my home, I was looking forward to my life at the Bannu club. I imagined how I will play squash, all day every day. How I will drill and train with Khurram. And how I will also find out what Khurram wants from me in return for winning my match with Fareed.

I continued playing squash. I was careful not to let anyone see me. What I didn't know was that there were people who stood outside the walls of our *kot* to hear me play. We found that out when, one evening, Baba was confronted at the mosque.

"They are asking me to put an end to Amina's squash. They are very upset that our daughter is playing a men's sport, wearing men's clothing, even if it is inside the walls of our own house," he summarized their objections. "They say that this kind of behavior sets a bad example for their daughters," he added with the pain of embarrassment clearly visible on his face.

Mamma's face crumbled and was awash with tears. "What are we . . . going to do now?" Her question broke up as she caught her breath.

"We will leave this village forever. And very soon," replied Baba matter-of-factly.

"Which side are our own relatives on?" Mather-Khubi asked, sounding extremely worried.

"They are the ones who are telling the rest of the village about Amina playing squash behind the *kot*'s wall and about her dressing inappropriately," replied Baba.

"We can't afford the opposition of the whole village, including our own close relatives," Mamma said, still crying.

"I will give up playing squash, I promise. You can tell them that," I told Baba, holding his hands tightly.

"I know these people. They will not stop at that. They have lost respect for us, and there is no need to live amongst them," he declared.

A few days later, Zameer came home with scratches and bruises on his face. He had gotten into a fight with some boys at school. They were teasing him about me and calling our family American lovers.

Baba traveled to Bannu alone without telling us anything about his trip. When he returned, his decision was made. "Pack up your things—only the bare minimum that you can't live without. We are leaving this Friday," he ordered.

"We will each have one box of our things, and then I will pack all our bedding separately. That is all we can take with us on the bus," he told us, giving a metal trunk to each of us that he had brought from Bannu.

Pushing her trunk away, Mather-Khubi declared, "Don't give me this trunk, I am not going anywhere."

"Oh yes, you are moving with us. You can't live here by yourself," Baba argued angrily.

"No, I can't migrate at this age. I will live here and die here. I can't move to a foreign land into foreign people. This is my village, and I want to be buried here in our family cemetery, alongside our ancestors. Don't ruin my end-of-life by taking me away from here!" Mather-Khubi yelled as she cried out loud.

Baba knew when to shut up while dealing with his mother. He left the house and was gone for the rest of the day.

Over dinner, Baba pleaded with her again, "Amma, please come with us. We won't be able to live in Bannu without you. You know that our lives are becoming impossible here."

"Brother, she has made up her mind and even your calling her Amma to butter her up won't melt her heart." Chacha said with a grin. He continued, "Don't worry, she can stay with me. I will take care of her. I am her son too. Go there and see how it works out in Bannu. Who knows, you might have to come back. If you do succeed there, then you can bring Mather-Khubi."

Baba didn't speak a word. It was hard to imagine her not being with us. Mather-Khubi had always been part of our lives.

Who will tell us those long stories in the sundalee? *Who will I cuddle up with? And who's soft gentle touch will sooth my nerves?* I asked myself. *And her naans—Mamma's naans are never as good as* her's.

Other than Mather-Khubi, little Siama was devastated by the news of our move. She had become very attached to me, and I was equally fond of her. She followed every move of mine and tried to spend every possible moment with me. I knew I would feel brokenhearted about leaving her.

"Aappa Amina, will I ever see you again?" she asked innocently.

"Yes, my darling, I will come to visit you frequently, and you will come to visit us. Bannu is not that far from here, and you can come with your baba every time he will come to visit us," I told her to calm her down and, more than her, calm myself.

"Will you still love me like the way you love me now once you move to a big city?" she asked me bluntly.

"Yes, even more, as I will miss you every minute of every day," I told her, hugging her tightly and wiping off her tears and mine.

We didn't have much to pack. Some clothes and few other things didn't even fill our boxes. Siama stayed at our house and slept with me. She looked so sad that just looking at her cute face brought tears to my eyes.

Baba rolled up our comforters and the bedding into two big rolls. Noor Chacha and Chacha helped us pack up. We woke up very early that morning. Mather-Khubi fried some *paratha* breads and eggs for each one of us.

"This will keep you full all day long," she promised as she asked us to eat quickly.

Both Mather-Khubi and Mamma had been crying all morning, while Siama was glued to me as if she was trying to absorb every minute that she could get with me. My heart sank as I looked around. I made a mental picture of every corner of the house to take with me.

As I stood at the door of the squash court, my mind drifted off into the chapters of my memory book, *My first scolding by Mamma for playing squash was at this door. Later the beatings that I got from her for the same crime; my first match with Zameer; my first match with Chacha; and then with Baba—my first wins against them; a*ll those events rolled by in front of my eyes like a TV show.

"Where is Amina? We have to leave. We will miss the bus." Baba's call snapped me out of my daydreaming.

The donkey cart had arrived, and Baba, Chacha, and Zameer loaded our luggage onto it. Mamma and I went around the house one more time to check. Mamma paused to stare at a few spots of the house and the *kot*. It seemed like she was also trying to capture her memories to take along with her.

"Mather-Khubi, please come with us. I beg you. I will not be able to live in Bannu without you. My heart will be torn between there and here," Baba begged-his voice crackling.

"Go on, my son. May Allah be with you at every step. May Allah bring safety and prosperity to you and to the rest of my family. I will pray to Allah for your wellbeing five times a day," Mather-Khubi responded, weeping even louder.

As the horse-cart rode away, the rising dust behind us blurred the image of our *kot*, but each one of us absorbed the last glimpses of our home before it faded away completely. Riding through the village, we passed by the hills where we used to slide and shoot snowballs. As we reached the field behind our school, I saw the corner where we used to play cricket and *pitho* balls. Then we passed by the village center and the village store, where, as usual, groups of men were standing outside, talking. The sight of those people got smaller until it also vanished.

We unloaded our luggage at the bus stop on the side of the road. Mamma cried all through the ride. As I saw the bus in the distance, my heart raced like I was in the middle of a big squash match. I was not sure if it was the anxiety of leaving my home or the excitement of heading to the Bannu Squash Club. My last evening at the club when Khurram asked me for something in return for winning my match with Fareed, was flashing in front of my eyes. I might find the answer to that question in a day or two. That thought was causing butterflies in my stomach.

"How many are you?" the bus conductor asked Baba.

"Five all together, three men and two women and this luggage," replied Baba, showing him the luggage.

"There are no seats on the bus—you will have to sit on the floor. I will put your luggage on the roof, there is enough space up there," he told us.

Since there was no other bus for the rest of the day, Baba had no choice but to agree. He bought the tickets, and we boarded the bus. Baba and Chacha helped the bus conductor move our luggage to the roof. We said our goodbyes to Chacha. While the two brothers embraced each other, Baba pleaded, "Take good care of Mather-Khubi."

"Don't worry about her. We will all miss you. Try to come and visit us as often as you can," Chacha replied.

"Yes, you also. Try to come to Bannu whenever you get a chance. We can play some good squash there," Baba told Chacha, smiling.

"Please promise that you will bring Siama with you every time you come to Bannu," I begged.

Mamma and I sat in the women's section in the front end of the bus on the floor, while Baba, Noor Chacha, and Zameer stood in the back half of the bus. As the bus drove off, the walls of our village started disappearing faster and faster. Pretty soon, the last of the *kots* went out of my sight. Fields and orchards, ditches and hills, forests and grasslands, small and big villages—all zipped by at a dizzying speed. Our bodies were taking quite a beating, absorbing the twists and turns and the bumps in the road. Sitting on the hard floor and holding the legs of a fellow passenger's seat, was very uncomfortable. I envied those sitting on soft comfortable seats.

We were not even halfway through when Mamma murmured, "My head is splitting with ache. Tie this end of my shawl around my head as tight as possible."

I immediately obeyed while balancing myself from falling on to other passengers.

"Let me massage your head," I offered.

I laid her head in my lap and massaged it as hard as I could while she murmured, "Too bad, Zameer couldn't come to the women's section here. With his massage, my headache goes away in minutes. He has a cure for my headaches in his fingers." I kept on massaging without saying a word.

"Here is some medicine, take it with a glass of water. The headache will be gone, *Insha Allah*," offered a lady on the front seat.

Her daughter brought some water from the jug and handed over the medicine. Another kind lady rubbed Mamma's head with her right hand and murmured some words while blowing repeatedly at Mamma's head. Something worked, and Mamma dozed off for the rest of the journey.

Upon reaching Bannu, Noor Chacha hired a taxi to take us to his house. Noor Chacha's wife, we call her Chachee Jan, had prepared dinner for us. While we sat down to eat, Mamma went to lie down; her headache was not all gone, and she was not hungry at all despite not having eaten anything all day. Their house was very small. It only had two rooms. Their three children were younger than us. They had emptied out and cleaned up one room for us. Baba rolled out our blankets and comforters to make two beds on the floor, one for Mamma and I and the other one for himself and Zameer. Right after dinner, we went to sleep.

"How do these city people live in such small places? In the village, people have more room to keep their sheep," Mamma commented before passing out for the night.

Although the bed was not comfortable, I slept deeply through the night. The next morning, right after breakfast, Baba left with Noor Chacha. His plan was to visit every school in the town to apply for a teaching position. I was counting hours and minutes until I could get to the club. I was dying to find out what it was that Khurram wanted from me in return for winning my match with Fareed. I was eagerly waiting to see all my squash partners and to just play some good squash. But Mamma didn't let me. She asked me to stay with her. We spent the day unpacking and setting up the room. In the evening, Baba brought enough groceries for both our families. Despite Noor Chacha's strong objection, Baba insisted on sharing the burden of our living expenses. Mamma and Chachee Jan prepared dinner.

During dinner, Mamma inquired, "Have you found a job?"

"No! But there is a potential position at one of the schools that I fully qualify for. One of their teachers is applying for another job. And as soon as he leaves, they will hire me to fill that vacancy," Baba shared his excitement.

Next morning, I got ready well before Noor Chacha to go to the club with him. I harassed him all morning to hurry up. Zameer wanted to stay home another day. As we walked into the club, every one of my squash partners greeted me warmly. Khurram came straight to me. "So that is it. Your family has finally done the right thing for you. You should have moved to Bannu a year ago but this is still good. I have designed a tough training program for you to make up for the lost time. And we will start right now and right here." Unable to control my giggle, I responded, "Thank you Master. I am fully ready, you tell me what to do and I will do it to the best of my ability."

With a grin on his face he reminded me, "Remember, you had promised to grant me my wish in return for winning that match with Fareed. And remember, I told you that I will ask for it on your next visit. Now that you will be with us permanently, I will ask you to fulfill your promise." He stopped. I waited for him to continue but he just looked at me as if he was expecting a comment from me. For a while neither one of us said a word. Then he continued with a serious face, "From this day forward, you will not address me as Master, you will just call me Khurram. I know that in your mind, by Master you mean your teacher but to me it sounds like, I am the slave-owner and you are my slave. From the very beginning, I wanted you to drop the word Master from your conversations but I didn't know how to tell you. I didn't want to make you uncomfortable by interrupting you repeatedly. And since both of your visits were short, I didn't deem it worth your while to make you concentrate on this issue. Now that you are here to stay, I will not allow you to address me as a Master."

I was surprised that after making such a big deal and making me wait for so long—that was all he wanted from me. I responded, "Yes Master, from now on I will address you as Khurram." He burst into laughter. "You called me Master again." I apologized, "It has become my habit. I will try my best, but you will have to forgive me if I make occasional mistakes, specially, in the beginning."

Weeks turned into months, but the exchange that Baba was hoping for—did not happen. He was getting desperate. Baba tried other avenues. He asked everyone at the club for help. Some of them came up with jobs that Baba found demeaning for his qualifications and family background. These were jobs of house watching, gardening, and driving.

"All of you pray that the teacher gets his dream job so that I can get his position," Baba reminded us every night.

He went to the school every day to check on the progress. One evening, he looked very happy as returned home. He gave us the good news, "The teacher has passed all of his interviews, and within days, he will get his offer and I will get his current position."

Seventeen

GOING GOT TOUGHER

Baba was gone all day. When he returned in the evening we could all easily see that something was not right. He looked miserable as he shared his painful experience with us, "The principal can't give me the job. He has to oblige a senior government officer who has asked that job for his nephew."

In a barely audible tone, he murmured further, "And that officer's nephew doesn't even fully qualify for the position." All evening, that was the only sentence that was spoken.

The situation at Noor Chacha's house was stressed. Mamma and Chachee Jan had gotten into a couple of bad arguments, and even their children showed attitude. The house where we felt so welcomed suddenly became very uncomfortable. I could see Mamma and Baba feeling the tension. Noor Chacha was still as loving as ever. But he was out all day. Zameer and I also went to the squash club. There, we helped Noor Chacha with his work, and for the rest of the time, we played squash—if and when we found empty courts. Baba was gone all day looking for work, but poor Mamma had to stay home and deal with Chachee Jan.

Then one day, I overheard Baba telling Mamma with a deep sigh of hopelessness, "I am running out of money, and if I don't find a job very soon, we will have no choice but to return back to the village." He was not ready to give up the hope, though, and continued to venture out every day in search of a job.

One evening, he looked very tired, his face and beard covered in dust. I knew that there was a lot of dust in Bannu, but it seemed like he had been rolling in dust all day. He gave the bag of flour and vegetables to Mamma and went to take a bath. After a quick dinner, he went to bed and fell deeply asleep in no time. That was very unusual for him. The next evening was a repeat of the previous one. I knew that something was not right, but he was not telling us a thing. After a couple of days, I confronted Mamma. "What is Baba doing? Why does he look so shabby every evening?"

"He is working on a road project, smashing rocks," she replied with a heart-piercing sigh.

I knew that it was not his body that was hurting, but it was most certainly his ego that was shattered. This noble khan from a highly respected warrior family was smashing rocks on the roadside. I went to his bedside and sat next to him while he was completely passed out. I held his hands and felt them. He had blisters on both hands. Tears started rolling down my face. I could imagine how he sat in the blazing sun, smashing those huge rocks with a heavy hammer. While he smashed the rocks with his hammer, the rocks, in turn, smashed the man inside of him. My crying got louder. I ran to Mamma, and putting my arms around her, I wailed, "I don't want to live here. I will give up squash forever. We will apologize to the people at home. They are our own people. They will forgive us. I can't bear to see Baba like this. This will kill him." I put my head in Mamma's lap and cried.

"Please, Allah, take my squash away. Better yet, take my life away. Punish me for what I have done," I prayed. I felt like running to Baba's construction site and smashing my wrist with one of his rocks. "My wrist—that Khurram thinks turns a squash racket into a magic wand—is the cause of all this misery," I said, howling a little too loudly. That woke Baba up.

"Amina, come here and bring some oil with you," he commanded. I obeyed right away. By the time I got to him, he had his glasses on and was pushing himself up to lean against the wall. "Massage my hands with this oil," he told me.

"I didn't want to wake you up," I said apologetically.

As I started rubbing the oil on his blistered hands, he continued, "This is not only due to your squash. The Taliban had made my life miserable. They were interfering in my teaching. They were harassing my students and me every day. They were planning on taking most of the older boys to the war and prepare the younger ones for their jihad. I don't mind working whatever work I find to take care of my family. Better times lie ahead," he said, holding my face between the palms of his warm hands and wiping my tears with his fingers. "I will find a teaching job soon. Then we will get our own house, and both you and Zameer will start going to school once again," he reassured me.

The situation at Noor Chacha's house went from bad to worse. Mamma and Chachee Jan quarreled every day, and their children teased us. Thank God for the club. My brother and I would find some refuge as we spent most of our time there. I played squash myself and watched matches between the best players at the club. That took my mind off all my problems.

I played another one of those tough matches. After retrieving a difficult drop, I lobbed the ball high into the back, but suddenly, the court grew darker, and I felt dizzy. After what seemed like hours later, I opened my eyes. I had fallen flat on the court floor. I came around when people splashed water on my face. Three other players had gathered around me. They were asking me questions, but I had no idea, and I couldn't think straight. Just then Noor Chacha, Khurram, and another player walked in.

"This is Doctor Sahib. We pulled him out of his match to come and see you," Khurram told me, visibly trembling.

"Doctor Sahib, I am fine now, I just felt all dark and obviously fell down. I want to finish my match," I told him to reassure all present.

He checked my pulse and looked into my mouth and eyes. He asked me to take some deep breaths. "Are you taking any medicine or drugs?" he asked bluntly.

"No, none whatsoever," I answered.

"Do you sleep well and enough?" he asked.

"Yes. All night," I responded again, feeling good about my response.

"Do you eat well?" he shot his next question at me.

"Yes, of course, I eat what the rest of the family eats, and why wouldn't I?" I responded to his question with a question of my own.

"What did you eat all day yesterday?"

"We had naan in the morning with tea. At night, we all ate naan sprinkled with salt, Mamma and Baba ate onion with it too, but I don't like onions with my naans," I told him.

"And what about the day before?" he asked.

After trying to think what we ate the day before, I told him, "Mamma and I picked some wild leafy grasses—you know those that look like small cups. Mamma boiled them, and we ate those with some salt sprinkled on them. We have been eating similar food for weeks now, but I never had this kind of blackout ever before. It can't be the food," I argued.

"You are undernourished. You can seriously hurt yourself if you train without proper nutrition," he explained sympathetically.

What must Baba's body be going through? He eats the same food, and yet he works such hard labor all day, I asked myself.

The news of my fainting circulated through the club. Several people asked me sympathetically if there was anything they could do for me. What could I tell them? They have all tried to find a job for Baba but with no success. What else could they do?

After finishing one of my training sessions, Khurram asked me, "I have more students than I have time to teach. I need someone to take on a few of them. You can do some coaching at the club, and you will get paid for doing that. I can transfer some of my junior students to you, and you can train and drill with them a few hours each day."

"That would be very good. I will ask Baba and let you know tomorrow," I told him happily.

"I am getting a coaching job at the club, can I take it?" I asked Baba in the evening.

"Providing for you is my responsibility. Am I not doing that?" he asked angrily. "As long as I am alive, my daughter shouldn't even think of taking up a job," he declared without waiting for my reply.

"I spend the whole day at the club. What is wrong with getting paid?" I asked.

"No. And if you bring it up again, I will stop you from going to the club altogether," he roared.

The next day, I told Khurram the whole story. After a brief pause, he came up with a solution.

"I think they are worried that you would be teaching men or older boys. And I wouldn't like that either. So I will give you all my girl students and the younger boys."

I dared not ask Baba. So I pleaded with Mamma, "I will only be teaching girls and young boys. Maybe you can talk to Baba."

In the evening, Mamma brought up the topic with him. Again, he was furious. Even Khurram's suggestion of me teaching children only, didn't calm him down.

Mamma pressed on, "Your daughter is following in your footsteps. You have spent your life teaching, and now she wants to do the same. She knows squash, and she wants to teach others."

"My daughter wants to teach others," he murmured. "Whatever money she brings, put it away for her future. I don't want any of her money to be used in our household. That is my responsibility, and I will fulfill it till I die," he said sternly.

Khurram handed over three girls and five young boys to my class. They were all beginners. He filled their ears with praise about me and my capabilities. Some of them were somewhat upset for being placed with a student instead of starting off with a teacher. But very soon, they realized that they were happier in my class than they were in Khurram's. I also did my best to teach them the techniques and the drills.

One evening, I finished my class late. It had gotten dark outside. I was feeling fearful thinking about my walk home.

Khurram guessed my unease and offered, "You shouldn't walk alone this late. It is not safe. I will walk you home."

I was relieved. I waited and watched Khurram teach and drill with his students. Right afterward, we left the club together toward my house. As we turned the second corner, three men approached us.

One of them asked us sternly, mostly facing Khurram, "Who are you two, and where are you going?"

Looking at their appearance and what they had stopped us for, I had no doubt that those were Taliban imposing their brand of morality on the city streets.

"She is my student at the squash club, and I am taking her home because it is too late for her to walk by herself," Khurram replied calmly.

The second Taliban man continued his questioning in an even harsher tone, "You are not allowed to walk with a man who is not your relative. If you two are married, then show us your marriage license. Otherwise, we will take you to the police station. You are committing a sin as well as a crime, and you should be punished for it."

Together, they lectured us, "This is a Muslim country, where girlfriends and boyfriends are not allowed, and we intend to keep it this way."

"Get the police here, we are not going anywhere with you," Khurram responded angrily.

Without saying another word, all three of them attacked Khurram. They punched and kicked him till he fell on the ground. He wrapped his arms around his head and face while they kicked him on his body. I screamed for help, but there was no one in sight. I swung my squash bag at one of them to get him away from Khurram. The bag hit his face. Now he was furious at me. He turned around and punched me a thousand punches. I firmly held the squash bag in front of my face, but several of his punches landed on my body. Even though his punches hurt me and I screamed with pain, I felt a sense of relief. I was at least able to get him away from hitting Khurram. This gave Khurram a chance to get up. With his face covered in blood, he kicked and punched them back. I came in again and swung my bag at the second one. He was hit in his face. He ran after me, calling me bitch, slut, whore, and a chain of nastier swear words. He ran fast, but he was no match for my fast feet. In spite of being hit and hurt, they didn't give up fighting with us. I opened my bag and quickly pulled out two of my rackets. I passed one to Khurram and held the other one tight in my hand. I swung the racket at one of the attackers, aiming straight at his face. He was hit. He was bleeding. Khurram hit the second attacker. Looking at the racket in our hands and seeing what it could do, they finally backed off. They didn't run away but dared not come near us. They just called us names and threatened to find us no matter where we hid. While they attended to their own wounds, we, holding our rackets out ready to attack them again, stepped back and ran straight back to the club. There, Khurram got his wounds washed and cleaned. I didn't have any cuts, but I had several scratches and bruises. Khurram needed bandages around his head and face. After resting a little, one of Khurram's students drove me home.

"These crazy Taliban are everywhere, and they do whatever they want," he said to me.

"I have only heard of this kind of lawlessness happening in Bannu, and today, it has happened to me," I replied, exhaling a big sigh.

As I walked out of the car after saying thanks and *Khuda hafiz*, I saw Mamma standing at the door. Her pose reminded me of the days when she used to beat me up for playing squash.

"Where have you been all this time, and whose car were you in at this late hour? Do you realize that I spent all evening crying and waiting for you, not knowing where you were and why you were so late? You have never done this before. I was worried sick for you!" she yelled into my face.

In response, all I did was to wrap my arms around her and howled on her shoulder.

"What happened? You will make me insane if you don't talk immediately," she said in a cracking voice with tears dripping down her face.

We both sat down on my bed. She poured some water for me, and I told her the details of the whole event.

She pulled my shirt up and looked at all the bruises on my body. "Are they hurting?" she asked me sympathetically.

"Only if you touch them, otherwise, I am not feeling much pain," I responded.

"I knew all along that your obsession with squash will come back to haunt us, one way or another. As if losing our home and settling down like refugees in a foreign land was not enough, now we have this to deal with. Who knows what kind of evil this encounter of yours with the Taliban will unleash upon us?" Then raising her hands towards the sky she prayed, "I beg Allah for forgiveness and pray for his protection."

"These are some nasty bruises. I will heat up some water. Go take a warm bath. Then I will make you a glass of warm milk with turmeric. That will take away your pain and the swelling," she comforted me.

"If I could find those Taliban men, I would strangle them with my own two hands. How dare they touch my girl? Didn't they feel any shame in hitting a girl on the street? Is this how they understand Islam? They will burn in hell for their sins, *Insha Allah*," she mumbled while putting a big pot of water on the stove for my bath.

"After your bath, I will make turmeric paste to put on your bruises. You will feel better by tomorrow," she said, hugging me and kissing my forehead.

"And yes, let us keep this between us. Don't let your father and brother hear about it. Who knows what they might do to get revenge from those Taliban for this insult to our family. At this time, we have enough worries and problems. We can't afford a war with Taliban," she suggested with teary eyes. "If we were home in our village, I would have gotten all the men from the whole tribe to go out, find those Taliban, and chop their hands off, those hands that touched and hurt my girl."

In response, I couldn't stop myself from wrapping my arms around her and sobbing uncontrollably.

Baba still hadn't found a teaching job. He had been working at one labor job after another. While at the club, my students were very happy with me. Their parents thanked me pretty much on a daily basis for teaching their children. Zoha had taken a special liking for me. Her father had been playing at the club for years. He wanted Zoha to play squash also, but he didn't enroll her in any lessons because there was no female teacher at the club. As soon as he heard of my class, he got her in. Zoha progressed through the lessons much faster than any other of my students. The number of students in my class increased steadily.

Eighteen

A NEW DAWN

Zoha's baba had used his influence at Zoha's school to get Baba a teaching position. Fortunately, a position opened up when one of their teachers left without much notice. The principal met Baba and immediately gave him the job. All that happened within a few days. One day, Baba was smashing rocks, and just the following day, with his blistered hands, he was teaching at a school again. Baba's dream had come true. With that, our living situation changed completely.

The first thing Baba did was that he rented a small house for us. While we had very few belongings, the house was filled with peace and tranquility. His next mission was to enroll Zameer and me into a good school as soon as possible. His own school was for younger children only and didn't have upper grades. Within the next few days, Zameer got accepted into a school of Baba's choice. But for me, he had to wait a little longer.

"Don't worry, Amina, I will get you into a school very soon," he promised as he left to take Zameer to his first day of school.

Noor Chacha was still very nice to us. He came to our house almost every other day. All he did was to talk about my squash with excitement. He would tell me how to deal with different people at the club. He had known them for years. He would tell me about the gossip at the club and, more importantly, all the things that were happening around the club. He told me about an upcoming interclub tournament.

One evening, as I entered the club, I saw Khurram anxiously waiting for me. Without even saying salaam, he told me the news, "We are going to have an interclub squash tournament. Among other clubs, the B team of the famous Peshawar Club is coming to play. You can only play against women. I know all the girls at the Peshawar B team. You will have no problem winning against them. You just need to concentrate and improve your conditioning a little more. And yes, try to eat good food if you want to work hard. We don't want anyone collapsing on the court floors. And remember this is an order for you from your Master," he added, laughing out loud.

I trained every day for the tournament. Since girls don't run outside in public, I used an old treadmill at the club. I noticed that, only after a couple of weeks, my game improved. I ran faster to chase the balls, and with my anticipation and conditioning, I was able to win many more points from my opponents.

During the tournament, the men from our club lost in the earlier rounds. But I kept winning my matches. I reached the quarterfinals, where I played against Nadia. She was the best B player from the Peshawar Club. By then everyone was talking about me—wondering who I was, where I trained, who my coaches were, who my father was, and, most importantly, what he did for a living.

The first thing I noticed about Nadia, as she entered the court was that she was extremely beautiful but she looked tired, and that was no surprise. She had played a very hard match earlier that morning.

"I think that your good conditioning will be your best ally," Khurram whispered to me.

After shaking hands, we started. I played long rallies; the idea was to make her more tired. In doing so, I lost the sight of winning points. Very quickly, I lost my first game to her.

"Stop drilling and start playing. Get some points, however you can," Khurram nearly scolded me.

In the second game, I scored points any which way. While the spectators applauded at some of my good shots, my club members were cheering at every single shot of mine. That support and encouragement boosted my confidence, and soon, the second game went to me.

In the third game, she started playing one excellent shot after another, and I had no answer for those shots. I couldn't do a thing, and she won the third game.

"Don't worry, she will lose her stamina. You just make her run as much as you can, but make sure to win points whenever you get a chance." Khurram came up with a new strategy.

I struggled, but Nadia seemed to be more tired than I was. With some luck and playing my level best, I won the fourth game. Now I saw my chance. *I must win the fifth and the final game to win the match*, I told myself, knocking my head with the racket strings.

However, my energy level had sunk to the bottom. To make matters worse, she played some very strange shots. I didn't know how to handle those. Her drops died in the corners, and the ball didn't lift at all. I felt exhausted. My feet felt like lead. My shots lost accuracy, and none of my strategies worked for me. I summoned all of my energy to win two more points, but she got to the match point. Again, she dropped the ball tightly in the corners, and my legs completely failed me; I didn't make it to the ball in time. I lost the point, the fifth game, and, with that, the match.

"Your lack of match experience cost you this match. You seemed like you were drilling with me rather than playing a competitive match. She has played in hundreds of tournaments, and for you, this was your first. You played well," Khurram said, trying to console me.

Patting my shoulder, Noor Chacha commented on my match, "You have made us proud. You have played a very close match against a girl who has had the best training all her life, and you have come from nowhere."

After the match, the players and coaches from different clubs got together for some tea and snacks. Khurram and I chatted with some of the people from the Peshawar Club.

"You know that our club is one of the top squash clubs in the world. We have had several international tournaments there in the last few years," one of the coaches told us.

Nadia added proudly, "Three of the world champions play at our club."

The assistant coach bragged, "We have our own doctors, nutritionists, and even psychologists there."

"Why do they have a psychologist at your squash club? Do your players have mental problems?" I asked innocently, but no one responded to my question.

"Our coaches are all internationally ranked players, and our trainers are the best in the country," remarked one of the other coaches.

"Do you have separate coaches and trainers?" I asked, giving him a chance to correct his mistake.

"Oh no, coaches and trainers are completely different professionals. A coach only teaches you squash, while a trainer works on your physical fitness exercises," he explained.

Then Nadia boasted, "That is why getting into our club is nearly impossible. In addition to very high fees, one must be from a noble background. Almost all of our members are very high-level officers from the military, the air force, and the government or are very rich businessmen." I felt very little listening to their description of the Peshawar club.

Baba fulfilled his promise and found a good school for me. Going to school every day was a strange feeling. I had forgotten how it felt to sit in a classroom, deal with the teachers, and make new friends. Although I could not be happier about being back in school, my mind was too occupied with the match that I had lost to Nadia.

Weeks had passed, but the memories of the tournament remained totally fresh in my mind. Those memories calmed me down when I faced any difficulty. And I was facing a lot of trouble at my school. I was starting my schooling after nearly a two-year break. Instead of going into the ninth grade, they put me back into the eighth grade. And honestly, I felt that I didn't even belong there either. Most of my classmates there spoke English easily, while I could barely read the alphabet. Baba was aware of my troubles. He immediately hired an English tutor for me to bring me up to speed with the rest of my class.

My English tutor advised me, "In addition to learning from your book, practice speaking English any chance you get with anyone who speaks English. Also, watch English TV shows—as many as you can."

I tried my best to follow her advice. I would sit with my English book in my hand, but instead of trying to read it over and over as my homework required, I would watch my squash match with Nadia in my head. That would comfort me tremendously, while the words on the book pages would be totally impossible for me to even pronounce.

Having gotten me a good tutor, Baba himself was not much involved in the matters of my school. Besides, his attention was divided over several other matters. He did not miss any opportunity to go to the village. He often took Zameer along. He missed Mather-Khubi and all other relatives too much. He also had to find someone who could take care of our orchard. The news from the village was not good.

Upon returning from one of his visits to the village, he described the situation there, "The Talibans have taken over the whole administration of the village. Our school has become a madrassa where they only teach Koran and the sharia, while all other education is forbidden. Women are completely locked up in their houses. People are forced to marry off their young daughters. Many of the girls—even younger than you—are now married, and some even to Taliban commanders who are much older than them," he said, facing me as he continued, "They have too much influence over the *jirga*, and most of the business is under their control. The Taliban are even spreading to the neighboring villages. The whole region is slowly but surely coming under their control."

That didn't come as a surprise. We knew that even in Bannu, Taliban could be seen roaming around and policing people into doing things only in the Taliban's ways. Women were beaten up if they went out without covering their hair fully. They had burned some of the cinema houses down. Men were beaten up for not wearing proper beards and proper Islamic attire at all times.

The Taliban delivered speeches and *khudbas* at local mosques. In those speeches, they told people to stay away from everything that they called un-Islamic. They had even attacked local shopkeepers for selling movies and songs on tapes and burned down their shops. They insisted that putting any pictures or posters of human or any living thing was un-Islamic. So they destroyed many such billboards and posters.

Baba didn't know this, but I felt the Taliban terror very deep in my soul every time anyone mentioned their name. The nightmare of what I went through while walking with Khurram, had left deep emotional scars.

Hearing the sad situation of my homeland from my own father was enough to depress me for my entire life, but again, my squash came to rescue. There were talks of an upcoming tournament at the Peshawar Club. Rumors were that they were inviting only the selected clubs. Since our club was at best mediocre, we were not expecting an invitation to play. However, some of our players planned on going there just to watch some high-caliber squash. I wanted to go and just visit the world-famous Peshawar Club.

"There is a tournament at the Peshawar Club, and some of the people from the club are going. I want to go too," I blurted the whole thing out all in one breath without pausing. I knew that if I paused, I would never be able to finish my sentence.

"What—you want to go to Peshawar for a few days with some people from the club? Are you completely out of your mind?" Mamma responded without even giving a second thought to my plea.

Not sounding all that angry, Baba added, "Peshawar is a very big city. We don't know a single soul there. You could be lost or, worse, kidnapped. It is not safe for you to go there."

"Can you take me there?" I begged.

After a brief pause, Baba explained, "No, I am taking some time off from the school to go to the village to see Mather-Khubi. After that, I will not be able to take even a single day off for a while."

Khurram even tried to have Noor Chacha influence my parents into letting me go. But Noor Chacha himself was against the idea. I just had to accept my fate and live on.

The club got much quieter as so many players left for Peshawar. I just drilled by myself or played with those who stayed back.

One evening, as I returned home after my practice, Mamma was hosting some ladies from the neighborhood. They were having tea and snacks. I said my *salaams* to them very respectfully.

"Where are you coming from at this time?" responded one of them bluntly to my *salaam*.

"I was at a friend's house," I lied.

Mamma had forbidden me to tell anyone about my squash. It looked like they didn't believe my lie, or maybe it was just my guilty conscience.

"Have you started looking for her?" asked one of them, pointing at me.

While I tried to decode her sentence, another one of them spelled it out for me. "She is what, fifteen, sixteen, isn't she? This is a good age to marry off your girls."

Sounding very worried, another one of the guest ladies added her opinion, "The situation in our society is going from bad to worse. You should fulfill your responsibilities earlier rather than later. A daughter is a very big responsibility. The sooner a girl goes to her husband's house, the better off you are."

Yet another one of them preached by quoting her Imam Sahib, "Keeping girls at home for too long makes Allah unhappy with you."

Mamma and I sat there speechless. I tried to change the subject, but they didn't let me. I remained respectful, but my mind wandered off. Instead of listening to them, I started thinking about my life. I was very happy to be in school, but it was all work and no fun. I had made some friends, but those girls played no cricket, no football, no *pitho* ball, or any other sport. Whenever I brought up the topic of playing a sport, they would all look at my face with astonishment. There it was all about studying and some socializing.

The studies were becoming increasingly difficult for me as the exams were fast approaching. Zameer and Baba started helping me prepare for the final exams. I studied long hours. Baba made good money tutoring kids in the evening, but then that didn't leave him much time to be with us. Mamma took care of the rest of the household. She enjoyed socializing with the neighbors. Zameer had made some friends. He played cricket with them almost every day. He also played some squash some days, but we all knew that his heart was not into squash.

Ramadan started. Fasting in Bannu was not the same as it used to be back home at the village. We badly missed the festivities of Ramadan. At the village, Ramadan used to be a full month of family feasts. At both, the pre-morning meal, the *sahri* and the breaking-fast meal, the *aftaar* in the evening, all the relatives from the whole *kot* used to gather in the courtyard to share food and just be together. Children did what they do best—just be rowdy. Even after the whole day of fasting, we would run around, play hide-and-seek, climb trees, or simply just scream and yell besides eating our favorite foods and drinking glasses of cold drinks.

In Bannu, we sat all alone, cooped up in our little house, to eat our *sahri*. In the evenings, at the *aftaar* time, we missed our relatives badly and thought a lot about the *aftaars* back home.

The traditions in Bannu were very different. In the pre-morning, about two hours before sunrise, some men would go around the neighborhoods, making loud noises. They beat drums, knocked at each door, sang holy songs, and announced loudly, "O people get up for the *sahri* meal. O people, get up to earn Allah's blessings, get up to fulfill your obligations of Ramadan fasting."

Mamma would get up first to prepare the meal. Some nights, Baba had to go to the bazaar to bring some milk or some other food items for *sahri*. Stores opened just for that during Ramadan.

"I have fried some *paratha* and eggs. Eat this with some cheese and drink a full glass of milk, and you will not be hungry all day long," Mamma would promise.

In response, we would complain, "This is a lot of food at this time of night, we are half asleep, and you are rushing us to finish before the siren goes off."

Sirens announced the end of eating time. As soon as we heard it, we had to stop eating whether we had finished our meal or not. Right after that, we would do our morning prayers. After all that excitement and hurriedly eating stacks of food, we would try to get some sleep, before having to get up again for school. By the afternoon, everyone would be hungry, thirsty, and tired. People would get irritated at the littlest things. We saw a lot of fist fighting between people during the fasting month.

Coming back from school and not being able to eat everything in sight would be the hardest thing to do. We desperately waited for the *aftaar* time. And it was always a very long wait. Those last few minutes felt like eternity. We would sit around the food and wait for the siren that announced the breaking-fast time—fully ready to jump at the food. The hardest thing to do for us was to control our thirst. We would drink water like there would be no tomorrow. And drinking that much water would ruin our appetites. With all the good food around and being hungry all day, it seemed like a miracle that we didn't eat the whole world. Soon after the *aftaar*, Baba and Zameer would go for *traveh* prayers to the local mosque, while the Mamma and I would clean up the kitchen area to start the preparations for the next meal.

Nineteen

BRIBING TO GET HOME

Ramadan, as difficult as it was in Bannu, was coming to its end. As we entered the last week of the fasting month, we started talking about our Eid visit to the village. Everyone was excited about our trip home to spend Eid with our relatives. I couldn't wait to see Mather-Khubi and cuddle up with her in the *sundalee*. Though her stories were not quite as exciting as they used to be, I still felt a sense of comfort listening to them. I looked forward to seeing Chacha and everyone in his family. Most important of all, I was looking forward to being with my beautiful cousin, little Siama. I missed how she called me Aappa Amina, which just melted my heart.

A taxi dropped us off at the bus station into a sea of people. Eid is always the busiest travel time. Baba frowned and sounded worried as he admitted, "All these people waiting for one bus is a bad sign. I doubt we will get tickets." And how right he was. Within minutes, the conductor announced the bad news, "All the buses for today are sold out already. You should get here early tomorrow if you want to take this bus."

Baba was unable to hide his disappointment, and frankly, nor could we. Meanwhile, Noor Chacha arrived at the bus station along with his family. The plan was that our two families would travel together.

"No tickets for the bus today," Baba told them.

Noor Chacha's children started crying. They had been so excited about the trip. Noor Chacha tried to calm them. "Sorry, children, we can't do anything about it, except that we will try again tomorrow. We will get here well ahead of time and buy our tickets."

Baba went around looking for a taxi to take us back to our house. Even taxis were hard to come by that day.

Suddenly, a young man approached Baba.

"Salaam, Master Sahib," he addressed Baba, holding his hand warmly. Baba paused; apparently, he didn't have any recollection of that student of his.

Noticing the blank look on Baba's face, he tried to refresh Baba's memory, "Master Sahib, you were my teacher at my school in Idak ten years ago."

"I realize that. Why else would you address me as Master Sahib? But I am sorry my memory is not as good as it used to be all those years ago," Baba responded with a smile.

"Sir, you look worried. Is there something wrong? I have connections here. May I be of some assistance to you?" he offered.

Baba explained the situation to him, "Yes, son, we are going home to the village for Eid but all the buses are sold out. Now we must try again tomorrow morning."

"Just wait here and I will see what I can do. God willing, I might be able to get you tickets," he reassured us. "How many passengers are you?"

"In total, we are nine people, four in my family and five in my brother's," replied Baba.

The man stepped away. We waited impatiently, giving up hope several times. In what seemed an hour, he returned.

"I can get tickets for the last bus today, but you have to pay extra money to the company manager."

"Yes, how much for nine tickets?" Baba asked him, taking out a stack of hundred rupee notes from his pocket.

The man then told us the bad news, "Sir, I can only get enough tickets for one family."

After a long pause, Baba decided, "In that case, we will all try tomorrow."

Noor Chacha interfered, "No, brother, you and your family should go. At least, some of us can get there today. We will catch the bus tomorrow morning."

After some hesitation, Baba accepted and gave the money to the young man there. Within a few minutes, we got our tickets and boarded the bus.

Thanks to the kindness of one person and the bribe that we paid, we made it to our destination. However, since we arrived very late in the night, we couldn't find a ride from the bus stop to our *kot*. We had to carry our luggage and walk all the way in the dark of the night. It was tiring, but no one complained. We were all happy to be in our village, heading to our *kot*. Chacha and Mather-Khubi came running to meet us. Little Siama had stayed up late, waiting for us also. After giving hugs and kisses to all of us, she came and sat right next to me, holding my hand tightly. We talked and laughed till very late into the night.

The next day, walking through the village to our orchard, we saw with our own eyes what Baba had been telling us for months. The whole society had changed for the worse. The Taliban had brought war into every house. The community was bitterly divided. Some people supported the Taliban, while others wanted them gone. American bombings had killed hundreds of people, including some we knew well. People who had lost relatives in these bombings were honor-bound to fight alongside Taliban against the Americans. There was also a bloody war going on against the Pakistan army for its support of the Americans. To make matters worse for us, the news of my squash had spread throughout the village, making us social pariahs.

We waited all day, expecting Noor Chacha and his family's arrival, but they didn't come. We went to bed worrying about them. Mather-Khubi stayed up to pray for their safe arrival. The following morning, while some of us were still asleep, there was a knock on the door. It was Noor Chacha and his family. Instead of being groggy for being woken up from our deep sleep, the whole house burst into jubilation.

Noor Chacha told us the story of their journey, "The next day, we arrived at the bus station early in the morning and waited there the whole day. There were four buses coming this way, two regular and two special ones for Eid only, but we couldn't get tickets for any one of those. We were about to leave the bus station when we heard a rumor that there might be a special night service. The rumor turned out to be true. We were very lucky to get tickets for that one. It took several hours longer because of the dangerous night driving, but we are all here safe and sound. The driver was a very good man. Her drove very carefully and patiently getting us here just before the morning prayers."

We were all one happy family gathered together for Eid. Mather-Khubi was absolutely thrilled. All three of her sons and their families were gathered in one house. Finally, the day of Eid came. Baba and Zameer and all the men from the *kot* went to the Eid prayers. Mamma cooked a big feast. She prepared several snacks and a big dish of halva with nuts and raisins because we were expecting many guests from all over the village to call upon us throughout the day. Baba, Noor

Chacha, Zameer, and Chacha returned, along with some of our close relatives and friends. Halva, snacks, and tea were served. All the children got Eid money from the uncles. The little ones went out to the Eid fair, where they bought small toys and sweets.

While snacking and sipping tea, the men had heated debate about politics—both local and international. Strong opinions were voiced against the Americans and the Pakistani government for supporting the Americans, while many supported the Taliban. To my utter shock, even Chacha was among those who were praising the Taliban. There was mention of Palestine, Israel, Kashmir, India, Afghanistan, Iraq, and Iran. Our life in the city was another topic that most guests talked about. Questions about our lives in the city abounded. Many of them expressed their concerns or pity at our lives away from home, away from our relatives, away from our place of birth.

Surprisingly, we didn't get as many guests as we were expecting. It seemed many of our neighbors, and even some of our relatives had decided not to call on us to wish us Happy-Eid. They were showing their disrespect toward us to punish us for my squash.

In the afternoon, Baba, Noor Chacha, and Chacha took all the boys and some of the girls to the Eid fair. There were magic shows, rides, toys, food and snacks to buy, and acrobats showing their tricks. We went to see the show called *The Cage of Death*. A young rider rode his motorcycle around and around on the wall and even on the ceiling of a huge steel cage. He went speeding around at least twenty times. We all held our breaths as his slightest mistake would have sent him falling down hundreds of feet to a certain death. After watching that show, we went on some of the faire rides. The scariest ride was a swing that went very high. I could see the whole village from up there. We stopped at a vendor who was making beautiful figurines with some kind of stretchy candy. Baba bought bird figurines for all the children. Most of the children promised that they will keep their figurine forever, but within minutes the birds started shrinking and soon they disappeared. No one could resist the temptation of licking and nibbling on those delicious treats.

There was a big crowd of people at the fairgrounds. Although we kept a close eye on the younger children suddenly, we didn't see Siama with us. We all panicked and started running back the way we had been walking. We had heard of horror stories of children getting lost or abducted at fairs like these. My heart was pounding with fear, and I was trembling with the thought that harm could come to my favorite cousin. Shivers went down my spine and tears down my cheeks. I was screaming her name and stopping people to ask if they had seen a small girl crying for her family. No one had seen her.

"How could have no one seen a little girl crying for her parents?" I was yelling in anger.

"Here she is! I found her!" I heard Chacha screaming.

I ran in the direction of Chacha's voice. There she was standing at a bangle vendor's stall, looking at a bracelet. I grabbed her and hugged her tightly. After getting my breath back, I noticed that she was looking at some bracelets. Those were, indeed, very beautifully decorated bracelets. With my Eid money, I bought three of those—one for me, one for Siama, and since Noor Chacha's daughter was there with us, one for her too.

After that scary experience, we all wanted to go home, but we heard a roaring lion from inside a nearby tent. The tent was painted with the picture of a lion in a cage. My cousins and I had never seen a real lion in our lives. We begged Baba to take us in. He bought tickets, and we walked into the tent. We were thrilled and fearful that we will soon see a live lion in a cage at only a few yards' distance from us. To our utter disappointment, there was no lion and no cage. We saw that they were creating the lion roar from a wire stretched inside a drum. A man was stroking the wire with wet fingers to create the sound of a roar. All they had was a man dressed in a lion costume, imitating the tricks that they do with real lions in a circus. We felt cheated and angry. Baba wanted his money back, but the vendor wouldn't even listen to Baba's argument. We walked out of the show even before it was half over. Baba didn't want to spoil our Eid fun.

The Eid holidays flew by. Saying our goodbyes was the hardest thing to do. Mather-Khubi was sad, and looking at Siama's face made my heart sink, but we had to leave.

Just before leaving, I said, "Look, we have exactly the same bracelets. Every time you see yours, you will think of me, and when I see mine, I will think of you."

"Aappa Amina, you are on my mind all the time anyways. This bracelet can't make me think of you any more than I already do. But I will treasure it because you have given it to me," she said, sounding much older than her years.

Twenty

A FOREIGN LANGUAGE

Two days after Eid, we returned to Bannu to the same old routine—school to squash and squash to home. Baba got as busy as ever, if not even more, as the exams' time was fast approaching, and his tutoring load increased to its maximum. I was not feeling very confident myself. My teachers had been warning me for months that I would fail if I didn't study harder and spend more time on studying. My tutor tried her best to help me improve, but I was not able to catch up despite my best effort. I was very afraid, and to take my mind off my troubles, I played even more squash. Squash worked like a panacea for me. It took all of my worries away. English was still my biggest struggle. I just didn't get the language. There are just no rules that I could memorize. Why doesn't "cut" sound like "put" except for the different sounds of P and a C? Why do we say "played" but don't say "goed"? I just didn't seem to get this strange language.

During the final exams, Zameer did well, but I did poorer with each exam. My science exam was difficult, but the next day, my social studies essay answers were a disaster. I was unable to answer a single question fully while most of my classmates found the exam fairly easy. Then came the day of my English finals, which I had been dreading that whole year; every page of my answer sheet was left mostly blank. I knew I was not going to pass in any of my subjects, but at least, the nightmare of exams was finally over. To distract myself while waiting for the results, I played squash full time. The announcements came. Zameer passed with a high position in his class. To my surprise, I passed math and science, but social studies and English were a different story. I failed the year and needed to repeat the grade.

Baba read my report card with the expression of disappointment mixed with compassion. He tried to console me, "I am very disappointed, but I do understand that it is not all your fault. Not having gone to a regular school for two years has left a gap that is not easy to fill. Most children have been learning English since the first grade, and you had barely learned the alphabet. I know that English is not an easy language to learn."

His tone completely changed as he remarked sternly, "You must promise to do better next year. I know you can do that. Get more tutors if you have to, but next year, you must pass."

At the club, Khurram had been anxiously waiting to find out my results. As I entered the club, he came running to me.

"So what happened, did you pass?" he asked, expecting to hear a "yes."

I told him, with the pain of failure clearly visible on my face, "No, I have failed in English and social studies."

"No, seriously! You are joking, aren't you?" he asked with a naughty smile.

"I wish I were, but unfortunately, no. I am sorry my grades in these subjects are too low," I replied.

Tying up his curly hair in his headband, he said, "Come here and sit down. We need to come up with a strategy to deal with your problems in English first."

"I have tried everything, including hiring a tutor, but it is just too strange for me, and I just don't get it right, no matter what I try," I said, not being able to hide my frustration.

"I know you better than you know yourself," he told me reassuringly. "There is nothing you can't do if you put your heart into it. We just need to come up with a system that works for you. You have learned the most difficult squash shot by drilling them hundreds of times. Why not try doing the same for English?" he proposed with optimism beaming from his eyes. "Get some English lessons on a tape and drill each lesson hundreds of times," he suggested.

I knew that whatever he has told me to do—has always worked for me. I was determined to try the drilling technique in English. I felt a wind of inspiration blow over me.

My tutor had told me the name of a course for learning English. Showing Baba the title I asked, "My tutor wants me to get this CD set to learn English."

"I will ask my student, Zulfi, to pick one up from his father's store," Baba proposed. I guess one good thing about being a teacher is that your students are from every field of life. And they are keen to oblige you.

I started my drills from TV shows. Instead of sitting down and watching a show quietly, I would pick one sentence and repeat it dozens of times. I began to understand the shows even less, but I practiced and drilled into my brain a few sentences from each show I saw. Within a week, my CD and a small CD player arrived. I skipped the first few chapters and went directly to the second level to challenge myself. I listened to one sentence; then I drilled it several times, trying to imitate the speaker. I worked with it for a couple of months. In the beginning, it seemed easy, but soon, it became horribly boring. I also didn't see any benefit. I memorized the sentences on the tape, but I could almost never use those in real life. There was a whole lesson on ordering food at a restaurant. *Why would I ever order food in English? How many waiters understood English in Bannu?* Then there was a whole chapter on asking directions in English. *When and where would I ever ask for directions in English?* I questioned the wisdom of my learning method. I was losing motivation. I wanted to stop but was afraid to face Khurram. He was so excited about this method. How will I tell him that he was wrong and that his system has failed for me? For no reason, other than the fear of facing Khurram, I kept on drilling the lessons from my CD. At the club, I tried my favorite sentences—most of the time to impress Khurram.

"I am feeling very tired today," I murmured one of my lesson sentences, not knowing that Khurram was standing right behind me.

"Then go home and rest," he responded with a big grin on his face.

"You know that I can never be too tired for squash. I am just repeating this sentence from my English CD," I explained.

Not being able to wipe off that naughty grin from his face, he replied, "I know that, I was just teasing you."

All through the first game, I kept repeating that sentence. "I am very hungry today" was my next sentence to drill during the second game.

"Now don't you tell me to go eat," I told Khurram to preempt him, noticing that oncoming smirk on his face.

"This is very good, just keep this up, you will soon begin to feel better at this language," Khurram reassured me.

At school too, I spoke those sentences whenever and wherever I would get a chance. It sounded very pretentious at times, and I felt embarrassed and odd speaking to my close friends in a foreign language, but I pushed myself. Of course, when it came to really expressing my feelings, I jumped back to my native Pashto, as English completely failed me there. Also, at home, I couldn't speak English because Mamma didn't understand a word of it. Zameer tried to speak to me in English, mostly to teach me; he also corrected my mistakes when he could. As time passed, I began noticing improvement in my English. I was gaining confidence using my sentences in different real-life situations.

After one of our training session, I sat down with Khurram and some of his students for lunch.

"Do you like this food?" one of his students asked me in English, to start a conversation.

"Yes, the very good food," I responded after translating the question into Pashto and then translating my response from Pashto to English.

"Tell us about some of the dishes from your village," another one of his students asked.

"We have the same dishes in our village as you have here. We and use a big flat plates, a some small plates, and a bowls made of metals or porcelain, same dishes as you have," I responded very proudly, after translating his question and my response. While I reassessed my words for correct translation, I noticed that everyone looked utterly confused.

"Enjoy your lunch," Khurram's student said to me, while everyone else stayed quiet.

I felt so proud about my conversation in English; I was making progress. I was filling up workbooks after workbooks and I was beginning to understand short sentences. I could read short conversations. The first conversation I fully understood was a joke in a joke book:

A man was driving extremely fast on a small road. A policeman stopped him.

Acting very innocent, the man asked, "Good morning, Officer. Are you stopping me for driving too fast?"

The officer replied, "No, sir, I am stopping you for flying too low."

I laughed about the joke for days, not because it was funny but because I was so happy and proud to have understood it entirely.

Twenty One

THE PESHAWAR CLUB

Other than training in the English language, I trained hard for an upcoming tournament at the Peshawar Club. For the fear of rejection, I didn't dare ask Baba if I could go. Since we were in summer vacation, Baba had a lot of free time. He had been taking trip after trip back to the village. He still had not found anyone to manage our orchard. We had lost the harvest for the whole year.

"Leaving the fruit trees unattended for a whole year is extremely damaging for the health of those trees," Baba worried aloud. He was desperate to line up someone for the next fruit season.

I had been on a lookout to catch Baba in his best mood. I wanted to ask for his permission to go to Peshawar. I knew well that I would have only one chance, and I was afraid to lose it.

With a big smile on his face, Baba announced, "I have found a reliable person to manage our orchard."

"Thank God. Allah wishes to save our trees," replied Mamma.

I seized the moment. "Baba, there is a squash tournament at the Peshawar Club, and they have invited our club to compete. The coaches have chosen me in the girls' team. Will you be able to take me there?"

After uttering my one long sentence in one single breath, I prayed hard that he wouldn't scold me too much for asking something so impossible from him.

After some thought and some mumbling, he replied, "We can all go. I also want to see Peshawar."

I couldn't believe my luck and murmured repeatedly to myself, "I am not dreaming. I am not dreaming. Baba is really taking me to Peshawar to compete in a squash tournament."

To prepare me for the tournament, Khurram had designed a program of training for me for the rest of the month. I played and trained nearly six hours each day while he drilled into my head, "Concentrate on the accuracy of your shots and improve your conditioning." Some days, I trained against two good players. They gave me the same shot hundreds of times, and I played returns. The training was brutal. Doctor Sahib advised me about how to keep my diet healthy for the intense training, while Khurram seemed very happy with my progress.

"In anticipation of precipitation on higher elevation, the administration reviews the conditions of nutrition, hydration, sanitation, and communication," I mumbled while doing my drills with Khurram.

Trying to control the burst of his laughter, he asked, "Where did you hear such a sentence? And do you have any idea what it even means?"

"I saw this in a newspaper, and I just wrote it down and must have said that a thousand times," I confessed. "What does this word 'antipation' mean?" I asked, trying to over-twist my tongue to pronounce it correctly.

"The word is not 'antipation'—it is anti-ci-pation." He made me repeat after him piece by piece. "I have heard this before, but I don't know what it means either," he admitted.

As the training for the day ended, he asked me to sit down on the chair in front of him. He took a deep breath before starting his sentence. "I have taught you all I can. You need a higher-level coach. If you stay with me, you will not improve any further."

I interrupted him, "There is no better coach than you in the whole town. I have to keep going with you. What other options do I have?" Without waiting for his response, I made my threat, "If you stop coaching me, my squash career will end."

My threat worked. His tone immediately became apologetic, and he tried to comfort me. "I am not stopping, but I am telling you that you need a better coach. This club is not right for you anymore. You can easily defeat the best players here. You should go to a new club where you can play with players better than you. That's how you move forward."

I returned home, not sure if that was a good or a bad news for me.

Instead of taking the bus, Baba hired a taxi all the way to Peshawar for the whole family to travel in comfort. The drive to Peshawar was rough but beautiful. We drove through the mountains, fields, orchards, and many small villages scattered on both sides of the road. There were also several tent-cities put up by the Afghan refugees. In Peshawar, we stayed at a hotel. The manager there was one of Baba's many students.

He personally took care of our every need and gave us the best rooms available.

The next morning, Khurram took us to the world-renowned Peshawar Club. I was scared yet also giddy with anticipation. The approach to the club was, indeed, worthy of its name. A long private driveway lined with tall cedar trees led to the entrance gate. The pillars of the entrance gate were no ordinary pillars that you see around. These were made up in the shape of two towering squash rackets crossing each other at the top. Two armed guards, dressed in traditional *Pashtoon* costume, attentively stood by, one at each post of the gate. Passing through the monument-like gate, I felt very small. A manicured lawn with plots of fragrant flowers decorated the passage to the entrance of the club building. I pictured squash legends, Jahangir Khan Hashmat Khan and Jahansher Khan, strolling around the thick carpet-like grass between the flowers. Khurram had many friends at the club and he introduced us to them with pride in his voice. There was a museum displaying squash memorabilia from all over the world. The building as well as the people there were intimidating, yet my dreams about this club were vivid ever since first hearing about it on TV.

While I was still catching my breath, I saw Nadia coming toward me. The match that I had lost to her, flashed vividly in front of me. Every shot of that match was engraved in my memory. She apparently didn't remember me, and I don't blame her. We greeted each other after being introduced. She looked stunningly beautiful. As I walked around, I witnessed some of the best squash talents ever. I had only seen such quality of squash on TV, and there I was, among the living and breathing players who I could touch and talk to directly if I wanted to. I realized how much more I needed to learn. Waves of inspiration gave me goose bumps. I noticed some girls playing as well. I watched them carefully and critically, but their level didn't seem to be too much out of my reach. *With some practice and hard work I can easily attain their level*, I assured myself.

Khurram introduced me to the top women players there. They greeted me nicely, but I felt certain arrogance in their voices and their body language. They barely talked to me beyond the formalities, and once they found out what club I played for, they suddenly had an urgent task that they needed to attend to.

I got a court to myself for a couple of hours in the evening to practice. I wanted to play with someone from the host club, but no one was available, and I, again, ended up playing and practicing with Khurram, using our normal routine. I noticed that several of the players stopped by and watched my game and drills. No one came up to me to make any meaningful conversation, except for the formal "well played" comment.

The next day, Baba, Mamma, and Zameer went to tour the city of Peshawar, but I came straight to the club. I wanted to spend as much time there as possible—surrounded by squash. I wanted to absorb the air of the club into my body. As I ran on a treadmill, Simin and Sonia walked into the gym. They were among the top twenty women squash players in the region. They were glued to each other. I wanted to say hello to them, but they didn't even give me a second glance. I shadowed them looking for a chance to have a little conversation. I caught them in the hallway of the changing room as we crossed each other in a narrow corridor.

"I am a very big fan. I have been watching your matches for years. Both of you play amazing squash," I quickly blurted out, holding their hands.

"Thank you," they responded in English with a smile.

"I have been playing squash since I was a little girl, and I want to play like you do. Do you have any advice for me?" I asked them.

"Practice and drill a lot," Simin replied, walking away.

My head was filled with lots of questions, but they weren't interested in talking to me. I sat down on the bench with my head in my towel.

"Are you all right? Do you need something?" Nadia asked me, tapping on my shoulder.

I immediately stood up to show my gratitude that she even acknowledged my presence and responded, "No, I am fine, I am just heading to the round-robins."

In the round-robins, I had a chance to ask any player of my choice to play against me. I realized that the competition was going to be very tough. I was very disappointed that Simin and Sonia didn't play. I played some good games against several women who were higher level players. Playing with men—well that was a different story altogether. After playing with them, I got the feeling that they were from a different planet altogether.

Throughout the evening, I kept my eyes on the coaches there. I wanted to play with one of them at any cost. I got my chance, and I challenged their head-coach Asmat to a game. I knew well that he would not be able to decline my challenge during round-robins. Since no warming-up time was allowed, we started our match right away. Asmat was the world-renowned coach at the club. Many of his students have become world-class squash players. Asmat and I played a three-game match. I applied all the tricks and expertise that I could muster, but they all failed me miserably.

"Well played. You have a talent in squash, but you need good coaching," he told me bluntly. He went on to warn me, "You should join our club. Otherwise, you will be wasting your talent."

Completely out of breath after playing three very hard games with him, I spoke in a broken sentence, "I hear . . . . it is very hard . . . to get into your club."

With a smirk on his face, he said, "I am sure I can pull some strings for you."

After playing with Asmat, my evening was done. I had accomplished what I had aimed for. I was tired. I got back to the hotel. Soon, Baba, Mamma, and Zameer returned from their day of visiting the city. They seemed very excited about their day. I felt envious listening to them, but I was certainly not sorry. My accomplishments of the day far outweighed any fun I missed by not going to visit the city.

For the next two days, it was all intense competition. Players from the whole region were participating. I had one tough match after another, but with a lot of luck, I made it to the fourth round—no small accomplishment on my part. In the quarterfinals, I played against Asma. From the little that I knew about her, she had been playing at the Peshawar Club since she learnt to walk. She had even made it into Asmat's class. I felt thorns in my throat.

"She plays hard smashes, which are fairly accurate, but she is not very consistent. She might play five great shots, but then she will hit two loose ones. You could certainly use that to your advantage," Khurram whispered to calm me down.

As I started heading to the court, I spotted Baba's sunglasses. Indeed, it was Baba sitting in the first row of the spectators. His presence brought a burst of confidence in me. The spectators' benches were completely full. I had never played in front of so many people, including some world-class squash players, but I was determined to ignore everything except Asma and her shots. She started off with her signature game, hitting hard and accurate shots. I tried my strategy to make her run, but it didn't work, and I lost the first game to her quickly.

"You have to drop and lob, back and forth. Mix your shots. She will return some good ones, but then she will return some easy ones that you could easily win points from," insisted Khurram.

I didn't agree and argued, "No, I have to play hard smashes to her to make her returns less lethal."

He tried to dissuade me, "She likes to play hard-hitting games, and she is very good at that."

I walked on to the court for our second game. I decided to ignore Khurram's strategy and just follow my instinct. As the match started, I hit some smashes at her. I got the feeling that she was enjoying the hard-hitting game, just as Khurram had warned me. She was able to dislodge me from the center, capturing it for herself. I managed to mix the length and the pace of my shots and fought to get into the court center. She was finding it hard to put in her best smashes. I won the second and then the third game, but by then, my energy level had sunk. My arms felt weak. She used this to her advantage and came roaring back, winning the fourth and the fifth games. I fought hard, not letting her take the match from me easily. Both the last games went to deuces, but the inevitable happened, and she won. Playing a hard game sapped all my energy and had cost me the match. What disappointed me the most was that I had come so close to winning the match. I stood there, lamenting, *Only if either one of those deuces had gone my way!*

"Excellent match, playing quarter finals and coming so close to winning against one of the best players in the country is no less than a miracle," Khurram remarked, trying to hide his disappointment unsuccessfully.

Baba came down and patted me on the back. "I didn't know you played so well. Don't worry about losing the match. You have proven to be a very good squash player." This was his first compliment on my squash game—a moment I have treasured all my life.

Asmat walked toward me. Clapping his hands warmly, he commented, "Well played. I must admit I underestimated you terribly." He turned to Baba, "Your daughter has a talent, and she can go distance if she gets good training."

Baba looked at me. He must have read the question on my face, a question that I didn't dare ask because I knew what his response would be. He thanked Asmat for his comments and ended the conversation. I wanted to stay the next day to watch the semifinals and the finals, but Baba had decided to leave for home. Coincidently, we left the hotel exactly when the semifinal match was scheduled to start. Asma was playing with the champion from Lahore—the girl that I would have faced—if I had won just one of those unlucky deuces.

Oh well, I will watch the video of the match. I shrugged.

Throughout the ride back, I analyzed and reanalyzed each and every shot of my game, trying to think what I could have done differently.

Twenty Two

NOT JUST A DREAM

The dream of moving to Peshawar Club had been haunting me since our return. One day, as we sat for dinner, I marshaled all my courage and asked my question, already knowing the answer. "Is there any chance of us moving to Peshawar?"

"Don't ask such silly questions. We are not migrating again. One migration nearly took our lives. We will certainly die if we move again," Mamma scolded me to shut me up.

Baba explained in a much gentler tone, "You know how hard it was for us to settle down in Bannu. Had Noor Chacha not been here, we could not have made it. Peshawar is a much bigger city, and we have no one there to support us. Our life is good in Bannu. We will need much more money to live in Peshawar. Besides, the expenses of that Peshawar Club are beyond my reach."

This made me sad, mainly because I knew how right he was, but I also knew that if I were to have any future in squash, I would have to be in Peshawar. Baba didn't leave any room to talk further about moving. However, the dream of playing squash there wouldn't die in me. My daily routine resumed. School, home, and squash were all I did week after week. Khurram and the rest of the people from our club returned with videos of the whole Peshawar tournament. Beaming with excitement and pride, Khurram surprised me. "Your quarterfinal match was shown live on TV, and I am still getting comments from all over the country."

Chacha came to visit, and the first thing he told us was that many people in the village saw my match on TV.

"How did they like it?" I immediately asked him.

Chacha explained, "Some people were happy to see their daughter on TV, but most were furious at you for playing a men's sport with men watching you and your hair not covered. And they were furious at your baba for not stopping you."

Mamma sounded very concerned. "Who are those people?"

As Chacha went through his list, each name was more shocking to me than the other. Many of those were the families of the boys from my school who used to play cricket and *pitho* ball with me. However, I had bigger worries on my mind, desperately wanting to move to Peshawar but not seeing how it could happen. I had a feeling, maybe a wishful thinking, that Baba was not against the idea altogether, but financially, he didn't know how to make it happen. A solution came to my mind, and I called Asmat immediately.

"I am willing to coach as many students as possible to cover my club expenses there."

He didn't sound impressed. Instead, in a very blunt tone he replied, "First, we have plenty of coaches already, and even if I got you some students, you would not be able to cover the membership fee for the club. Listen, as promised, I can get you in as a member, which is not a trivial matter, but you will have to take care of the finances."

I had explored every avenue and didn't know what else to do. All roads seemed blocked. My difficulties were consuming me so much that I couldn't concentrate on my schoolwork at all. *I have got to do better at school*, I told myself, knocking my forehead with my knuckles. I was improving in English but was still way behind. At the Peshawar Club, everyone spoke English most of the time, while I was struggling badly. First, I was trying to avoid conversations with people because of my English, and when I had to talk, I was translating their sentences from English to Pashto and then translating my reply back from Pashto to English. This was certainly embarrassing.

Being so engrossed in my worries, I was losing focus even during my training. One day Khurram seemed a little preoccupied. He didn't talk much during our drills. "Wait for me in the lobby after changing," he instructed after finishing one of our sessions. As I walked to the lobby, he was already sitting down and waiting for me with an empty chair opposite to him. "Sit here," he ordered very directly. Without wasting any time on formalities he grumbled, "There is something very wrong with you and you are hiding it from me?"

I didn't respond and just sat there with my sight fixed at a crack in the floor to avoid eye contact with him. I felt a lump in my throat that completely choked any sound from coming out, but tears rolled down my cheeks, completely betraying me.

He brought some water and in a gentle tone, said to me, "Tell me what is bothering you, and I may be able to help you out." Looking into my eyes, he told me, "You are miserable, and I can't stand to see you this way."

"Asmat has been pushing me to move to Peshawar. I know that this is an amazing offer, but I don't want to leave our club here in Bannu," I confessed.

"Look, Amina, you must move. If you want to take your squash to the next level, you cannot stay here with me. I can't teach you anymore, and this club lacks the facilities that you now need to advance," he told me sympathetically.

I told him my second concern, "I feel terrible asking my family to move again after knowing what they went through when we moved to Bannu. Baba has a good job, and he will not find one like that in Peshawar."

After staring at the ceiling for a few moments, he floated a new plan. "Why don't you, Zameer, and your mamma move, while your baba stays here in Bannu?"

"Khurram, it is not as simple as you make it sound. Baba doesn't make enough money to pay for two homes, one for him here in Bannu and one for us in Peshawar. And most certainly, he will not be able to afford paying for my club membership and coaching expenses," I confessed reluctantly.

Now he was quiet. He seemed to have no solution. As I got up to leave for my tutoring class, I said *khuda hafiz* to him. I was almost out of the door when he asked, "Have you tried finding a sport sponsorship from a company or a business?"

Though I got to my teacher's house in record time, I was still pretty late. She scolded me. I couldn't hear a single word she taught me that afternoon because my mind was so preoccupied with what Khurram had said.

When I got home, Mamma was watching a religious show on TV. "Come and listen to what Imam Sahib is saying. He always has good things to tell."

"Okay, but after this, I want to watch an English show," I said, knowing well that she didn't understand English at all. I felt very selfish.

After the show, I did my homework. Baba was busy with his tutoring, and Zameer was out playing cricket. At night the four of us ate our dinner together. I couldn't think of anything other than finding a sponsor.

At the club, before starting our training, Khurram asked with a chuckle, "Have you solved all your life problems?" I was not amused.

"Here is a sample letter. Write one like this and send it to as many companies as you can find all over the country. When the time comes, you will need letters from me and Asmat, commenting on your talent. That will help," he explained. The letter was in English.

"How will I write all that English?" I fretted.

Over the next several days, I managed to write a letter and showed it to my English tutor. She burst into laughter after reading the first few sentences. "I am a squash talent." I had written.

"No, Amina, you are not a talent, you are a girl." She corrected my first sentence and wanted my whole letter rewritten. Together we worked on the letter in next two sessions. It was then suitable to send. I showed it to Khurram, and he was also impressed.

I sent letters to every company and institution that I could find the name and address for. I looked through every newspaper and magazine. I asked everyone for more names of businesses, and I didn't miss a single contact that I could find. Khurram gave me some old phonebooks with many more business names and addresses. I even wrote down the names of the companies that advertised on TV and sent them my letter. Zameer also helped me. Months passed, but there was not a single reply of any kind. Every day I wondered if my letters were even reaching people. Someone should reply, even if only to tell me that they don't want to sponsor me. After several months, one reply arrived.

The first phrase was "We regret to inform you . . ." The letter further explained that since they were sponsoring some cricket teams, they had no money for any other sport. It was a big disappointment, but I felt some encouragement. *At least, I got a response*, I assured myself. I felt jealous of the popularity of cricket in our country for the first time. And then a second response came. This one started off more positively, saying that they do sponsor squash players, but only men because men are higher on the squash ladder. That letter hurt and upset me.

Completely drowned in my disappointments, I walked into the club. Khurram greeted me at the entrance. I casually headed to the changing room. As I came out, Khurram was waiting for me at the court door.

"I have been trying to introduce you to someone very important, but you seem to be ignoring us," he complained with a smirk. In response, I profusely apologized for my behavior.

"This here is my coach who taught me squash. We haven't seen each other for years, and today, he just surprised me," Khurram introduced his friend to me. Turning toward his coach and pointing at me he said, "This is Amina. I have been coaching her for a couple of years, and she is already the top player at this club."

After saying our salaams, the coach complimented me, "I have seen your games, you have talent, and I see potential in you to become a first-class squash player. You should move to the Peshawar Club. They can make you."

Khurram told him the whole story and how we had no success in finding a sponsor.

After a brief pause, he asked, "Khurram, do you remember Shahid?"

"Which Shahid?" Khurram asked, trying to concentrate.

"I trained him in the same class as you. I used to scold him for not moving in the court. He was a little pudgy," the coach said to tease Khurram's memory.

Suddenly, Khurram was excited. "Yes, now I remember him. Where is he these days? He left our club before finishing his training with you, didn't he?"

"You two obviously have a lot of catching up to do. I will leave you alone while I go do some drills," I excused myself, but they were too involved in their conversation to even hear me.

As I started walking toward the courts, I overheard Khurram's coach, "He is the manager of Habib Bank in Peshawar. Go see him there for Amina's sponsorship. He must remember you, and I will write a note also. Just show him that. I think that he will do all he can. Besides, he loves squash."

Hearing my name along with a possibility of a sponsorship from a big bank, I became all ears. I bombarded him with questions about Mr. Shahid and his bank. We concluded that we must meet him as soon as possible. I practically sprinted all the way home. Baba and I cross-checked my list, and to our disappointment, we found out that I had already contacted the Habib Bank in Peshawar, but they never responded to my letter. I told Khurram that the Habib Bank lead may not pan out for us after all. He also got worried but then thoughtfully suggested, "To be on the safe side, we should take the coach with us when we meet Shahid. He would not be able to say no to his teacher as easily as he might brush us off."

Within a few days, Khurram gave me a letter, "Manager Shahid Sahib wants to meet with us. You and I should go to Peshawar to see him. Coach will join us there."

This was the first good news after a very long gloom. I was again going to present my case in front of an authority, just the same way I presented my case for a girls' school to our *jirga* all those years ago. I was ready for it in my heart.

At home, I showed the letter to Baba. Staring at the letter, and to my utter surprise, Baba said, "This might be a good contact. Go meet him soon. Zameer will go with you, and I will pay for your expenses."

Within a couple of days, we showed up at Shahid's office. As planned, Khurram's coach met us there. The office was beautiful. The whole building was nice and cool—it felt like walking into a heaven from the hot hell outside. The air-conditioning, the lights, and the furniture were all top quality. Manager Shahid was thrilled to see his coach, and he remembered Khurram well. He immediately ordered his assistant to bring cold drinks for all of us. After some reminiscing, my squash came up. Both Khurram and his coach bragged about my talent and potential.

I was overwhelmed. I didn't know what to say. I just blurted out, "I can play a match for you down at the Peshawar Club so you can see for yourself how good I play."

As soon as I uttered those words, I began to question the wisdom of my statement. But fortunately, Manager Shahid didn't take it as bragging on my part. Instead, he brought up the topic of his own membership at the club.

"I am a member at the club, but I rarely find time to go and play," he admitted.

"What can you do for a budding talent like hers?" the coach asked Manager Shahid point-blank.

"You are my teacher. How can I say anything but yes? Your wish is my command," he replied, holding the coach's hand. "I can get her the membership through my bank. We have a special contract with the club," Manager Shahid boasted.

I was about to jump with joy, but the coach was not satisfied. In his authoritarian tone, he demanded, "See if you can get her a sponsorship that pays her living and coaching expenses."

Shahid paused for a little bit. He scribbled some numbers on a sheet of paper. Then he called for another one of his assistants. They exchanged some words, and then turning toward the coach, he said, "My dear Coach Sahib, I am not sure how, but I assure you that I will—one way or another—cover her coaching expenses. I can promise you that much. However, as for her living expenses, I have absolutely no authority to approve that at my level."

Khurram raised his concern. "Her father can't afford her living expenses in a big city like Peshawar. How will she live in this city?"

Shahid remained quiet. Writing more numbers, he said, "I have to send a special request to my head office in Karachi. I promise to use all of my contacts there to get this approved, but this will take time."

We said our salaams and left his office. I just simply don't have the words to describe how happy I was that day. Although we didn't get my living expenses promised but just securing my club membership and the coaching fees was nothing less than a miracle for me. And then I was very confident that Manager Shahid will use his influence at the head office to get my living expenses approved as well.

We waited to hear from Manager Shahid. Days turned into weeks, and then weeks became months. Nothing was moving. All we could do was to make phone calls to the bank. And their response would be the same every time, "We have talked to this officer or that officer and the file has been moved from that office to this office." Getting no definite response was making me furious.

I felt like running to Karachi myself and telling those people off. If they don't want to approve my request, then they could at least let me know. Why was I being ignored? I was afraid and couldn't wait much longer. *What if Asmat changes his mind or some other adverse event happens?* These thoughts would send shivers down my spine. Baba was also very concerned about the progress of my application with the bank. He asked me every day if I had heard back. Then he came up with an idea.

"Amina listen, you, your Mamma and your brother should move to Peshawar, while I stay here. I don't want to lose a secure job. Who knows how long it might take me to find another one in Peshawar? I can provide for the family's living expenses, and the bank will cover your club expenses."

I was totally astonished because Khurram had suggested the same idea months ago and I was too afraid to even mention it at home to my family. And there I was hearing the same suggestion from Baba.

Twenty Three

BABA'S SOLUTION

In the next few weeks, Baba made several trips to Peshawar, and using Asmat's connections, he found small quarters for us near the Peshawar Club. For himself, in Bannu, he found a room in a neighbor's house, where he could live and continue tutoring his students.

Mamma was concerned and expressed her opposition to the arrangement. "Who will cook and clean for you?"

Baba was ready with his response. "I will pay extra, and my host family will provide my meals."

Mamma raised her second concern. "Where will you get all that money to pay for two households and also pay for someone to cook your meals?"

Baba replied sternly, "I will just add another tutoring session to make extra money for these added expenses. I will provide for the family, it is my responsibility and not your place to think about it." Turning toward me, he issued his threat. "There are only a few months left in the school year. The final exams are approaching. All I want in return is for you to pass your exams so that you can get into a college in Peshawar. If you fail this year, the whole plan is off. And you, Zameer, you are performing excellent in school. Keep up this fine work, and your dream of going into the engineering college will soon come true. Just remember, admission to engineering colleges is extremely competitive. You must score very high marks to get in. But the way you are doing in your school, I have full confidence that you will get in for sure."

Zameer couldn't be happier. He had been lamenting about the Peshawar College of Engineering and about becoming an engineer since he started his college in Bannu.

Over the next few months, I concentrated on my studies. I cut down my squash hours to a minimum and worked extremely hard on my schoolwork. English drills had taken the place of squash drills. I practiced math, memorized science, social studies, and Islamic studies every day. I had a good feeling, and most of my teachers were happy with my progress.

I was so excited to move, but when I thought about leaving Bannu, I would get a lump in my throat. *My friends at school are going to go their own ways after this year. I won't see them anyway*, I consoled myself. But I felt especially sad about leaving my club and the players there who trained with me for hours each day. *Then there is Khurram and all that he has done for me over the years. Without him, I would be nowhere in squash. And he has not only been there for me in squash. He is the one who got me those students to teach to make some money when we desperately needed some. He also got me going in English and then finally he has arranged for me to get this sponsorship for the Peshawar club. What will I do without him?* I pondered.

All in all, Khurram had been a strong pillar in my life. I felt such comfort looking at him, talking to him, and just simply being around him. I didn't want to imagine my life without him. He had promised me that he would stay in touch, but I also knew that once you are out of sight, you are out of mind. Or as they say in Pashto, "Once out of sight even a mountain doesn't exist. That thought bothered me to tears.

In addition to imagining my life without Khurram, I worried about the problems that I was creating for my own family. Playing in Peshawar Club meant that my lifelong dream was about to come true. Similarly, Zameer was totally thrilled to move. Going to the Peshawar College of Engineering, then just the life in a big city—he couldn't wait to get there. The story with Baba and Mamma was entirely different. They were worried about the family being split between two cities.

Mamma kept moaning, "Baba will be here all alone. There will be no one to take care of his meals. Who will do his laundry and set up his clothes? Who will make his bed? And who will clean his place?"

While Baba didn't say it as much or as often, he did express his concerns a few times. "Your mamma will have to run the family without me. Zameer is still young and immature. He can't assume the role of the head of the family. Most importantly, what will people say about me not being there for you all?"

I could see the grief on my parents' faces increase as the day for our move came closer.

Knowing that the only thing that might put my moving plans at risk was passing the exams, I doubled my effort on my studies. At home, I got

Zameer to help me explain anything that I had trouble with. I worked at my maximum with my tutors. At the club, Khurram was always there for me. Instead of squash drills, he did hours of English and math drills with me. He helped me memorize dates in history, formulas in math, and sentences in English. During my squash lessons, he would ask me to recite stories in English or quiz me on dates of events from my history lessons.

The exams started. I was very afraid, but as the exams rolled by one after another, I started to get a good feeling. I was confident that I was doing fairly well. The last one was the history exam. I came home from the examination hall and went straight to bed. I slept all evening and then all night. The next morning, I felt refreshed. All that puffiness under my eyes that Mamma had been worried about was gone. After lunch at home, I left for the club. Khurram was there teaching his students. I sat outside the court and watched him drill, feeling overwhelmed by a sense of gratitude toward him. *What would I be without this man coming into my life?* I questioned again and again.

As soon as he turned around and saw me sitting outside the court, he immediately stopped what he was doing. With a big smile on his face, he came to me and said, "Are you still alive? You had disappeared. During your exams, I understood when you didn't show up at the court, but what happened to you after the exams? Why didn't you come?"

I explained, "The last paper was only yesterday morning, and I slept all evening and all night like a dead person. If the world had ended yesterday, I wouldn't have known."

"Okay, all right. How are you feeling now? Have you recovered? How did your history paper go? Did you remember all the dates of the important events? What year did the Muslims of India fight the war of independence against the British Frangie?" he asked me, still smiling wide.

I replied, "Yes Khurram, that did come up in one of the questions, and I had it right. The year was 1857, wasn't it?"

"Are you sure you didn't write 1957? In your drills, you kept on making that mistake," he reminded.

That evening, I didn't do any drilling. I played friendly matches, first against Khurram and then against other men, until late into night.

For the next three weeks, I waited anxiously for my results to come out. During that time, I slept extra-long hours and spent good quality time with my family. The remainder of the time, I spent playing squash from morning until late evening at the club. I had to also teach a lot of makeup lessons to my squash students. I had postponed most of my teaching for until after the exams.

The results were out. With a throbbing heart, I looked into the newspaper. Name after name, I went down the list of candidates who had passed. There I was. I showed my name to Baba who was looking at the paper from behind my shoulder.

Sounding happier than I had ever seen him, he said, "You have passed with good grades. This will get you into a good college in Peshawar. The move is on. Get ready, pack up, and we will leave as soon as you all are ready."

Within a week, Zameer's results were out too. He had scored very high grades. Looking at his grade card, Baba couldn't contain his excitement. He nearly shouted, "My son has scored the highest grades in the district! These grades will get you into any college that you want to apply to. For sure, your plan to become an engineer is on track now."

Zameer was calm as he shared his future plans, "I will apply at the Peshawar College of Engineering. It is one of the best engineering colleges in the country."

In two days, we packed up the whole household. By early afternoon, the truck driver honked. We were still running around, gathering our boxes. Baba had hired two men to do the loading. Noor Chacha also helped. The truck was all packed up in a few hours. We were all set to leave.

Noor Chacha said his goodbye to all of us. Giving me a pat on my shoulder and tears in his eyes he said, "I am losing my second home, but I am very happy. This is exactly what I wanted for you from the day I realized your talent."

Although we didn't live in that house for very long, it still felt sad to leave it behind. Mamma cried, and I tried to hold my tears. Unfortunately, or maybe even fortunately, we didn't get much time to say farewell. The truck drivers kept on pushing us to hurry. Since the moment he arrived at our door, he kept on repeating his plea, "We must leave. It is already very late. I will have to return late tonight, and the roads are not safe after sunset."

I hoped that Khurram would come to say goodbye. But he didn't. As the truck rolled away, my eyes remained glued on the path to our house, still hoping.

Twenty Four

ALL NEW START

Baba stayed with us for a week. He got us all settled in during that week, buying us everything we didn't have, but were going to need in our new place. He had to fill out the forms for both of our colleges. There were many documents involved, especially for Zameer. Baba went around to different government offices, obtaining all those required documents. Zameer got accepted into the famous Peshawar College of Engineering. I got into a government college for women. Both colleges were similar in their looks. They were both old, red-brick buildings with arches, lawns bordered with flowers and rows of shady trees. In my college, mulberry trees lined one side of the lawn. It was called the mulberry quarter of the college. The first time I walked under the shade of those trees, my mind wandered off to our orchard back in the village and our mulberry trees there.

Baba left after finishing all that he had to do for us. For the first two or three days, it felt similar to those days of our village life when he used to go to the city to do something or to visit Noor Chacha and his family. It didn't take long before we felt the pain of his absence. Sitting down for our meals and looking at his empty spot would kill our appetites. The first few times, I just got up without finishing my meal and went away sobbing. Anytime that I took my mind off missing Baba, I would just miss Khurram and my life at the Bannu Club.

I felt badly torn. One half of me thanked Allah several times a day for granting me my dreams, the dreams I never believed could come true. There was a time when I went on hunger strike, demanding merely a fifth-grade schooling for me. And here I was now, going to a renowned college. Not only that, I had also become a member of the famous Peshawar Club. If anyone had told me that these two events were going to happen to me in my life, I would have scolded them for trying to enchant me. While at the same time the other half of me felt miserable. I had suddenly lost the most important men in my life—Baba and Khurram.

Being overloaded with college studies and squash training was a blessing in disguise for me. It took my mind off missing Baba and Khurram. At the college, I had to find out my classes, buy books, sit through lectures, and finish loads of homework every single day. At the club, I had to play matches and participate in group drills. Our capabilities were being assessed. After going through all that testing and drills, they had put me in Bilal's class. Bilal was a second-level coach. He took students who had potential to become professional players and gave them extensive coaching and training. Very few students qualified to enter his class. It disappointed me that I didn't make it into Asmat's class. Asmat was the highest-level coach at the club and, for that reason, in the whole country.

Baba came for what was supposed to be his weekly visit after missing two weeks. The same day, Chacha also came from the village to visit us in Peshawar for the first time. He brought Siama and Shaaz with him. We hadn't seen them for nearly a year. Mamma cooked Baba's favorite saucy beef with potatoes. Since we didn't have our own tandoor, Zameer had to run down the street to pick some naans from our local tandoor just as we sat down to eat. Baba stayed for only two days. There seemed something different about him. He had new sunglasses that suited his face better than his old ones, but he looked tired and weak.

Chacha looked very different. He had grown a beard and shaved off his mustache. He talked about his support for the Taliban.

When the conversation turned toward my squash, he shocked me. "The people in the village are against your squash, and they are right. Girls should not be running around among outsiders, doing men's activities. You should give up squash. Otherwise, you and your family may have to pay a very high price," he warned me at the end.

Facing Siama, he continued, "You are a bad influence on Siama already. Her mother has caught her a few times hitting squash balls in the court. She has gotten a few beatings already, and I hope she learns her lesson."

I looked at him in disbelief. *This is the same uncle of mine who got me into squash to begin with. Without his training, I couldn't have made it past our homemade court. It is he who used to practice squash shots with Siama as soon as she was able to hold a racket in her hands. How could he make such an about-turn?*

Baba changed the topic of the conversation. He asked Zameer and me, "How are your studies at college? Are you both concentrating on your education? Don't be lazy, work hard, and get good marks on the tests and exams."

"I am happy. It is a very good college," Zameer replied.

"I am not asking if you are happy. Are your teachers happy with you?" Baba asked, sounding more like a teacher than a father. "Amina, have you started your training at the club?" He wanted to know.

"Yes, Baba, Asmat has assigned me to his assistant, Bilal," I answered.

"Why is Asmat not training you? He promised to coach you when he first asked you to move. Is he not honoring his own words?" Baba inquired, pushing his sunglasses up on his nose.

"Asmat is the head coach. He has a team of coaches, and he assigns players to different coaches according to their abilities and their needs. Bilal is a senior coach, and he doesn't normally take newcomers, but in my case, they have made an exception," I explained proudly.

"But Asmat should have kept his word," Baba insisted.

"My next promotion will be to Asmat after I finish my program with Bilal," I told him, trying to control my excitement.

Mamma wanted to know how Baba was faring in Bannu. "How is your room? Do you get your food on time? Is your host family treating you well? You are paying them a lot of your hard-earned money. Are you getting a good return from them?"

Baba didn't seem too keen to talk about his life. He brushed off Mamma's queries by a short reply. "Yes, I am managing. As for my meals, they bring me my dinner on time, but I eat it after I finish my last tutoring class."

Mamma got more concerned than she already was. "But then doesn't your dinner get cold? You have never eaten cold meals all your life. You don't even like taking naans stacked up on the plate. You only eat the ones that come fresh out of tandoor. Then how do you handle cold food?"

"I am fine, don't worry about me," Baba closed the topic.

Siama slept in my bed throughout their stay with us. The two of us would talk till late into the night.

"Aappa Amina, how did you play squash at home? Didn't your mamma scold you and beat you?" she asked innocently.

I knew exactly what she meant. "Oh yes, I got my share of scolding and beating from Mamma, but thanks to your baba and mine, I kept on playing, mostly secretly, until Mamma gave in. But remember, I had the support of Baba and Chacha."

"My baba has changed. Before, it used to be only Mamma. Now he doesn't want me to play either. And even if I somehow sneak out to the court, I have no one to play with," she lamented, sighing deep.

Feeling her pain, I advised, "If you really like squash, you should keep playing. You will have to hide it from your parents, and just remember— you must be ready to get scolding and beatings if you are caught."

Gently stroking her cheeks with the back of my fingers, I whispered, "I will take you to my club tomorrow if Chacha goes somewhere. I will teach you some shots there that you can practice by yourself when you go back to the village. You don't need anyone to play with you."

In the morning, Siama and I got our chance. I took her to the club and taught her how to hit straight drives.

"At home, you should practice this shot as much as you can. This is the most difficult shot, and if you can get this right with consistency, then the rest of the shots will come much easier to you," I advised her while she smiled with a sparkle in her eyes.

Baba was leaving for Bannu. Mamma washed and ironed all of his clothes for the whole week and packed him some food to take along.

As we said our goodbyes, Baba said, "Study hard. Do well at your college and make me proud."

Before saying *khuda hafiz*, Mamma reminded him, "Please eat your meals properly and on time and don't let your food get cold."

All through the week, Siama remained right by my side. I didn't miss any chance to sneak her out of the house to my club to teach her some squash shots either. She was an eager student, and she wanted to learn squash at any cost. The week flew by. I had so much fun with my cousins. We talked, goofed around, and ganged up against Zameer and Shaaz. After they left, it felt very lonely but only until I jumped back into my usual activities.

Getting around in the city was a challenge. Some girls were dropped off and picked up by their parents or their drivers, but most of the girls took taxis to come to the college. Baba had arranged one for me too. The taxi would take six girls; every day it was the same driver and the same girls. We addressed our driver as Salman Kaka meaning Salman uncle, with respect. He was a gentle and a caring person. Often, I would ask him to drop me at the club. He didn't mind picking me up at the club to take me home whenever he could.

"Don't walk alone, it is not safe. Ask your brother to come and walk you home," he would repeat now and then. As if I needed a reminder on that subject. Who would have known it better than I? I dared not walk with someone from the club after what happened to Khurram and me when he walked me home in Bannu. The Taliban situation had only gotten worse. Thank God, neither the club nor my college was too far from our house.

Twenty Five

BASED ON LIES

I was trying very hard to adjust to the life at the club. While there were many highly accomplished players, I noticed a big difference in their attitudes compared to the players in Bannu. Everyone was glued to their clique. It was tough trying to make friends. I was ready to do anything to join Simin's group. She was always surrounded by Sonya, Asma, and Nadia. They would stick together from the minute they walked into the club until they left. I had admired them since my first encounter with them back at Bannu Club when they came to play a tournament. Since I rubbed shoulders with them several times a day, I wanted to have them as friends.

While Sonya and Simin played a friendly match, both Nadia and Asma sat outside the court and watched. Boldly, I walked to the front row and sat right next to Nadia. She didn't seem to mind my intrusion as she continued chewing her gum. I admired Nadia's beauty, her light brown hair a little longer than her shoulders in the back and bangs on her forehead with her almond-shaped green eyes.

"That was a great shot. Don't you think so?" I asked Nadia

She replied, "Yes, that is a typical Simin shot. Those who have seen her play know this."

"I would have played a drop shot," I commented on the next one.

"Oh, by the way, I am Amina," I introduced myself at the first chance I got.

"Where are you from?" Asma asked.

To start a conversation with Nadia, I tried to refresh her memory. "I played for the Bannu Club where I lost against you in a tournament."

Nadia remarked, "I play so many tournaments that it is hard to remember all of my opponents."

"So you have moved from Bannu, I guess," Asma added.

"Yes," I said, smiling and happy that they were talking to me.

"What brings your family to Peshawar?" Nadia asked. "I bet your baba has been transferred from Bannu to Peshawar. My uncle is posted in Bannu. He is using every possible connection of his to get a transfer to Peshawar also. Army officers don't like Bannu very much."

I clarified, "No, my baba is not in the army or the air force."

"Then what does he do?" Nadia asked abruptly.

"Oh, he works at schools," I said, thinking quickly, trying to come up with something more glamorous. "I mean he has a school business." I tried to modify my response because I knew that if I told them the truth, they would never want to deal with me.

"He owns English-medium schools all over the country," I further explained to glamorize Baba's job.

"What schools and in what cities?" they both asked, sounding very excited.

"He has schools in every city with different names," I replied after some fast thinking.

"My cousins go to a very good school in Islamabad. Maybe your baba owns it," Nadia remarked.

Before I could come up with a reply, Asma interrupted, "My cousins go to a very posh school in Lahore. I will find the name of their school and see if your baba owns that one."

"What about in Peshawar? Which school does he run here? Nadia asked.

"He hasn't opened one in Peshawar yet, but he is thinking about starting one here too." I crafted another reply after some quick thinking. I was surprised at how quickly I was making up lies after lies.

They bought into my deception and were excited to talk to me.

As Simin and Sonya came out of the court, Nadia introduced us, "This is Amina. She has moved from Bannu, and her father owns English-medium schools all over the country."

They also accepted me very warmly.

"I have seen you play with Bilal. You are very fast," Simin commented on my game.

"Time to go home, our drivers must be waiting for us. Do you need a lift?" Sonya asked me.

"Oh no, my baba sends me his car, don't worry about me," I told them, trying to avoid showing them where I lived or how I get to and from the club. Lucky for me, Salman Kaka came to get me well after all the girls were gone.

"What's in your mouth?" Mamma asked.

"Chewing gum," I answered.

"What is a chueen-gom?" She wanted to know.

"A kind of sweet that people in the city chew," I explained.

"Are you sure this is not *niswar*, the chewing tobacco? That is the only thing that some people chew. You are too young for that. Only men and very old women chew *niswar*. You will get a terrible headache," she warned.

I explained further, "No, Mamma, this is not *niswar*. It is kind of sweet candy that mostly children chew. It tastes very good."

I took one out and gave it to her to let her taste it. She looked at me strangely but didn't say much.

Next morning as I was leaving for college, she confronted me again. "Why are you going out with your hair all loose? Why haven't you made your braid?"

I protested, "Why can't I leave my hair loose? It is covered under my chador anyway. Other girls come to the club with their hair not tied in a braid."

"No, I don't want you to walk around with your hair flowing all over the place. Make a braid or I will make it for you," she threatened, continuing angrily, "Do you not realize that you are some sixteen-seventeen-year-old grown woman? All other women your age are married and are having children. They are running the whole household. Here you are—you haven't even learned to respect your own body and your appearance."

I argued for a few more minutes, but she was in no mood to give in. I quickly made a braid and left for the college. After I got out of the taxi, I undid the braid and let my hair loose. My friends liked it very much. They all told me how it suited my face.

Sumaira recommended, "You need to have your hair layered."

Shereen agreed and even offered, "I can cut it for you. I will bring my scissors and comb tomorrow. I do it for all my friends."

"No, I want a straight shoulder length at the back and straight cut across my forehead. Can you do that?" I asked.

"You mean bob cut in the back and bangs on your forehead? Yes, that is even easier," she responded. "However, make sure that your parents are not one of those who are strongly against girl's hair-cut. Some parents don't allow their daughters to cut their hair. I have gotten in big trouble before," Shereen warned me.

"Oh no, my parents are very modern. They won't care," I lied, knowing very well what kind of trouble I could get myself into.

I entered the club lounge very excited to see my new friends. At the other end of the lounge, I heard overly excited Asma, yelling, "Amina, over here! Come here, we have saved a seat for you. I have brought some warm samosas, and we have already ordered teas for all of us."

The samosas were delicious, and so was the company. I was with four of my favorite women in the world. After our teas and samosas, we headed to the courts. We played friendly games in a round-robin style, where the winner stayed on to play with the next player. All of them beat me easily.

The next day was the same, except that instead of samosas, there were some European chocolates that Nadia's baba had brought from one of his overseas trips. I had never had those sweets before. I didn't really like them, they were bitter, but I still ate my share.

To impress them, I lied again, "Oh yes, these are excellent, my baba also brings some when he goes abroad?"

"Your baba goes to Europe?" Simin asked with fascination.

"Yes, about once a year at least," I replied.

"Has he ever taken you there? Nadia asked me.

"Yes, many times," I responded quickly.

"What countries have you seen?" Nadia wanted to know.

"Oh, I have seen many countries: London, France, Paris, New York, England, and so many more." I rattled off every name that I knew.

"How lucky you are, my baba is only allowed to take Mamma but not the children," Nadia sounded envious.

I couldn't get over how beautiful Nadia looked. I wished I could get a haircut like hers.

That became our routine. After each one of would finish our training with our coaches, we would meet in the lounge, chitchat with one another, eat snacks that one of us would bring and drink hot tea from the café. We would talk about our squash, our college, and mostly about our families. And then end the evening with a couple of hours of friendly squash games. But somewhere deep inside me, I feared that, one day, my lies would be exposed. I became very cautious about everything I said or did.

"I miss my baba a lot. He is always traveling, but when he is with us, he is all mine. I feel his love deep inside my heart. He started me off with squash, and without his support, I couldn't have gotten anywhere in this sport," I told them, reminiscing about Baba and desperately missing him.

"I wish I could say the same about my baba. He is very busy all the time, but even when he is with us, he is not really with us. He is involved with his own things. I don't feel that close to him," Nadia admitted with teary eyes. "The same is true for Mamma. She is always busy. She is rarely home. Most of the evenings, she is gone to some function or a meeting," Nadia added.

"Who cooks your meals? Who takes care of the children and the family?" I asked.

"Our housekeeper, our cook, and other servants, of course!" she replied while all four of them stared at me with bewilderment at my question.

Each one of us talked about our parents, but I got the feeling that my baba cared about me much more than any of theirs. Just that thought brought tears to my eyes. Except for Baba not being around every day, my life was perfect. I couldn't have wished for anything more.

As I walked into the lounge, I saw them all there sitting around our usual table. Waving the bag in my hand, I screamed, "Have you ordered the tea? I have some hot samosas here."

"Yes, tea is coming soon, just come and join us," Asma instructed.

"What is your home address?" Nadia asked pointedly.

"It's 205 Court Road," I responded.

"Is it that green house with a C-shaped driveway?" Nadia asked.

My heart pounding out of my chest, I replied, "Yes, that is our house. How do you know that house?"

Completely ignoring my response, she asked her next question, "Who is Mr. Shamsi?"

My face turned red hot. *How does she know our landlord?* I wondered. I felt like someone had stuck my face into the mouth of a tandoor.

"I don't know any Shamsi. Who is he?" I shot another lie to hide all of my lies.

"My parents and Mr. Shamsi's families are close friends. They were at our house for dinner, and he told us all about you and your family. You live in their servant quarters, and your father is a schoolteacher in Bannu," Nadia announced my social death sentence.

"You have been lying to us for months. We have no respect for you. You are a liar and a cheat. We don't want to have anything to do with you," Nadia declared their communal decision.

Tears of shame rolled down my cheeks, and without saying a word, I dashed out of the lounge, walking straight home. I didn't even care if Taliban stopped me for walking alone on the street. Reaching home, I ran straight to my bed.

I will never show up at the club ever again, no matter what happens, I promised myself.

Hearing me cry so loudly, Mamma ran in. "What happened? Why are you crying?" She repeated her questions a dozen times in half a minute while shaking me violently.

I contemplated if I should tell her the truth about my lies or lie to her too. Surely, I could not tell her the whole story either. With what face would I tell her that I had been making up lies about my own family?

"Nothing. Nothing." I snapped at her.

But she was not ready to let it go. She stood there and insisted on knowing what had happened.

"My friends have said some nasty things to me to hurt me very deeply," I responded angrily while still crying uncontrollably.

"What could they have said that made you so upset and sad?" She wanted to know.

"Please don't ask me that," I repeated again and again.

But she did not accept my response. Slowly but surely, she extracted most of the details of the day's events out of me.

"Your baba and I have taught you one thing all your life and that is to be truthful, and here, you lied about your family and your baba," she scolded me harshly. "Aren't you proud of your baba for all that he has done for you? Do you know of any other father in the whole wide world who has sacrificed so much for his daughter?" She shamed me with her questions.

I wanted to die. I wished deeply that the earth would split and swallow me alive so that I wouldn't have to face another human being ever again. I wasn't sure what I was more ashamed of—that I lied to my friends or that I lied to raise the status of my family. I couldn't fall asleep. I spent half of the night sobbing and the other half figuring out how to face those girls again.

I will go to the club and tell them exactly why I did what I did and will apologize for telling lies. And then leave it up to them, I decided.

I knew well that unexcused absence was not tolerated at the club. But I just didn't have the courage to face those girls ever again. I shivered when I thought about being expelled. Gathering all my courage, I pushed myself into the club after several days of absence. Bilal greeted me at the entrance, wanting to know why I had been absent all those days. I got away by making the excuse of being sick. After all, I had become an expert liar.

All four of those girls were sitting at their usual table, eating their snacks and sipping their tea. I ignored their presence and walked straight to the changing room. Over the next days and weeks, they taunted me at every chance they got.

"Here's the princess of the Court Road mansion" came one heart-piercing remark, along with a burst of laughter, as I passed by their table on my way to the changing room.

"No! No! She's the maid of the Court Road mansion, living in the servants' quarters" came the follow up taunt.

I didn't hear the rest of their remarks as I dashed away as quickly as possible to avoid their sights and sounds.

We only live in the servants' quarters, but we are no servants of Mr. Shamshi, I said angrily in my own head. *How dare she call me a maid? But then I have earned this*, I thought, feeling the guilt of all my lying.

Nadia mocked me loudly enough so that I could hear it clearly at the farthest end of the hall. "Yes, London, Paris, England—definitely in her dreams while washing dirty dishes for Mr. Shamsi and his family."

Again, the others laughed uncontrollably, making me feel completely humiliated. Their taunts were taking a toll. I had to drag myself to the club every day. Every fiber of my body resisted going there. However, some unknown force kept pulling me in the club's direction.

Twenty Six

DRILLS AND THEN SOME MORE

Bilal started my training. He matched me up with different players and started taking copious notes. I didn't mind this arrangement as I got to play with some of the best players at the club. He wanted to identify my weaknesses and then design a specific training program for me.

I was also getting accustomed to college life, which was so different from the life at the school. We had much more freedom. We ran from one class to another, and on the way, if we decided to miss a class or two, the professors didn't scold us. Learning my lesson from what happened to me at the club, I decided to come clean with my college friends.

Gathering all of my courage and preparing myself mentally to face the worst consequences, I told them the truth, "Shereen, thanks for the warning. You're right, my parents would not allow me to get a haircut." And to change the subject quickly, I proposed, "Let's go to Café Lalazaar for tea."

"No, please, don't do that again. You tempted me into missing this class yesterday, and if I miss today's class, then I will be left too far behind," Sumaira resisted.

"Oh, come on. Don't try to be Ms. Goody Good. Be a little daring. This is college, and you're not a schoolgirl anymore where your teacher will complain to your mamma," Shereen mocked her to shut her up.

"Oh well, we will ask for the notes of both today's and yesterday's class from some other girl," I convinced them as we walked toward Lalazaar.

My group of friends at college was very important to me. I had to make a major effort before I succeeded in joining the group. Almost everyone was already part of one group or another. There were girls in close-knit groups who stuck together because they had all come from the same school and possibly had been friends since their childhood; they didn't let anyone new into their groups. Similarly, there was a group of girls whose fathers were officers in the air force or the army. They didn't mix with the others. They didn't think of the rest of us as worthy of their notice. They spoke English with one another and even with the teachers during the classes. It would intimidate the rest of the class; most of the other girls were not confident enough to even talk to them casually. I was fully aware of my shortcomings in English. Although I was beginning to understand fairly long sentences, I was in no position to hold conversations.

"Why do you play squash? That is not a women's sport," Sumaira confronted me judgmentally.

"Your body will be ruined and you will not be able to bear children," Shereen chimed in.

"If you continue for too long, you will lose your femininity and start to look like a man," added Rafia emphatically.

I have seen sportswomen on TV, and many of them are very beautiful. Why haven't they lost their femininity? I questioned the wisdom of my friends' argument and concluded that they were wrong. But I didn't know of any female athletes who had children.

Maybe Shereen is right, but I just cannot give up squash, even if I try to. I know that much. Our family has migrated twice because of my squash and is living apart, leaving Baba all alone. With what face will I tell Baba that I want to stop playing? I reflected.

Bilal asked me to meet with him at the court. I changed and got there. As I stood in front of him, not knowing what he wanted me for, he laid out my training plan. "I have decided what drills I want you to start your training with. There are some drills that I want you to do alone. There are some that I will do with you, and finally, I have a list of drills that I will make you do with one or two partners."

None of this sounded too special to me. Khurram had done all of those drills with me from the beginning. As we started my training, I became aware of my weaknesses. Every day he divided his students into groups of three each to practice with one another. He sat outside and watched us. He made us change our roles from feeder to receiver every few minutes to keep us on our toes constantly.

"No slowing down, this is not a walk in the park—go faster. Speed is critical!" Bilal would yell. He was very strict; I missed Khurram.

"Start the next drill. Don't just stand around. No sleeping on the court. Go home and sleep in your bed. Vacate the court!" he would scream into his megaphone.

Each session would be three very long hours. We were only allowed one bathroom break and two water breaks. At the end of each training session, I would feel like I was going to collapse. We counted the minutes and seconds. At the end of each session, everyone would just plop flat on the floor outside the court. He hated that.

He would command, "Don't lie down. Get up and jump ropes. Don't let your bodies cool down too much."

We jumped rope for ten minutes in between the sessions and both at the beginning and at the end of the day. Even skipping ropes had to be done at the maximum capacity. Bilal never relaxed his rules. After each training session, we could barely move. I dreaded going to the training.

"Now she wants to become a squash champion. In her dreams! I will never let that happen. I will tell my baba to forbid Asmat from accepting her into his class." Nadia remarked spitefully as I passed by.

That got me worried. I wanted to get under Asmat's coaching from the day I started at the club.

What can I do about her? I can't go begging her to forgive me. I explored my options.

Their taunts kept on coming. "Father is the owner of English-medium schools all over the country—and the daughter can't speak a word of English," Sonya sneered as they all laughed sarcastically.

"He must be a janitor at a school in some village, and the daughter here has promoted him to the level of owner of not one but all the schools in the country." This vicious statement came from Nadia.

They could call me names, and I could keep on ignoring them, but things changed that day when they insulted my baba. I felt like scratching their pretty faces and yelling into their ears, "You can't show me one father in the whole world who could measure up to mine!" I knew in the heart of my heart that if they didn't stop soon, one day, I would tell them off, no matter what the consequence would be.

As I went to sleep that night, their voices echoed in my ears. *I have to stop them. I should talk to Bilal. Maybe he will tell them to stop. But what will I tell him about why they are doing this to me?* I contemplated.

No. I will have my revenge on the court, I decided. *I will thrash all of them one by one.* I could see myself doing just that with my eyes closed.

Other people at the club were not all that friendly either. Everyone was very competitive. Interactions were mainly limited to squash. My bitter experience with Simin's group had taught me the lesson that I needed to learn. I kept my interactions with the club members at the level of a formal "hi and bye" and just concentrated on my squash. Besides, there were few opportunities to socialize. Training was extremely strict. From the moment we entered the club until the time we left, we drilled and practiced. If we were not on the court, we lifted weights, ran on a treadmill, or jumped rope in hundreds of repetitions. The only time we sat down was when we watched videos of our own plays or of other players to learn how to do a shot correctly.

Ramadan came around again. Fasting was harder than the previous year. Most people at the club fasted all day and then did their routine practice, although the coaches became somewhat lenient. We had a special training schedule for Ramadan. Most of the practice took place in the evening, closer to the end of the day. After a couple of hours of training, the desperately awaited siren would announce the breaking-fast time. We would all sprint to the water pitchers and gulp water faster than our throats could swallow. A big spread of food would await us. Club members would bring in different dishes for everyone to share. Different mixes of sweet-spicy fruit salads, fresh fruit, warm samosas, veggie *pakoras*, baked patties, kebabs, and different pilafs would fill the table one end to another.

"Don't eat too much, you have several more hours of training left, and it is not easy to play on a full stomach," Bilal would warn loudly and repeatedly.

As Ramadan wounded down, we became excited about Eid. Baba made plans to take us home to the village to celebrate Eid with the rest of the family. I couldn't wait to see Siama. *She must have grown quite tall in all this time*, I imagined.

We were yearning to see Mather-Khubi too, but we were afraid to face other relatives and the neighbors. By then, the entire village had found out about my squash and looked down on our family. What worried me the most was Chacha. He had warned us that we might get into serious trouble because the village frowned upon my playing squash.

Baba arrived on an early morning bus from Bannu to join us in Peshawar. From there, he hired a taxi to take us to the village. He wanted to get to our destination before nightfall. The driver seemed to be a decent person. During the trip, he told us about his family, and Baba told him about ours. His name was Nisar. He was a family man with four children. The landscape had changed drastically since our last visit. We saw military camps, tanks, armored trucks, and uniformed soldiers hiding in bunkers. We were driving through an active war zone.

As we passed by a village, where most houses had been destroyed. Nisar told us, "There are daily battles between the Taliban and the Pakistan Army with heavy losses on both sides. Often, innocent civilians—including children, women, and old folks—lose their family members, their belongings, and their lives."

I couldn't resist comparing the miserable scenery that I was seeing to the days when children could play until late at night, sometimes even miles away from their homes without any worries.

It was already late when we arrived at our village. Nisar seemed nervous about driving back at that hour.

Judging the situation, Baba offered him, "You will not be able to make it back before very late tonight. You should stay with us and leave in the morning."

After declining a couple of times, he agreed. Baba opened up the back room for him and gave him bedding and blankets. Mather-Khubi had prepared dinner for us. Baba took some food to the guestroom to eat with Nisar. Mather-Khubi was thrilled to see us, but Chacha didn't come to greet us. Not being able to see Chacha and his family upon our arrival broke my heart. And not being able to hug my darling Siama brought tears to my eyes.

Getting up in the middle of the night to eat *sahri* meal before starting the fast is the hardest act of fasting. Yes, indeed even harder than going through the day without a drop of water. All that rich fried food has to be eaten quickly before sunrise and then drinking as much as your stomach can take is not easy. Our guest Nisar was also up and ready to leave for his days—work, but Baba persuaded him to eat *sahri* before leaving. Again, he accepted after declining a few times. On his way out, he dropped Baba and Zameer at the mosque for the morning prayers.

Life at the village was full of fear. I noticed people looked at the sky while walking, as if, any minute, the American drones or Pakistani air-force planes would appear out of nowhere and bomb any house, any gathering, and even children's playgrounds. People were extremely wary. Even in our house, Baba had a thick bunker built for Mather-Khubi, and we stayed there most of the time because it was the safest place. Chacha and his family had also converted a room into a bunker. Mather-Khubi told us that in every home, there was one. People throughout the village were always on edge. Any loud noise and people would run for shelter. There were trenches throughout the village center, around the mosque, the madrassa, and the village store. People bragged about their trenches and told stories of how those trenches had saved their lives.

Chacha and the rest of our relatives were still not talking to us. He wouldn't make eye contact with us, even when we bumped into him around the *kot*. He was dressed like the Taliban. I yearned to go to him and give him a hug, but he didn't even respond to my salaam. Mather-Khubi told us about all the gossip that was circulating around in the village. Baba sat quietly, upset, while Mamma cried loudly. Zameer and I didn't know what to think.

Siama sneaked into our house to be with me every chance she got. And yes, we sneaked into the court and played squash almost every day. She had mastered a few of the shots that I had shown her. She had excellent anticipation of the ball, and her footwork was beautiful. I wished I could have taken her with me to Peshawar.

I joked, "If you get a beating today, I will cry as loud as you just to share your pain."

Sounding very determined, Siama responded, "I don't care. I am ready for any pain as long as I can play squash with you."

Twenty Seven

CONDOLENCE VISITS IN PLACE OF EID FAIR

Like most years, that year too, no one was sure if Eid would be the following day or a day later. Immediately after sunset, everyone went outdoors to look for the new moon on the horizon. Some said that they saw the crescent, while others said they didn't. After breaking fast, all the men went to the mosque for the *traveh* prayers. At the mosque, they announced that since the moon was not sighted, Eid would not be the next day, as we were all hoping, but would be a day later. We had to endure one more day of fasting. We were very disappointed. We couldn't wait to wear our new clothes that Baba had brought for us. My outfit had beautiful embroidery on red cloth, and Mamma's was green. That extra day of fasting felt like a torture. Mather-Khubi and Mamma prepared food all day, not only for breaking fast but also for the Eid day.

Our wait was finally over when we woke up in the morning and it was indeed Eid after all our longing. Baba and Zameer took their Eid baths, put on new clothes, and went to the mosque for prayers. The rest of us started our day by cleaning up the house. Then we laid out the food in the sitting room. I placed the plates, glasses, spoons, and the jugs of water for our guests. At last, we changed into our new outfits. I kept looking at myself in the mirror.

"You just look like a doll," both Mamma and Mather-Khubi kept telling me again and again.

Siama sneaked in to show me her outfit, which was also a gorgeous dress full of embroidery. "Aappa Amina, I have never seen you look so beautiful. I wish I could look at you all day long, but I have to run back. Baba will be home, and he will be terribly angry at me if he saw me with you here," she told me, looking sad.

Baba and Zameer returned after visiting some of the village elders on their way home. We said Eid Mubarak to one another. Baba gave us our Eid money, and we embraced each other to wish happy Eid. Baba looked upset, but he didn't say much.

"The village elders and the people that we met out there were very unkind to Baba and even to me," Zameer whispered. "They told Baba off and made very sarcastic remarks about our family and about your squash," he continued in a barely audible tone. "One of our uncles shouted directly at Baba, telling him that our family had brought disgrace and dishonor to the whole village and ruined the good name of our tribe forever."

We waited the whole day for someone to come and wish us happy Eid, but no one stopped by. Even Chacha didn't come to greet us on Eid.

"Two of my sons are not even wishing each other Eid Mubarak while living under the same roof," Mather-Khubi moaned all day with her deep, painful sighs.

The Taliban now controlled our once-beautiful village. Hundreds of unknown faces were seen congregating around the mosque and the village center. Many of our old neighbors had left. All of the girls my age were married off and having children. Several of them had become the second or third wife of much older men or the Taliban commanders.

The Pakistan Army and the Taliban engaged in regular battles, in which thousands of people had been killed on all sides. Then there were drone bombing by the Americans with its own toll of heavy losses of life and property. The villagers debated in angry arguments about every topic, except for the drone bombing. People were angry about it and wanted revenge. Even Zameer argued that avenging the death of innocent people would be the right thing to do. I shouldn't have been surprised by Zameer's comments since he had taken a special liking to Chacha on that trip. While Chacha was not talking to the rest of us, Zameer had been spending a lot of time with him.

Instead of going to the Eid fair that children look forward to the whole year, we went for condolence to the families of the people who had died during the past year. We called on several families, including the family of Zameer's childhood friend, Riaz, and his father, Naeem Khan. We used to address him respectfully as Naeem Chacha. This family was neither related to us, nor was it one of our close neighbors, but our family had known them for generations. Riaz and my brother, Zameer, had been friends since they started school. They were inseparable during those days, and their friendship had not wavered. Riaz got married the previous year. Baba and Zameer attended his wedding. I remember how Zameer talked about the wedding for months.

In a drone attack, his whole family got killed—his mother, his sister, his new bride, and even his newborn baby. Naeem Chacha and Riaz were at the mosque for their evening prayers when the bomb fell on their house. We sat down and started small conversation with them.

Staring at the floor with visibly teary eyes, Naeem Chacha commented, "Riaz's sister was about to get married, and we were all preparing for her wedding. Now she is no more."

Riaz stayed completely quiet after saying his formal salaam. There was a picture of his smiling baby on a side table. We sat for a few minutes of painful silence and then said the prayers for the deceased. Before leaving, we told them to be strong and patient. Mamma and Baba tried, without success, to console them.

Baba had his own worries, which he had not shared with us. Our orchard had been turned into a tent city. Since Baba was not there to stop them, hundreds of Taliban had occupied our orchard. They had pitched their tents, settled their families there, and put up a mosque for themselves. Baba had been trying for almost a year to have them evicted. The squatters had threatened Baba with dire consequences if he tried to remove them from the property. Baba had been pushing the *jirga* to intervene. The *jirga* had met several times to debate Baba's complaint but were unable to make any decision. All *jirga* members accepted that the orchard belonged to Baba, but then they were divided after that. Some members were outraged at the Taliban for illegally occupying someone's property, while others were sympathetic. They didn't want to uproot the holy warriors and their families, especially the war widows and their orphans.

Baba had been taking time off from his work in Bannu to attend those *jirga* meetings. No wonder he had been skipping visits to us in Peshawar.

"Since we don't live here anymore, we are not getting full support from the *jirga*," Baba suspected. "No matter what they think about the Taliban occupying our property, most *jirga* members don't want to confront Taliban—either out of fear or out of sympathy for them," Baba concluded, setting his sunglasses higher on his nose.

"And who would want to destroy a mosque where people have been praying for months? Not even I could do that. Wouldn't that be a sin?" Baba wondered aloud.

To save himself from taking another trip from Bannu, Baba requested the *jirga* to meet while we were there. They agreed to meet on Friday. That forced us to extend our stay for two more days. Baba missed two days from his work. Zameer and I missed a few days of college.

"You all should pray that the *jirga* accepts my appeal today," Baba told us before leaving to attend the meeting.

Mamma and I went to the rooftop to sit in the sun and watch for Baba's return. I knew every scratch and every bump of that rooftop. I had spent countless number of hours up there, waiting to fetch the ball when Baba, Chacha, and Zameer played squash. While Mamma's eyes were fixed on the street, I couldn't take mine off the squash court.

Inside the house, I found some old rackets and a few squash balls. I entered the court and started hitting the ball. Since no one had taken care of the court in over a year, the walls and the floor were crumbling. Many of the balls didn't come back straight because the plaster on all four walls and the floor had chipped at many spots. The size of the court was very different. For the first time ever, I became aware of how bad that court was. It was just a corner of the *kot*, with four walls and calling it a squash court was a stretch of imagination. I slammed the ball harder. Mamma watched me with no expression on her face. For one second, that stare sent a shiver down my spine. "She is not stopping me from playing squash anymore." I reassured myself.

"Do you see Baba?" I asked her while continuing my shots. She didn't reply, and I continued hitting the ball.

As the sun started setting, I suggested, "It is getting dark. Baba will stay at the mosque for the evening prayers. Let's go in and start dinner."

In the kitchen, we finished cleaning up first, and then Mamma kneaded the dough for naans. I washed the vegetables and cut tomatoes and onions. While waiting at the tandoor for our turn to bake naans, Mamma started chatting with the aunties gathered there.

One of them asked, "Are there tandoors in Peshawar, or do those poor souls eat English-breads only?"

"The homes are very small, and there are no backyards. How could they have tandoors?" another auntie answered for us.

Then more questions came: "You don't have any relative there—who do you talk to all day?" "Do people there speak the same language as we do, or do they have a different language?" "What kind of clothes do people wear there? Do women go out without covering their hair?" "Do the city-women wear such tight clothes that their body shapes can be seen by other men?" "If there are no backyards, then where do they dig their wells for water?" "Do men and women walk together on the streets?" "How can you live in such a foreign land where nothing feels your own?"

Mamma briefly acknowledged some of them and ignored others. As soon as our naans were done, we said *khuda hafiz* to all and left the tandoor. Dinner was ready, but there was still no sign of Baba. Mamma started talking to me about my college and what I liked about it. Our conversation ended up being about squash. Mamma still shunned me for playing squash. She didn't understand what I would do with it or how it would shape my future. Just as our discussion got heated, Baba and Zameer walked in.

"What did the *jirga* decide?" Mamma asked without saying her greetings.

"I am very hungry, bring out the dinner," Baba replied.

"What happened?" Mamma repeated after serving the food.

"There were long debates. The members were divided into two groups. One side was telling us to give the orchard to the families of the holy warriors, as charity to please Allah, and since we don't live here anymore, why do we need the orchard? While the other side was insisting that allowing the Taliban to continue occupying our orchard would set a wrong example. Anyone of the villager could be the next to lose his property in this way," Baba summarized the hours of arguments.

"How can they expect us to give up our property that has been in our family for generations?" Mamma demanded an answer.

Baba happily told us the *jirga's* final decision, "Allah has answered our prayers. The Taliban have been ordered to remove all of their homes from our orchard, except for the mosque. No one supported demolishing the mosque."

I was thrilled. While Baba and Mamma talked some more, my mind wandered off to the hot summer days of my childhood that I spent working in that orchard. I could almost feel the cool breeze passing though my hair while standing under the shade of our trees. The taste of the sweet apricots and mulberries were still fresh in my memory. The squatters had chopped down many of our trees that we had nurtured with our bare hands.

Good or bad, our time at the village came to an end. As we loaded up our luggage in the taxi, I saw Siama sitting in her doorway, crying. She was not allowed to come out to see us off. All through the drive, I couldn't shed the image of her sad face.

Twenty Eight

CONSUMED WITH REVENGE

The memories of my trip were distracting me miserably. I was unable to concentrate on my lessons or, for that reason, on anything else. Sad faces of Naeem Chacha and Riaz and the pictures of the Riaz's baby haunted me. My friends asked me repeatedly if all was well with my family, but I said nothing to them. I didn't want to spoil their happy memories of Eid celebrations by sharing my painful ones.

Right after my last class, I headed straight to the club. Calm came over me as I entered the compound. Seeing all those familiar faces and hearing the noise of squash balls hitting the walls was a soothing distraction. There, I saw Bilal and Asmat talking to each other. I said my salaam to them. They responded warmly.

Bilal continued, "I hope you have had a good Eid and restful holidays. You have a grueling training ahead of you because there are several tournaments coming up back to back, and I want you to play in all of them."

Asmat added, "You have just turned eighteen this year. You could still play in "nineteen-and-under" league for another two years, but I want you to try out in the open competitions against ladies of all ages. That way, you can accumulate points and get into a strong position to compete internationally. You will have an excellent age advantage. You will be among the youngest competitors. Most of your opponents would be nearly a decade older than you."

Forgetting every other aspect of my life, I drilled and drilled each shot for hours each and every day. I especially concentrated on the shots that I used to be afraid to play. Any time that I didn't spend inside the court, I worked out in the gym. I used every exercise machine at the club. The training was grueling indeed. Several times each day, I got the feeling that my body was about to shut down before completing my routine. But I would push myself beyond my limits by doing those last ten squats or those impossible twenty more sprints across the court. My motivation, each and every time, would be the same—my revenge on Nadia and her group on the court. Their insults and taunts still rang in my ears, and the resulting fury of mine kept me going.

I started to feel stronger and faster both inside and outside the court. Bilal seemed satisfied with my progress but occasionally commented, "Your shots are improving a lot, but what worries me is that you don't put them together that well. That is critical during a match. Remember, playing squash is like knitting a carpet. No matter how tightly you tie each knot, you can't create a colorful, solid carpet without knowing how to put all those knots together."

The first competition was among all the teams from the northern region. Hundreds of players from all around the region surrounding Peshawar gathered at our club. Khurram and his small team from Bannu also came. I felt more confident having him around. I was impressed by the talent present there. Many of the players had come up playing at public park courts with no training or coaching whatsoever. They were all men. Women could never play in those public courts. I played my matches and won them one after another. I kept a close watch on Nadia's ratings. I was totally consumed by the fixation of playing a match against her and defeating her decisively.

I got my wish granted. I breathed a sigh of relief when I saw my name against her on the next round. I went home to rest well, but my heart throbbed with anxiety. I went to bed but couldn't fall asleep for hours. The thought of defeating her and then celebrating my victory over her kept me up till late. In the morning, I got to the club well ahead of my match. I saw Khurram running toward me. That put a smile on my face.

Out of breath, he asked, "So have you heard? I am so sorry."

I looked at his face, trying to figure out if he was just trying to pull my leg. "What have I heard?" I asked him, looking confused.

In a very sympathetic tone, he told me, "Has no one told you that you have been disqualified from this tournament?"

"No. What are you talking about? I have won all the matches and next, I am playing against Nadia," I nearly shouted at him.

He explained, "To be able to play in this tournament, you must have had a National Squash Association's ranking. And you don't have one."

Trying unsuccessfully to control my tears, I asked, "But then how was I able to play all those matches over the last two days?"

I saw Bilal walking toward me from the other end of the lobby. I saw a ray of hope. *He must have cleared things up for me, and he is coming to discuss the strategy of the match.* As he got closer, I tried to read his face expressions. They were more of disappointment, anger, and frustration rather than of relief or content.

He explained apologetically, "This tournament is relatively friendly, and most of the time, they simply ignore the small laws and bylaws, unless someone raises an objection. I didn't even remember this rule, let alone remind you of it."

By then, I was crying fairly loudly. I pleaded with him, "Please try to do something. I will talk to Asmat. I am sure he can use his influence to bend the rules a little. You know that I have trained extremely hard for this day. You can't take that away from me just like that. Nobody told me about this ranking thing. Please. Bilal, go and talk to the organizers."

"Amina, all morning, I have been running around, talking to one organizer after another. They all say that now that the objection has been filed, nothing can be done," he assured me.

Bilal left, but Khurram stayed with me to console me. He wondered, "Who could have filed the objection, and why?"

I knew the answer well but couldn't share that with him. I had never told him about my issues with Nadia and her group. Khurram tried his best to calm me down. He got me a glass of tea from the café and made me drink it on the spot. While I drank tea, he advised me, "You should register for ranking today and play every match and competition to gain your ranking at the NSA." While he was speaking to me, I saw Nadia walk by. She looked at me with a bold smile of victory on her face. Khurram didn't see that as he continued, "Within a few months, you will move up the ladder. It is very important for you to become a ranked player. All the national tournaments have that requirement. That would be just a formality in your case, as you can easily beat most of the players in the whole region."

He always knew what to say to calm me down, but I was completely devastated. Inside me, I was raging with anger toward Nadia.

Imagining her face in my teacup, I said, "Fine, you got your way this time, but you will have to face me, sooner or later, on a court. Now you have only increased my wrath."

Since I was disqualified, Nadia moved to the next round unopposed.

The event of my disqualification left a deep scar on me. But it also increased my determination to defeat her and defeat her soon. I got my chance. Within months, another tournament, open to all ages, was upon us. No ranking was required. Players from all over the country arrived. It seemed the who's who of the squash world was under one roof in Peshawar. Spectators came from all over the country—army generals, air force officers, politicians, and prominent businessmen. Manager Shahid from the Habib Bank met with me personally. As the bank was my sponsor, I had to wear clothing with their emblems all through the tournament. He ordered banners to advertise the bank with my picture on them. The first few days were relatively eventless. I made it to the fifth round.

Right after winning my qualifying match, I dashed off to see the ratings ladder. There was a crowd gathered around the rating board, but somehow, I squeezed through the crowd to find out who I was playing against in my quarterfinal match. It was to be Nadia again.

"Not only I, but the whole club is looking forward to your match with Nadia," commented Bilal, smirking while making his prediction. "I am so excited that one of my students will be competing against one of Asmat's. I am sure that mine will certainly win." I felt the pride in his voice.

As I turned around, I saw Nadia walk by us. I continued my conversation with Bilal. I wanted to see if she would initiate any conversation. "Hello," she said, nodding to Bilal. She completely ignored me while she casually talked to Bilal. I turned toward Khurram and started a conversation with him.

The match started almost two hours late because some of the other matches went longer than their scheduled times. Entering the court, we shook hands with each other without even saying our greetings. Then we both shook hands with the referees. After winning the toss, I served. I didn't know what I was hitting or where I was hitting. All, my mind could see was Nadia sitting with her friends and passing those hurtful remarks. She took full advantage of my disarray and won the first game.

"What are you playing out there? This is certainly not squash. You have lost this first game, and if you don't wake up, you will be out of this tournament," Bilal warned me during the break.

"I can't lose against her. Period!" I yelled at myself.

In the second game, she let her defenses down. I didn't give her any breaks or breathers and, surprisingly, thrashed her. She barely got four points, and I won the second game with my head spinning. Now I knew what to do. I repeated the same in the third and the fourth games.

Throughout the match, she kept on asking for lets against me from the referees, and they kept on granting her. I protested on several points, but the referees seemed like bent on rejecting those. They, however, rejected my own requests for lets on several occasions. But I didn't let their unjust refereeing get to me. I just wanted to win at all costs.

As I played the match point, the whole crowd roared at my shots. With a brutal smash at the lower left side of her body, I won the match. She was in shock. She had never seen and experienced that side of me. We shook hands without either one of us saying a word to the other.

"Amazing match, you didn't let her settle down at all. Good strategy," Asmat congratulated. "Excellent training with Amina, in such a short time too," Asmat commended Bilal, shaking his hand.

My semifinal round was against Madiha from Lahore. She was a ranked player and known for her consistency. But my eyes were on the finals. I knew that I had to win my match against Madiha to get to the finals. Simin was a clear favorite to reach the finals, and I wanted to play against her. I had to have my revenge against her at every cost.

The semifinal match went up and down for me. I won the first game, but then I lost concentration, making silly unforced errors. I came very close to losing the match before reversing the tables in my favor. I barely won the match. Nearly two hours of brutal squash and I had won only due to my sheer determination. All those matches were being shown on Peshawar TV. I was dying to know if the people at the village had watched my matches. Reporters and photographers were buzzing around me.

I had reached the finals and was set to play against Simin. As the match started, she behaved a bit more civilized than Nadia did during her match with me. Upon entering the court, she shook my hand, wished me good luck, and apologized to me. "Amina, I am sorry for joining Nadia and the others in teasing you about your family." Her apology shook my concentration. I wondered about her intentions, and even the thought of her being my friend again crossed my mind briefly.

It could be her apology or my lifelong admiration and respect for her that I didn't feel the same vengeance against her that I felt against Nadia. I wanted to win the tournament. I reminded myself that Simin did insult me and my family when she had a chance to stop the others.

My game was erratic. I played a bunch of smart shots, winning impossible points, followed by some very sloppy shots that Simin made me pay for dearly. Simin was also nearly ten years older than me. I was making her run back and forth on every shot. She was getting tired and losing concentration. After easily winning the first game, I lost the second.

"You have to make her run—make her tired. This is the only way for you to get points. She is getting tired, but you have to use that to your advantage," Khurram whispered to me during the water break.

I served a high lob to push her in the back court, and then with a very deceptive wrist shot, I dropped the ball in the opposite front corner. She made it there just in time to lift the ball, which I smashed into the other corner. With that winning shot, I defeated Simin and won the championship.

During the prize ceremony, the governor of the province gave me the trophy and my first-prize check. He praised me for my hard training and my dedication to the game of squash. Seeing Simin receive the second prize and Nadia not even anywhere around the podium was a much bigger reward for me.

Twenty Nine

CELEBRITY

All of a sudden, I had become a celebrity. I began getting invitations to attend functions at the governor's house and at the mansions of those high officials from the army and the air force. TV channels began calling our house. Newspapers and magazines were publishing my pictures and interviews. Several companies contacted us to cast me in their advertisements.

At the college too, attitudes had changed. Girls who would never even glance at me—were trying to find lame excuses to talk to me. Even their parents wanted to meet with me and invite me to their mansions. The teachers were extra polite. I was fully enjoying my celebrity status, knowing well that I deserved it and I had earned it with my hard labor and determination. But not even for a minute did I ever take all the credit for it. I was always mindful of the tremendous sacrifices that my family had made for me. I also did not forget my humble beginnings at that homemade court back in the village.

I desperately wanted to know how the people of my village felt about my success, but unfortunately, I had no contact with anyone there. Baba was the only one who used to go to the village often enough, but he didn't share the feelings expressed by our villagers about my squash. Even my immediate family had not been involved in my celebrations. Baba still lived in Bannu and visited us for one day every two or three weeks. Zameer was rarely home, and Mamma didn't talk about my squash ever.

We moved into a much larger and better house. During one of my TV interviews, the manager of a local car dealership gave me a new car as a reward for my achievements. He had been a member of the Peshawar Club for years and had been following my progress over the last several months. He was thrilled that I had won those tournaments for our club.

I wanted Baba to move in with us. After much thought and choosing my words carefully, I asked Baba, "Can you please move in with us? We need you here."

"What am I going to do about my job and my tutoring?" he asked me rather sarcastically.

"You could find a teaching job in Peshawar," I suggested.

I dared not tell him that he didn't need to work since I was making more than enough money for the whole family. He still wanted to provide for the family and would not hear of me supporting us financially.

"I need someone to be with me when I travel to different cities for tournaments or for interviews and photo sessions," I pleaded.

"Take your mamma with you," he replied bluntly.

"Mamma has never been involved in my squash. I want you to manage my squash career," I insisted.

He didn't seem to be too keen to talk about my request. The matter just got put off.

As I rested at home for a few days, I noticed that both Mamma and Baba were preoccupied. Baba was dealing with the situation of our orchard being occupied by the Taliban, and Mamma was dealing with Zameer's demand that she allow him to join the Taliban at the village. I was not fully aware of the gravity of either of these situations. I knew that Zameer had been going to the village very frequently and that Mamma was upset about it, but I didn't make anything of that. Zameer grew a beard and dressed in traditional *shalwar* and *kameez* instead of his jeans and T-shirts.

"Talk to Zameer and tell him not to join the Taliban. I have only one son, and I can't lose him," appealed Mamma.

"Zameer, how can you even think of joining the Taliban? Don't you remember their atrocities? How can you forget the acid-splashed faces of those girls? Don't you know that they have taken over our orchard and they have made Baba's life a living hell?" I bombarded Zameer with my questions and outrage.

Zameer started off gently but soon burst into anger. "Amina, remember, as children, we used to role play Shabaz Khan and Syed Ahmed Shaheed, two of the famous war heroes of our history who fought Frangies all the way till their last breath. You used to say that if Frangies ever came to our region, you would go fight against them. Now Frangies are here, and you are stopping me. The whole family of Naeem Chacha and Riaz was murdered by one single bomb. His innocent baby, who hadn't even uttered his first words, and his sister, his mother, and his wife . . . What was their crime?" he asked angrily.

"Riaz and Naeem Chacha are alive, but every single day they wish they had also died alongside their family-members. Their lives are more painful to them than their deaths could have ever been." He continued with teary eyes. "The only purpose in Riaz's life now is to avenge the massacre of his family. I can't abandon my closest friend, who is like a brother to me, in his time of need. I want Mamma's and Baba's blessings to go to the war, but I will go even without that. I would like to have their approval, but I know that to do good deeds in the name of Allah and to serve humanity, you don't need your parents' permission."

The thought of my own brother joining hands with the Taliban sickened me. I knew that the Taliban were not after some noble quest but were involved in horrendous atrocities against innocent citizens. "You might get killed," I told him, stating the obvious.

"Martyrdom, especially in self-defense, is the biggest honor a man can wish for," he chanted as his face lit up with excitement. "My only concern is that the Pakistani authorities might harass my family. Some of my friends' families have been arrested and tortured," he told me, sounding very worried.

To take my mind off the troubles at home, I left for the club. I played a few games with Bilal. Afterward, we just sat outside the court and started talking. Meanwhile, Asmat joined us.

"Your victory in Peshawar squash open automatically qualified you to compete in the upcoming tournaments in Islamabad and Karachi. Islamabad squash open is dominated by the northern region players, and you have played with most of them. However, the Karachi open has a totally different character to it. There are many more internationally rated players in Karachi, and you will have a much tougher competition," Bilal cautioned me while Asmat nodded in agreement.

Asmat started taking a greater interest in my training while keeping Bilal as my direct coach. Khurram also joined in fairly often.

"I would like you to be one of my coaches, Khurram. Neither Bilal nor Asmat can do what you have done for me and can still do for me," I pleaded.

"I cannot leave Bannu, but I assure you that you will find me in your corner at every major competition," he promised.

"Thank you. You have provided me with the emotional support that no one else can." I smiled with gratitude.

"You are in excellent form. I have no doubt that you will prevail in Islamabad and possibly even in Karachi."

Once again, he knew what to say to me. Baba accompanied me to Islamabad, and so did Asmat and Bilal. Khurram joined us the following day.

Simin, Sonya, Asma, and Nadia were also on the girls' team from Peshawar, with Asmat as our coach. Islamabad is a beautiful city. Surrounded on three sides by high lush green mountains, the city is very well laid out and extremely clean. I had never seen such shopping centers, hotels, and restaurants in my whole life. I couldn't believe that a city like that existed in the same country where my village, Idak, exists. Sadly, I didn't have much free time there. In addition to training and matches, I was overwhelmed by the media. I had to give one interview after another with TV, radios, newspapers, and magazines.

"How can a girl from North Waziristan become a squash player of your caliber?" This was the question that every interviewer asked me.

"I have had full support of my father and uncles. Without them, I could not have even held a squash racket, let alone compete in national tournaments" would be my usual reply.

I won my early rounds without any trouble. All the girls from our team, except Simin, were out before reaching the higher rounds. To Simin's and my surprise, we met in the semifinals. As the match started, I delivered. From the very beginning, I dominated. Simin seemed disheartened and didn't play her best.

"You are not even trying," I heard Asmat telling her during the breaks.

My straight-set win over Simin even surprised me. I should have been thrilled, but I was not. I was very disappointed because I knew that Simin didn't play her level best in the match between us. I wanted to compete against the real Simin and not against her diminished form.

My final match was against the champion from Multan, the number three player in the whole country. For years, she had played national and international tournaments, ranking among the top fifty worldwide. For that match Asmat, Bilal, and Khurram were all in my corner.

"She is very experienced, but don't let her intimidate you," advised Asmat.

Khurram said it best, "Just ignore everything that you have heard about her, and simply concentrate on your shots and your strategy, don't worry about who she is. You are at your best when you play your natural game."

Our match went up and down several times. We played the fifth and final game with two games to each one of us. Both of us fought hard for each and every point. The spectators were roaring throughout the match. After two deuces, I got the advantage. I drove her off the center with a back-wall shot, but she asked for a let, which the referee granted her. I protested, but my protest was overruled. Once again, we had a deuce. I was losing concentration because I was exhausted. *Two more points*, I demanded of myself. Summoning all my strength, I mixed drops, lobs, and smashes in a quick succession. She was exhausted too, and that proved to be too much. She ran forward for the drop and then back for the lob but couldn't return my smash. I won—I had won the Islamabad open.

Baba walked into the court and wrapped his arms around my head. "That was the best squash match I have ever seen," he said, grinning.

Khurram, Asmat, and Bilal also congratulated me warmly. Khurram looked extremely happy. Unfortunately, all the girls from our team had left earlier. I wished Nadia could have seen my match. That would have been another slap on her pretty face.

"Next stop: Karachi," Asmat told me, expressing his thrill at my victory.

"No, no, the real next stop is the world cup in Sydney next winter!" exclaimed Bilal.

"Their winter or ours?" asked Khurram.

"Their winter and our summer, of course," replied Bilal.

"What do you mean? Do they have summer in Sydney when we have winter here?" I asked, looking at their faces in confusion.

"Yes, their seasons are opposite to ours." I took Khurram's word, but my confusion was not resolved.

Asmat interjected, "Get a good rest, take a few days off, and then start your training in high gear. Winning the Peshawar—and the Islamabad-opens has moved you up the world squash ladder. After you win Karachi, your rating will rise into the top hundred worldwide. This automatically qualifies you to play in Sydney and other international tournaments in the future."

"I am yearning to spend the next few days at home doing nothing," I told Baba during our drive back to Peshawar.

"You need to rest for a few days. Don't get burned out," he advised.

As we got home, Mamma greeted us at the door. She said her salaam to Baba, and turning toward me, she announced, "My champion daughter! I saw all your matches and interviews on TV."

Hearing that sentence from Mammas' mouth meant so much to me. To celebrate, she had scrumptious lamb kebabs waiting. Only the three of us sat down to eat dinner. Zameer was not home much anymore.

"You missed my match in Peshawar. I wished you had seen my game there," I told them, trying to make them feel guilty.

"*Insha Allah*, you will have many more similar and even grander tournaments, and I will attend the next ones," Baba promised.

"Why did you have to go to the village three Fridays in a row?" Mamma inquired.

"The *jirga* has been meeting every Friday to discuss what to do about our orchard, but I am afraid there is no hope," he said with a heavy sigh. "How can I blame the *jirga* when my own brother and my close relatives are against us and they support the Taliban?" he wondered, sighing again. "I have found an influential fellow villager by the name of Riaz Khan. I don't know him that well, but I knew of him from years ago. Now he is also a lower-level Taliban commander, and he has good contact with the leaders of the squatters."

"Will he force the squatters out for us?" Mamma asked.

Baba clarified, "No, he has promised that if I pay off the squatters, he will make them leave our orchard and buy them some other parcel of land to live on. I will give him the money, and he will pay them off. He is asking for a ridiculous amount of money, but I think that no amount of money is too much for our beloved orchard. I have pulled out all of our savings as well as I have borrowed money from the parents of most of my students. I will pay them back in tutoring."

Thirty

A TRIP TO HELL

As Baba talked about his upcoming visit to the village, I blurted out, "I have some down time. I want to come with you."

"I am not sure if you will enjoy your visit. Mather-Khubi has been asking to see you, but then you will have to face the others. Your chacha will not talk to you, and neither will he allow his family, including Siama, to come and see you." He didn't sound very excited about my proposal but also didn't reject it either. I took it as a yes.

"We will leave in the morning. Shall I tell the driver to be ready for the trip?" I asked.

"No. Taking a new car on this trip is very risky. Carjacking is very common these days. I have arranged for a taxi for myself already," he replied.

The two of us left in the morning. Once again we drove through the war zone. There were military compounds and military traffic everywhere. We were stopped, our luggage was searched, and we were interrogated several times during our journey. The village looked markedly worse than it did around our Eid visit. Many more homes and *kots* had been destroyed either by the shelling of the Pakistan Army or by the American bombing. I saw a deep ditch at the spot where my school used to be. The spot had been bombed several times. I recalled how children ran and squealed during the breaks at school. I couldn't even see the playground where we used to play cricket and *pitho* ball. Now our village was overtaken by strangers carrying guns.

As our taxi pulled in, Mather-Khubi came out to greet us. I ran into her arms. She had a scarf tied around her head because she had a bad headache. Nobody else came to greet us. We ate our dinner sitting in the *sundalee*, which Mather-Khubi has especially prepared for us during the evening. I had forgotten how good it felt to crawl into the *sundalee* and how quickly it warmed cold feet and the rest of the body. Mather-Khubi described various scenes of devastation that she had experienced.

"During one of the battles, a bomb fell on the neighboring *kot*. I was only a few arms' length away. I escaped being crushed under a falling wall by only a couple of finger widths," she recounted.

"Please come and live with us in Peshawar. Now we have a big house, and the life is good there," I begged her.

"My age is not suited for wandering around. I can't leave my home and settle elsewhere in a foreign land."

Her reply had not changed over all those years. The warmth of the *sundalee* and the fatigue of the day's journey weighed on me. While talking to Baba and Mather-Khubi I fell asleep.

Next day Baba went out to meet his contact about the orchard. Mather-Khubi made tea and prepared fresh naan for me. I loved fresh naan with butter for breakfast, and she remembered. At the tandoor, some of my aunts and my cousins were also waiting to bake naans. Most of my cousins at the tandoor were much younger than me. All of those that were closer to my age were married and had gone to their husband's homes. The aunts made sarcastic remarks about me. They talked to one another loudly enough to let me hear their nasty comments.

"I would hate if my daughter played a man's sport mixed with other men without even a chador," one sneered to a neighbor, making sure I heard her statement.

"Some parents have no shame in seeing their daughter on TV showing their uncovered hair to the world," chided another.

"That is what happens when you don't get your daughters married at the right age. Then it gets too late, and no one wants to marry your daughter," a third admonished.

Several times, I caught Mather-Khubi looking at me from the corner of her eye without saying a word. She must have been noticing the embarrassment on my face. Although she didn't say that, the expression on her telltale face was betraying what was in her mind, *"This is why your mamma and I tried so hard to deter you from playing squash. If you had only listened to us, you wouldn't have to sit through this insult to yourself and your family."*

Right after breakfast, Siama showed up. She had been waiting for Chacha to leave because he had forbidden her to see me. We shared a long hug.

"I have missed you," I told her, kissing her chubby cheeks.

"I think of you several times a day. It is not fair that Baba does not let me be with you," she confided.

We talked all day long, even while we ate our lunch together and during our squash practice.

"I've perfected all the shots that you taught me. Please teach me some new ones," she requested humbly.

I demonstrated two new shots for her to practice by herself. We had to finish. Chacha was expected to come home earlier that day, and we didn't want to be seen together by him.

I returned to my house and waited there for Baba to come back and tell us how his meeting with Riaz Khan went. Mather-Khubi and I talked while waiting for Baba. It was late afternoon, and Baba was not back. I was getting worried, and even Mather-Khubi, who was very calm and content most of the time, looked nervous. We went on the rooftop to wait for Baba. From there, we could look for him walking home. It was already late afternoon, and there was no sign of him as far as our eyes could see. Mather-Khubi called in a young cousin of mine from the *kot*. She gave him some dried mulberries and told him to go look for Baba in the village center. He ran to the village center and returned fast.

"Some people near the mosque had seen your baba going off with someone," he reported to me. It came as a bit of a relief, but we were both very concerned about his safety. He had gone out with a huge amount of money. What if someone had robbed him or, worst, kidnapped him? Bad thoughts were streaming through my mind one after another, and I was unable to think of anything else.

A few hours later, Baba showed up with a bag of groceries in his hands. I put my arms around him and cried tears of utter relief. Mather-Khubi scolded him for making us so worried.

Baba looked very happy as he bragged, "I have given the money to Riaz Khan, and he has promised me that, soon, we will get our orchard back."

"Fantastic," I said expressing my pleasure about the good news.

Baba shared the pomegranates and oranges that he brought for us. We sat around the *sundalee* to eat our dinner of fresh naans from our own tandoor, kebabs, and grilled tomatoes while feeling hopeful about our orchard.

Our time at the village came to end, and we packed up for traveling back to Peshawar. The taxi driver showed up on time and helped load our luggage into the trunk. I slipped into the backseat, and Baba opened the front door to sit on the front seat.

"No, sir. Sit with the lady in the back," the driver stated.

"As you wish," Baba complied and sat next to me on the back seat.

Saying goodbye to Mather-Khubi was so hard. Baba gave her some money just moments before our taxi drove off, so that she wouldn't have a chance to refuse.

Suddenly, our taxi stopped at the mosque and another person got in.

"Why are you taking another passenger? I am paying for this whole taxi, and I don't want to share it with a stranger," protested Baba.

"Sorry, sir, I will return late at night, and you know how unsafe it is to travel alone that late. I am taking my brother with me." explained the driver.

"What choice do we have? It is not easy to find taxis in the village," I whispered to Baba.

The taxi driver began driving terribly fast. It frightened me because those roads were not meant for such high-speed driving.

"Slow down a little. Otherwise, you will get into an accident," Baba warned him.

He slowed down, but within minutes, he picked up speed again. We reached a main intersection where he should have gone straight. Instead, he turned left.

"You were supposed to go straight. Why did you turn? This is not the right way," Baba questioned, sounding very alarmed.

The driver ignored Baba's protests and drove even faster. Baba yelled again his voice cracking and his hands shaking violently with fear.

The man in the front seat turned toward me. Pointing a gun straight at my head, he said in a menacing way, "We are taking you to a safe house where we will keep you till our demands are met by the Pakistani government. Both of you cooperate and no one will get hurt."

The taxi stopped, and a second stranger jumped in. He forcefully blindfolded us and tied our hands behind our backs. As they drove, I had no sense of direction. The road felt unpaved, like a mountain road, with steep hills and lots of turns. After a fairly long drive the car stopped. I heard the sound of a gate opening.

"Mister, get out and hold your daughter's hand. We will take you to our commanders," he ordered.

After going through several turns in a hallway and up some stairs, they removed the blindfolds from our faces and untied our hands. Three men were sitting on chairs with their guns parked right next to them. Several heavily armed men stood attentively behind them. Looking at their outfits and listening to their language, we had no doubt that they were Taliban. The men sitting in the chairs seemed to be commanders or the superiors, while the armed men standing attentively behind must have been fighters or the soldiers.

"Salaam alaikum," one commander said to us respectfully.

"Walaikum salaam," we replied in one voice.

I started sobbing with fear, but Baba stayed amazingly calm.

Thirty One

DEVIL'S GUESTHOUSE

"We have brought you here, and we will keep both of you here in this house. We will make some demands to the government, and once those demands are met, we will release you," the commander explained. "If you cooperate, and if the government agrees, this can end soon without much hardship to you and to us." He spoke without any emotion, as if he was buying and selling livestock.

"Please let me call my family in Peshawar about what is happening," Baba pleaded.

"Your family has already been informed that you are both safe and sound with us," the commander countered.

"Can you please let me talk to my family on the telephone?" Baba begged.

After a brief consultation among themselves, they rejected. "No!" one man yelled. "It is too much of a security risk. We can't jeopardize our safety."

Baba pleaded, "Why us? You must be mistaking us for some high-level army officer. We are nobody. This is my daughter, and I am a poor schoolteacher. The government will not care about us."

"Tell your daughter to stop crying. No one can hear her for miles around here," one man on a chair told Baba, sounding irritated. He continued, "We know very well who you are. Your daughter here is the famous squash player. I know squash—I used to play in Peshawar. The government will certainly want to get her out of here."

They got up to leave, but before heading to the exit, they warned us, "We are leaving, but there are plenty of guards around both inside and around this building. Don't try to escape. The guards have the orders to shoot and kill you if you try to run from here. Furthermore, if by some miracle, you do manage to break out of this house, the surrounding forest will kill you. There is nothing for hundreds of miles, except for the dense, cold forest."

They locked the door from outside. In the room were the three empty chairs, a table, and two beds. There was a bathroom serving the room. Neither the room itself nor bathroom had any windows.

"Thank God, we are safe. Stop crying now. We need to think what our options are," Baba consoled me, gently stroking the back of my head. I only howled louder, hugging Baba very tightly.

At nightfall, the door opened, and two armed men came in. "Here is some food and water," one said, setting it down on the table. His partner stayed by the door.

"I don't want your food!" I yelled angrily.

Without saying a word in response, they left, locking the door behind them.

"Come and eat something," Baba pressed.

"No, I am not hungry. I can't even think about food," I said darkly, frowning at him. Baba took a few bites of food and left the rest on the tray.

"I hear some men talking. There must be at least two guards outside," I speculated.

Baba guessed, "We are either on the second or third floor of this building."

We laid down on our beds but neither one of us could sleep for even a moment throughout the night.

"Will they kill us?" I quietly asked.

Baba whispered back, "They want us alive to get their demands. Killing us will get them nothing."

Somehow or another, even that longest and the darkest night of our lives passed. The feeling of not knowing what disaster could befall us, and the fear of our lives ending any minute, kept us on pins and needles all through the night.

At daybreak, the three commanders returned. They gave us the day's newspaper to hold below our chins, and then they took our pictures and video-taped us for a short time.

"Can we talk to our family? They will die worrying about us. Please let us talk to them, even if only for one minute," Baba begged again.

Once again, they ignored our appeals. By then, our biggest worry was whether they had informed our family or not. Being unable to find out the answer was greatly aggravating Baba.

When the guards brought in our breakfast the next morning, Baba greeted them nicely with a salaam. That surprised me. I didn't understand how he could control his anger and act civilly toward the men who were prepared to take our lives.

One guard whispered, "Mister, don't say salaam to us. We are not allowed to speak to you, not even to reply to your salaam."

The door was ajar, so I tried to peek outside. There were two chairs at either side of the door for the guards. I also saw sunlight through a corridor. While eating breakfast, we heard the guard's words clearly.

"If we can hear them, then that means they can certainly hear us too. We'll have to be very careful about what we say to each other," Baba warned me.

The door opened again, and a commander came in to tell us, "We have made our demands to the Pakistani government, and we have given them one week's time to release our brothers from their jails."

"And if the government doesn't comply?" Baba asked, shifting his sunglasses higher.

"You better pray that that doesn't happen," he snapped.

"Your daughter is famous, which makes her a very important person to the government. They will be under pressure to make a deal. You are no ordinary, unknown people," he touted.

"Please, for god's sake, allow me talk to my family. I need to tell my wife that we are okay. I will not tell her any other information. Allah be my witness, I promise," Baba said humbly.

One of the commanders appeared at the door. Without saying a word, he handed a phone to Baba. The second commander instructed, "You have one minute to talk. The phone will turn off automatically." The phone was ringing. They must have dialed Mamma's number before handing the phone to Baba.

"Amina and I are all right, don't worry," Baba reassured Mamma without pausing to hear her voice.

I got the phone from him. As soon as I heard Mamma's voice, I started crying uncontrollably. "Mamma, I'm all right." I barely spoke one sentence between my sobs. The commander snatched the phone away from me and left the room.

The one-week deadline came and went, but nothing changed. We thanked Allah every day for being alive. To us, each day was a gift. Those people could have killed us any minute. After Allah, our lives were in their hands. The same commander came in every few days to take our pictures or to make more videos of us.

"Can we have something to read? Some newspapers, magazines, or a copy of the Holy Koran please," Baba asked him.

"No newspapers or magazines," he snapped.

"Then a Koran with Urdu translation," Baba requested.

We got our Koran the next day. Baba read it aloud in Arabic following every prayer. His reading of the Koran soothed my nerves, but his intended audiences were the guards, not me. He was hoping to win their sympathy by letting them listen to his recitation.

"Salaam," said Baba, nodding to the guard who brought us our food.

"Walaikum salaam," he replied for the first time, much to our surprise. "I have been listening to your Koran recitation. It is beautiful," he whispered before leaving our room and firmly locking the door.

We had been observing the pattern of how the rotation of the guards was set up. Two men seemed to have the responsibility of watching us around the clock. One was in charge of the day shift and the second one for the night. They each had their own assistants. Those assistants changed from shift to shift. Mostly, we saw new faces serving in that capacity. The man in charge carried the gun and kept a very close eye on our movements. His younger-looking assistant performed small chores like putting our meals down, picking up the used utensils, and locking or unlocking the door. Although they never revealed their identities to us, we overheard the names by which their partners called them.

The guard in charge of the day shift was Rehman. He was fairly tall and well built. He was also very strict with us. He never smiled or showed any kindness toward us. Even with his assistants, he was cold and harsh. Faisal was the name of the guard in charge of the night shift. He was also tall and muscular, but he was more kindly in looks and gentler in his manners with us. He looked much younger than Rehman. We were more relaxed around Faisal, whereas, during Rehman's shift, we felt jittery and afraid.

"Our bodies ache from sitting on the bed all day and all night. Please allow us to take a short walk from time to time," Baba requested the next time a commander came by, but he ignored Baba and left without uttering a word.

Days passed, and we almost forgot about our request to walk around. One day Rehman ordered us to follow him. We obeyed. We followed him to the rooftop where we saw sunlight for the first time after being locked up in that windowless dark room. Being out in the open air was refreshing, but we were shaking with fears.

Have they brought us into the open to execute us? It was an extremely scary thought, and Baba looked very nervous.

"You have half an hour up here on the rooftop," Rehman gruffly said.

Baba and I started a brisk walk to get as much exercise as possible. We looked around, assessing our chances of escape.

"Baba, you guessed right, our jail room is on the second or third floor. Jumping off the building is out of question. We are surrounded by mountains and forest, with not a single house or road in sight as far as we could see in every direction. If by some miracle, we escape from this building, we cannot get away without a car." Intense hopelessness overwhelmed me. Just then the guards ordered us back in.

We were adjusting our lives according to the situation. We spent all day and night in that windowless jail room. Our only relief was to talk to each other. I brought up my squash a lot. The Karachi tournament was approaching fast. I wondered if I would be able to play in that tournament at all and whether or not we would even be alive by that time. My body was losing strength due to lack of training, but there was nothing I could do about it, except reminisce. I described stroke by stroke all of my important squash matches to Baba.

"Come to the club with me right now, and I will show you where and how I defeated Nadia." Then my heart sank as the reality hit me. We were prisoners and not even free to so much as to leave the room—let alone go to the club in Peshawar.

Baba had opened up to me also. He told me about his schools and his tutoring, about dozens of his students, his experiences fighting in the war, his training, and his childhood. For the first time ever, he talked to me about his wedding to Mamma. He was avoiding the topic of Zameer though. I had a strong sense that he was worried sick about the danger Zameer was putting himself in. I wanted to know what Baba thought and felt about this.

"I am so afraid for Zameer's life," I deliberately opened the topic.

"I also worry about him," Baba agreed, trying to put a brave face.

"Then why don't you stop him from joining the Taliban? Why should anyone support the Taliban? Look what they have done to our society. Look what they have done to us, keeping us locked up in the middle of nowhere. Who knows, they might even kill us here," I whispered angrily.

"I wish my only son didn't have to put his life out there, but someone has to fight this war. Our lives and our children's lives, our ways, our resources, and, most importantly, our religion are all under attack. We must fight this war," Baba said passionately, to my surprise.

"This must be Allah's will, and only Allah knows the wisdom in it. My father and his brother gave their lives, and I lost one eye fighting. We became American allies to defeat the Russians. All our training and supplies were given to us by American officers. Now my only son is fighting against the same Americans."

He lowered his sunglasses to show me his collapsed eye for the first time ever. The sight of his face with a big bright twinkling eye and just a plain wrinkled scar in place of the other eye shocked me senseless. I started crying uncontrollably. All my life, I had only seen Baba's face with dark sunglasses. For the first time, I understood why he wore them. I was sure Mamma and Mather-Khubi must have known, but no one in the family ever talked about Baba's eye.

Tears dripped down my face as Baba shared his life story with me for the first time. "I was younger than Zameer when my father, his brothers, and all the men from our tribe went to fight against the Russian aggression in Afghanistan. I wanted to go with them, but Mather-Khubi didn't allow me. After my father and one of his brothers were martyred there, Mather-Khubi ordered me to go avenge the spilling of their blood. I joined mujahedeen in the war against the Russians, and I didn't return until we defeated the Russians. Many times during that war, I came close to death, but you only die when Allah calls you back. Even when I was injured during a battle and lost my eye, I didn't come home." Baba argued to my utter surprise. I couldn't understand how he was supporting Taliban in spite of suffering the worst nightmare at their hands.

The guards had become much more lenient toward us. Not only Rehman and Faisal engaged in conversations with Baba, they even allowed their assistants to interact with us. Mostly, they would talk to Baba about Koran and other religious matters. Baba answered their questions very patiently and calmly. After all, he was a teacher at heart. They talked to us about our lives and told us about theirs. We intentionally avoided the topic of my squash altogether. We were afraid that they might also consider my playing squash as a sin. Baba, however, talked to them about Zameer a lot.

"We are holding the family of a *ghazi* who is fighting in the war on our side," I overheard one guard say to the other.

Thirty Two

YOU ONLY LIVE TWICE

We were eating our lunch when we heard a car stop outside the house. Then we heard men running up the stairs. Our door opened, and half a dozen men barged in. They ordered us out at gunpoint. We obeyed and were escorted out of the room. With no idea what the commotion was all about, we feared the worst. We saw Rehman and his assistant standing at attention with their guns. Soon, two Taliban commanders arrived on the scene. The guards tied our hands behind our backs and made us stand against a wall on the rooftop. As I looked at Baba, I saw a deadly fear in his eyes. The two commanders began arguing aggressively with each other.

"The government is buying time by delaying the talks. Weeks have passed, and they have not accepted a single one of our demands. We should kill the hostages to teach the government a lesson!" yelled one of the commanders with spite.

"If we kill them, then we'll have nothing left. We will ruin our chances to get our brothers freed," argued back the other one more calmly.

The spiteful commander declared his verdict on our lives, "Remember what Imam Sahib told us after the Friday prayers . . . Killing kafirs has very high reward. These two are kafirs. She commits sins by playing and mixing freely with men, and this man doesn't stop her."

"They are not kafirs. They pray five times a day, and you should listen to his recitation of the Holy Koran," challenged Rehman.

The commander completely ignored Rehman's argument in our support. Our end was near. Reciting all the suras of the Koran that I had memorized, I kept my eyes on Baba so that his face would be the last thing I would see before dying. I wanted my last words to be the name of Allah and the verses of the Koran. I begged Allah to forgive my sins. Then everything around me started spinning. I was nauseous and ready to vomit. Baba tried to calm me down, but he was not calm himself; his hands were trembling, and his voice was shaking with terror. The quarreling between the two Taliban commanders led to a fistfight between them. Several armed guards intervened to separate their fighting superiors. The hostile commander grabbed his gun, and with no warning, whatsoever, he aimed directly at us. Baba fell to the ground, pushing me down. With a lightning speed, Rehman pushed the barrel of the commander's gun up in the air. I looked at Baba, and he looked at me, neither of us knew if anyone got hit. Either due to Baba's swift action or that of Rehman's, we remained alive. Baba's nose was bleeding, and I was bleeding from a cut on my upper lip. We had gone down face first to the ground, not being able to use our tied-up hands. Everything was over in seconds. Baba and I made eye contact. We were too afraid to ask each other if we were shot. We didn't dare move even when the commotion was apparently over. After his failed attempt on our lives, that commander stormed down the stairs, furious. The other commanders, along with their guards, followed him. They were all gone, except for Rehman and his assistant. They got us up on our feet, untied our hands and escorted us back to our jail cell. Baba thanked Rehman profusely for saving our lives.

With tears running down my face, I added, "Thank you, brother, for what you did. We are forever indebted. I pray from the bottom of my soul that Allah may reward you and your family for your kind deed."

We both knew we had gotten a second chance in life. Reflecting on that, I seriously questioned my wisdom in playing squash. *Since the day my elders first saw me holding a racket, they have been telling me to stay away from it. I have uprooted my family from our village and then split them. Baba lives in one town, and the rest of us are living in another. Baba left his elderly mother behind when she needs him the most. His own brother, the rest of his family and the entire clan has rejected us. Our beautiful orchard has been snatched away from us. As if that was not enough, we are now in this hell as hostages where our lives could end any moment. If we die, who will take care of Mamma? Zameer is still not standing on his own feet yet.* I concluded that my squash was casting a curse on us.

As the Taliban commander said, playing and freely mixing with men made me kafir, and kafirs will burn in hell fire for eternity. Not only myself, but I have also made Baba a kafir, and because of my obsession with squash, his soul will burn in hell. Perhaps Allah wants me to go back to the traditional life of a good daughter, accept the first suitor that comes my way, and bring up a God-fearing family, I reflected. I wanted to tell Baba that I will quit squash forever if we made it out alive, but I couldn't find the courage to say it.

Another week passed, each day dragged by slowly. After all our talking, reading of the Koran, praying, and eating, we still had so much time left, and we didn't know how to fill that extra time. By then, we were convinced that even if the Pakistani government met the Taliban's demands, they might kill us anyway. There were still those who wanted to collect their reward in the afterlife by killing a sinner and her father.

Baba and I started to talk more and more about finding a way to escape. We believed that it was worth taking a risk, since the chance of being released was slim. We fantasized about ways to escape. The house was completely secure. We didn't see any possible way out. There was only one door, and it was locked solid. The rooftop was three stories high, so jumping over a wall was not a possibility. We studied the walls below and saw no windows or doors or any other anchor points to help us climb down. And the two guards—they were always out there. Nevertheless, we considered escape routes at every opportunity.

We made it a routine to sit near the door and talk loudly so that the guards could hear. Baba recounted our family history. He described the details of how our great-grandfathers fought in different wars against the British, and how he himself bravely fought in the war against the Russians. I was hearing most of these stories for the first time from him. Mather-Khubi had narrated many of those, but coming from him, those stories had a different meaning for me. He also talked about Zameer joining the Taliban and how he was fighting somewhere out there. We were sure the guards were listening to Baba's talks.

One afternoon, as we walked on the rooftop for our daily parade, a guard questioned Baba about the Russian war stories. "Mister, did you fight on the Kandahar front during the Russian war?"

"I trained for a short while in Kandahar, but for the war, I was sent to the northern border," Baba replied casually.

Despite their strict orders to the contrary, the guards engaged in conversations with Baba. He told his war stories to them. Without adding a word, I would listen, only asking questions occasionally just like the way the guards did.

Thirty Three

NOT EVEN A GOODBYE

The door opened. Surprisingly, Rehman appeared without any assistant. He allowed us to do our routine rooftop walk. As usual, Baba told me his Russian war stories. When our walk was over, Rehman ordered us back into our room and locked the door behind him. He was alone again in the evening as he brought our meals. When he left, I didn't hear the latching of the lock. I was sure. Patiently, we ate our dinner and did our regular nightly prayers. Baba started reciting Koran afterward. I tiptoed to the door and tried to sense if anyone was there on the other side. Even after minutes of eavesdropping, I didn't hear a sound. I signaled to Baba that there was no one there. He came to the door and nodded in agreement. With shaky hands, I pried the door open and looked out. The lights were on. Baba opened the door wider. No one was in sight. I had my shawl and a thin sweater on. Baba had his blazer. Gathering strength and courage, we went to the rooftop. There was no one else anywhere.

"We are on the third floor. The only way out for us is to climb down the building. We need to find a rope," he directed.

"Let's pull the ropes that tie the bed net to the bed frame and knot them together," I suggested.

We accomplished that part quietly, hoping the ropes would be long and strong enough for our descend down two stories. Quickly, Baba found an anchor and tied the rope. After pulling several times to feel the strength of the knot, Baba told me to slide down first. Without knowing how far the rope reached, I went down. We didn't have time to think. With little light from the stars and a new moon, I couldn't see what was below. The rope was dangerously short. My only choice was to let go. Not thinking too much, I did just that. I fell from a significant height but, luckily, didn't get hurt. It was Baba's turn. I waited to help him, fearful that he would tumble for sure. We both knew how crucial it was for us to keep extremely quiet. Any noise could have been our death sentence. I whispered to warn him about the reach of the rope. He released his grip at the end of it, and I grabbed him with all my strength. He lost his balance a bit but because of me he was fine too. We ran eastward between the trees as fast as we could. I was frightened out of my mind of snakes and scorpions beneath us and bullets from guards above. We had hardly any light, and it was bitterly cold. Before long, we'd stepped into puddles. Having only flimsy shoes, our feet got soaking wet. Our clothes were also not enough; Baba's simple coat was not keeping him warm, and I only had my light sweater and the chador.

"Are you cold?" Baba asked.

"No, not if we keep running," I answered.

"Run carefully. If we fall and get hurt, our lives could end in this wilderness," warned Baba.

We ran, alternated with brisk walks, for at least an hour, maybe longer. We couldn't see signs of human life in any direction, except for a ray of light from the house we had escaped. That sole light served as a beacon to run away from. My heart pounded. We knew that losing our way might bring us back to the Taliban. Heading straight due east we climbed the hill. As we reached the top, we searched desperately for any sign of life around us.

We started going down the hill, but then Baba had a change of heart. "Let's stay on the ridge and not go down," he said.

"We should keep going due east because we don't know which direction the ridge runs," I argued.

"If we go down now and reach the valley, what if we hit a stream there, how are we going to cross it at night?" Baba reasoned. "Also, from this hilltop, we have a better chance of seeing farther and finding a house or a road," he added.

So we continued walking on the ridge, trying to look for something somewhere.

Suddenly, I saw a faint light in a distance. I looked at Baba. He was looking in that direction too.

"Do you see that light down there?" I asked him with hope in my voice.

"Yes, I just hope that it is real and not a trick of our imagination," he replied.

We took off hastily down the hill, both of us trying to see more than what our eyes could show us. As our speed increased, we slipped and stumbled repeatedly. We had fallen so many times, we had lost count. Somehow, our bodies were not even registering the pain. We practically ran toward the light, keeping our eyes fixed on it. Soon we could see that it was coming from a building.

"What kind of building is it? Is it Taliban territory? Or are these simple villagers, living there in the middle of nowhere?" I posed the questions without expecting any reply from Baba.

"Generally, people don't live in such isolation in Waziristan. There are always several homes in a community. But this looks like a single light. What could this be?" Baba contemplated. "It has to be some kind of Taliban hideout."

As we got closer, I felt nearly paralyzed with anxiety. Slowly, we approached the building. With such faint light, our eyes were focusing amazingly well. It was a small building in the middle of the forest. A perimeter of a few hundred feet had been cleared of trees and shrubs, and the area was surrounded with barbed wire fence. We still didn't have any idea what it was.

Baba speculated more, "If this is a Taliban hideout, then we are doomed. If it is a house of a regular villager, they might shoot us, mistaking us for a criminal or Taliban. If it is a military post, they might also shoot, suspecting us as suicide bombers or Taliban terrorists."

After some quick thinking, we came up with a plan. Baba proposed, "You hide here in the forest, while I go closer and scream for help. If they capture me, you walk away and try to find some help elsewhere."

"I think I should go, and you should stay behind. They are less likely to shoot at a woman," I argued back. Baba gave in.

Leaving him hiding, I advanced and screamed, "Help! I need help. I am hurt. Please, somebody help me for god's sake."

No response came. I moved closer to the fence and repeated my plea by screaming even louder. Still, there was no response of any kind. Then suddenly, another light came on. I could see the silhouette of a person trying to see me from a window. I kept on screaming.

"Who is there?" a man's voice yelled out.

"I am Amina. I am hurt, please help me," I answered.

"Are you alone?" he asked warily.

"Yes, I am all alone, hurt, and cold. Please help me. In the name of Allah, please help me," I begged.

I still didn't know who the man was. Was he a Taliban commander or a military soldier? Then I heard nothing for a while. I screamed again.

"Stay where you are and don't move," the man commanded.

A gate opened, and a truck with bright headlights rolled out. There were more men in there, and they were all carrying guns. The truck drove toward me and abruptly stopped. Although the headlights were glaring, I could see men pointing guns right at me. "Take your chador off and put your hands up."

I realized that it was a Pakistan Army compound, and the soldiers were in civilian clothes. Relief came over me. The headlights were so bright I couldn't see in the cabin of the truck. Slowly, the truck moved to where I stood. It stopped again, but this time, two men and a dog jumped out. The men took cover behind the truck doors, pointing their guns at me, while the dog sniffed at me. As their dog returned to them, the men walked toward me with their guns still pointed. They asked my name, my father's name, and where I lived. One of them made a phone call. He relayed all my information. He took his time.

"You may put your chador back on. This is Pakistan military post, and we will help you as soon as we get orders from our commanding officer."

Hearing these words, I nearly collapsed. *Should I tell them about Baba? What if they are Taliban pretending to be Pakistan military?* I held off.

"Get into the truck," he commanded.

I readily obeyed. In there, they asked more questions and continued relaying on the phone what I said. The truck returned to their compound. We all went together into an office where several men in Pakistan army uniform were waiting for us. A chair was provided for me and a blanket to wrap around myself. While I contemplated telling them about Baba and his hiding place in the nearby forest, a man kept on talking on the phone with his superiors.

"Yes, sir, I will ask her," he said into the phone.

"Are you Amina who was kidnapped by the Taliban? Is your father with you?" he asked me, putting his hands on the phone speaker.

Not to raise any suspicion, I quickly told them about Baba's hiding place and why he was hiding. They wanted to go look for him.

"I must come with you. Otherwise, my baba won't know whether you are the army or the Taliban trying to recapture us," I told them.

"Yes, of course," the officer agreed.

We drove out again into the forest. I jumped out of the truck and called Baba.

"We are safe, this is Pakistan military, please come out!" I yelled and screamed with excitement.

Baba came out of his hiding place. The soldiers pointed their guns at him, but he hurried straight toward me. We hugged each other like two people meeting after many years of separation.

The truck reentered the camp where two officers welcomed us. They gave Baba a blanket, and both of us got hot tea to drink. All the officials present wanted to know about our ordeal. They had been working to finding us. One of the officers who saw the Taliban videos had recognized me from watching my matches on TV.

"Your kidnapping has been big news. From ordinary civilians to the top political leaders, all have condemned it. We had orders not to spare any efforts to find you," an officer told us.

They served us a meal, and two younger officers gave up their beds for Baba and me to sleep for what was left of the night.

In the morning, an officer spoke, beaming at us, "Ironically, this unit was set up to find you. Instead, you found us."

That afternoon, we were transported to a larger military post in Peshawar. Mamma and Zameer were waiting for us there. I buried myself in Mamma's arms. We both sobbed. Zameer gave me a hug and kissed my forehead.

At the second military post in Peshawar, we were questioned about every event that happened to us during our captivity. They asked us about the guards, the commanders, the house, and the surroundings. We gave them as much detail as we could muster.

An officer explained our security arrangements, "Your escape has not been announced to the media yet. We don't want to alert the Taliban. We need to take additional security measures for you before we let you return to your home." Some of the officers had their pictures taken beside me and asked for my autograph.

Thirty Four

MY PLEDGE

The chief officer gave us his list of instructions: "We are putting two soldiers to guard your house. Soon, you should hire your own guards. There are many safety features that we are adding to your house. Also, you must not travel around unprotected. Always travel in a car, even if you only go out of your house to the next street corner. Always have a guard accompany you."

A few days later, on the evening news, we heard about our escape. With that, we began to receive visits and phone calls from all over the country. We even got a call from the president of Pakistan. He congratulated us on our escape and expressed deep regrets about all the trouble we went through during our captivity. TV and newspaper reporters were lining up to interview us. The attention was exciting in the beginning, but after a few weeks, it became very unpleasant to be constantly intruded on by strangers.

The very next day, Chacha, Shaaz, and Siama showed up at our house. It was a wonderful, pleasant surprise. We could not get enough of hugging one another and cried happy tears.

"Please forgive me. The thought that I hadn't talked to you for years kept me awake night after night. I fought with my Taliban commanders. I have decided to break all relations with them," Chacha announced, putting his arms around me and Baba.

Siama squeezed in between and grabbed a hold of me. She held me tightly, and we cried together.

Khurram came to see us as soon as he heard of our escape. "Thank God, you are safely back at home. We feared the worst," he said, shaking Baba's hand warmly.

"How did the Karachi tournament go?" I inquired, getting into their conversation.

"They regretfully announced your absence and prayed for your safe return. The champion from Karachi won the tournament, defeating Simin in the finals. You would have won the tournament without a doubt," he said.

Thanks to Manager Shahid of Habib Bank, who came to our rescue again, we moved into a larger more secure house and hired a driver and two armed guards. He authorized loans for me to cover all those expenses. Baba was afraid to leave us by ourselves anymore. Since Zameer was not living at home, Baba left Bannu and moved in with us. As expected, he didn't find a teaching job in Peshawar, but he easily found students to tutor for four to five hours in the evenings, making enough to take care of the family financially.

After several weeks, the military and the police gave us permission to go outside of our house. Their guards were gone, and our own guards had taken their place. As I went back to my college for the first time in months, I found some of my friends. Again, we ended up at Café Lalazaar instead of our class.

Everyone wanted to know all about my kidnapping, but I tried to joke it off. "We were both guests of Taliban for several months, and when they got tired of feeding us, they let us go."

I yearned to go back to the club and play some fast games, but I had made a promise to myself, and I had asked Allah for forgiveness.

I don't know if it came out of my mouth by mistake or was it my inner voice, but I impulsively ordered the driver, "Turn into the club," as we were about to drive past the club entrance.

Inside the club I received the warmest welcome. It was evening, the club was full. Friends and even my fiercest opponents were there. Bilal and Asmat came running out of their courts to meet with me. We all sat in the café and talked mostly about the kidnapping.

Asmat was very excited about my squash. He sounded worried. "You must start your training right away—missing the Karachi tournament has adversely affected your ratings. You will have to play in every tournament possible to make up."

I stayed quiet. I didn't have the heart to shatter his excitement by telling him that I was leaving squash forever.

As we said our *khuda hafiz*, I gathered all my courage and murmured to Asmat, "I have decided to give up squash."

His reaction was very surprising, almost as if he was expecting this from me. He remained calm and said, "I can't even begin to imagine the ordeal that you went through. I admit that this would have broken most people's resolve. Please don't make any decision under these circumstances. You must wait and let your emotions settle down."

Over the next few days, I visited the club every day and on some days, even twice, but I was true to my pledge. Anytime Asmat would see me, he would repeat his advice, "You should start your training. The longer you wait, the worse it is going be for you." But I was resolute.

One afternoon, as I entered the club, Manager Shahid was waiting for me. He greeted me very warmly. He ordered food from the café, and we sat down for a meal. We talked about our lives, mostly mine and mostly about my horror during the kidnapping.

He then came to the point. "You must start your squash training. Asmat has told me that you want to stop playing. You will have to reconsider. Not only your future will be ruined, but also your life will be in danger. Think about your financial situation and all the earnings from squash. This will all be gone. How will you afford to live in a safe house and pay for the guards and the driver? This is all possible because of squash."

"I have made a pledge to Allah, and I can't break it," I replied without giving further explanation. He appealed to me to reconsider, and we said our *khuda hafiz*.

Sitting around surrounded by squash and not being able to play was pure torture for me. I saw matches, and I cheered for one or the other player. I even advised them what shots to play, but I didn't get on the court myself. I would see Simin, Shazia, Asma, and Nadia play against one another and then brag about how well they played. It would tempt me to jump into the court and show them some real squash.

My attention was all focused on a fast match when I got a tap on my shoulder. I turned around but saw nothing, so I continued watching. Then came another tap on the other shoulder.

Turning my head further, I found Khurram standing right behind me, smiling.

"What are you doing here on earth?" I asked him in English, trying to rein in my excitement.

"I was born on this earth—where else can I go?" he replied in English with a loud laugh. "I have been standing behind you all this time, but you were too engrossed in that match."

As always, I was thrilled to see him and forgot all about the match I was so intensely interested in.

"What brings you to Peshawar?" I asked him, trying to suppress my giggle.

"Why, must there be a reason to come to Peshawar? Can't I just stop by?" he joked back. "By the way, the correct expression is 'what on earth are you doing here?' not 'what are you doing on earth?' Try to drill in the correct expression," he whispered. "What match are you watching? I bet you could beat them, even if both of them played together against you. It's a matter of fact."

"Oh, Khurram, I am sorry, I can't play squash anymore." Then I explained my pledge to him.

"You have no right to make such a pledge on your own. Your squash is not all yours. Yes, Allah has given you the talent, but what about the tremendous sacrifices your baba has made? Have you given any thought about all the time and energy that your coaches and trainers have spent perfecting your skills? What promises have you made about all my dreams for you?" He barraged me with questions, to which I had no answers.

Before I could say a thing, he stormed off. This was very strange. I had never seen that side of him. Khurram had gotten frustrated with me hundreds of times, but he had never turned his back on me.

He doesn't understand. How can I play? I have made a pledge to Allah. And who knows, even if I tried, I may not be able to play anyway. I am too shaken by my ordeal. My nerves are not under my control, I admitted to myself.

I looked for Khurram all over the club, but he was nowhere to be found. I opened my cupboard and looked at my rackets and gear for the first time since before our kidnapping.

"No, I can't play." I shut the cupboard. "He doesn't understand me and I don't care."

I left the club and went home. Mamma had dinner ready, but I didn't eat a bite. I went straight to bed instead. I stayed up most of the night, contemplating Khurram's reaction. *Why is he so angry at me? He has no idea what I have gone through.*

I turned around toward the wall and closed my eyes, trying to shut my mind off. I just wanted to go to sleep. But every time I closed my eyes, I couldn't get Khurram's picture out of my mind. The scene of him sitting opposite to me and asking me angrily—what right do I have to give up squash—kept playing. And each time, I failed to answer his question.

Is it possible that he might be right and I, indeed, do not have that right after all? I questioned my decision for the first time. *How could I promise something to Allah which is not all mine? Where do Khurram and his plans for me fit in this decision of mine? What about the sacrifices Baba has made, the hard work of my trainers, coaches, and Manager Shahid, who persuaded his superiors to make Peshawar Club happen for me in the first place?* I brooded until I dozed off.

Arriving at the club earlier than usual, I opened my locker with trembling hands. There I was, face-to-face with my favorite racket. I could almost hear all my rackets complaining that I had abandoned them.

I picked up my favorite racket and hugged it tightly, mumbling, "How could I abandon you? You are the one that got me my victory against Nadia and Simin. You won me the Peshawar and the Islamabad tournaments. You have always been there for me whenever I needed you. How did I even breathe without holding you in my hand for so many months?"

I swung the racket in air, immediately feeling complete again. Taking the first open court, I started hitting a ball and felt that all my hand-eye coordination had disappeared. My feet were like bricks. I missed every single ball that bounced back to me. I put the ball away and did some stretches. After that, I did half an hour of sprinting in the court, first without holding a racket then with a racket in my hand. I ran from corner to corner, from wall to wall, from line to line. I picked up the ball again, and after warming it up, I hit my shots. I was slow, but I could feel my rhythm returning. Just then I heard a knock at the door. It was Asmat.

"Can I join you?" he asked me, entering the court.

"I don't think that you want to play with me. I am completely useless. I am not even getting my shots right," I countered.

"Don't worry about that. Let us just hit some balls. Can you turn your competitive switch off and just do some warm up drills with me?" he taunted me with a devious smile.

I gave in, and we started hitting back-and-forth shots. We had barely warmed up the ball when Khurram showed up at the door.

"Can you please excuse us?" he asked Asmat as he entered the court.

He pulled out a coin and asked me if I wanted heads or tails. I chose tails.

"Why did I even ask? I should have known. You always ask for tails," he said, smirking while tossing the coin in the air. "Heads it is. Sorry. It is my serve," he declared sarcastically.

He served, and I missed; he changed the side and announced the score 1-0. He served his second volley and counted 2-0, even before I returned the shot. Then came 3-0, 4-0, 5-0, and pretty soon, it was 11-0. I looked at his face, wondering what he was trying to do to me.

"One game to zero for me, going on to the second game," he announced the scores, sliding his headband up a little.

On his next serve, I jumped and smashed the ball into the front corner without knowing what I had done. He gave me the ball and announced the score as 1-0 for me. Something clicked in me, and I played without planning or thinking. I played as if I was continuing after the tournament, as if nothing had happened, as if all those terrible months had been erased out of my memory. In the end, Khurram won.

"I haven't won against you in years. I am so proud of myself," he told me, leaving the court with a sly look on his face.

Thirty Five

ASMAT KHAN THE GREAT

In the evening, I returned to the club to just work out. Asmat approached me again.

"Meet me in the competition court in exactly half an hour," he casually remarked as he walked by.

I was very reluctant to play against him, but some part of me was also excited about playing a competitive match. As we started, he won point after point. I messed up shot after shot. He was irritated by my mistakes, and I felt ashamed at my performance. *I have to concentrate harder. Getting to play against Asmat is no small matter. I can't jeopardize this rare opportunity.*

My shots improved, but my mind wandered off to other things very easily, and again, I played some dumb shots. The match went up and down. I lost to him, but I was able to keep the scores close.

"I will take over your coaching. We will still keep Bilal to also train you, but I will create your training program," Asmat notified me. "I have also asked Khurram to join your training team, but due to some family commitments he will not be able to move to Peshawar. However, he has promised to be there for you whenever you need him." Asmat didn't accept students easily. He had made a big exception for me.

"Asmat Khan is my coach," I repeated the sentence several times to make myself believe it.

Zameer was gone for longer and longer periods at a time and only came home for a couple of days after many weeks. He told us that he was training to fight against the Pakistan Army and the foreign invaders, both in Pakistan and in Afghanistan. In addition, he was getting a thorough education in Islam. He was happy about that, but I was disgusted. I knew that he was on the path of certain death, and any day, any minute, he could be the target of a drone attack or might die fighting on the battlefield. He had become very strong in his beliefs. He continually opposed my playing squash and questioned why I couldn't be like other girls who get married and bring up good devout Muslim children. Baba and Mamma tried their best to persuade him to stay home. But I knew that, at some level, Baba was proud of Zameer. Mamma cried with fear whenever anyone mentioned Zameer's name.

I went to the club regularly. It must have been Satan, the devil, who had broken my resolve to stop playing squash. I had tried again and again to forget about squash and not even go in the direction of the club, but some unknown force just pulled me back into it. Who else could that have been other than the Satan?

My full-time training with Asmat began. He made me practice very hard. Each move and each shot had to be drilled for hours each day. My muscles were getting trained to play most of the shots by themselves without me thinking of what to do. Asmat called it "muscle memory," and he used that word over and over. Everything was about muscle memory to him. I was also putting in plenty of weight training and conditioning. The trainers in the gym were top people who knew exactly what was needed and made me do those exercises vigorously. In some drills, I had to compete against Asmat and Bilal at the same time. That was excruciating. Those two together made me run ragged. My chest ached after only twenty minutes of doing that drill, but they never relented.

Asmat found matches for me on a weekly basis. There were tournaments sponsored by businesses, the army, and the air force. Then there were exhibition matches. Although these matches didn't affect my rating, they gave me excellent practice at playing high-level players. I got paid handsomely. I also played for my college team, and there were several intercollegiate competitions. My schedule was overloaded.

Chacha brought the whole family to visit us. Siama's visit gave me respite from my hard training and busy schedule. Chacha had bad news about our orchard. Although the *jirga* had decided in our favor, the squatters were not leaving, and the *jirga* had no means to enforce their decision. The village was not going to war against the Taliban due to many reasons. The village couldn't afford another conflict, especially not for those who didn't even live among them anymore.

Baba's man, Riaz Khan, had taken all that money from Baba for nothing. Chacha used his sources to find out what Riaz Khan had been up to, and he discovered a disturbing secret. A gang of powerful men, including some Taliban leaders, had conspired to take our orchard. First, they got squatters to camp there, knowing well that Baba was not there to resist. Then the gang instigated the squatters to fight against us at the *jirga*. Even after the *jirga* decided in our favor, the gang kept the squatters there because the *jirga* had no means to enforce their decision. They knew that Baba didn't have the power to fight against them.

We were shocked beyond belief when Chacha told us, "Riaz Khan is in with the gang. The land values have gone up in the village, and your orchard is worth a lot of money. The gang is just using the poor squatters, but eventually, they will kick them out and seize the land. They will sell it at a very high price and pocket all the money."

Baba was furious at Riaz Khan who conspired to take over the orchard and who embezzled a huge amount of our hard-earned, mostly borrowed money.

"There is nothing we can do about it. We will have to leave it to Allah to do justice," Baba consoled us.

Baba wanted to break every link with the village and never even face in that direction, but for his mother, brother, and the rest of the family's sake, our ties to the village couldn't be broken completely.

"The justice system in the village has collapsed. These people—some of them have known me all my life—are doing this to us and all that just for money. Money is what you don't take to your grave, but your bad deeds, you do. They don't have the same emotional connection to that land as we do. The orchard is my link to my forefathers," mourned Baba.

As expected, Siama remained right by my side. She followed me to the court and spent every possible minute around me. I played only a little squash with her because of my grueling training schedule. She had improved immensely. She had mastered the shots that I had taught her, and she had learned new ones.

"My baba plays squash with me, and I drill all the time," she told me proudly.

"She has a talent that rivals yours. She needs coaching. What are you doing about that?" Asmat asked me after observing her play with me.

"She lives back in the village, and there is no coaching at all for her," I responded.

"I think we need to get her over here and train her. She might follow your footsteps and even surpass you," he remarked.

"Coach Asmat Khan said Siama has a tremendous squash talent and needs proper coaching. He will help her into the club. Why don't you leave her here with us? She has no school at the village. We can get her into a school here, and she can play squash," I asked Chacha and Chachee together.

Baba went a step further. "I think that you should all move here. What is left in the village? It is all ruined—both of your children have no future there."

"Our forefather's memories and our family *kot* are keeping me there. If I move, our homes will be taken over by others, and we will lose all our connection to our roots. Our ancestors are buried there. The *kot* is the only connection that we have left with our ancestors' land—with our motherland—and that would be all gone. You know what happened to your orchard after you left. And the most important reason of all is that Mather-Khubi is not leaving the village in her lifetime."

Baba agreed with him. He then suggested a compromise, "You are right, one of us brothers has to live there. What about leaving both Shaaz and Siama here. We will send them to a school here. What future do you see for them, living in the village under today's circumstances?"

After dinner, Siama snuggled next to me in bed. "Aappa Amina, I will die of excitement if I could come and live with you. I will play squash every possible moment of my life all day long," she whispered. "Pray as hard as you can that my baba agrees to leave us here," she said, squeezing my hands hard.

The next day, I went to the club, and Siama tagged along. I went through more excruciating training. Siama followed every move I made, like men follow their imam during prayers at the mosque.

The following morning, Chacha announced, "After carefully thinking about the situation of our village, we have decided to accept your offer. We will leave Siama and Shaaz with you. I will pay for their expenses here. We will come and visit them every chance we will get and we will have them come to visit us as often as they would like."

"Dear brother, these are our children too. We are very blessed financially, and you don't need to pay us for feeding and housing them. However, if you insist, you can pay for their schools, although I will be happy to pay for that as well," Baba generously offered.

Chacha and Chachee put the right hands of Siama and Shaaz in Baba's right hand to officially hand over their guardianship to Baba.

"Teach Siama all you want, but I don't think she can ever reach your level," Chacha whispered to me.

Only I knew how wrong he was.

Thirty Six

DESTROYER FROM WAZIRISTAN

"You have an invitation to play at the Tehran open. This tournament is not as important as some of the other squash events, but this will be a fine opportunity for you to play on an international level. The prize money is not big, but you will play some great matches there. Squash is very popular amongst Iranian women, and some of them are very accomplished players," explained Asmat as he handed me my invitation.

"Most people go from Tehran to play at the Sharjah open and then to the Cairo cup, which takes place a week later. If you want to play for the Cairo cup, let me know. I will arrange to get an invitation for you."

"How important is it to play at Cairo?" I wanted to know.

"Cairo cup is much more prestigious than the Sharjah open, but the prize money is not as high."

"Are other members of our club going to any of these tournaments?" I asked.

"Depending on her ratings—Simin might qualify, but as of now, I doubt it. However, three of the men players will go to one or more of these games, especially Sharjah, because of the money."

Iran was my first trip abroad. Baba and Bilal accompanied me. I wanted Khurram to come too, but he was not free. As our plane lifted off from Peshawar, I saw the ground fade farther and farther away; houses, buildings, and roads grew smaller, and my view of the city grew wider. Soon, I could see the entire city below me. Looking from above made me feel like an angel watching people as they lived their lives. The airplane then flew over the ocean. I felt strange yet exhilarated. I had never seen the ocean before. It looked like a canvas with an empty background—waiting for the rest of the picture to be painted by an accomplished artist.

On our drive from the airport to the hotel, I got to see different parts of Tehran—a strikingly beautiful city so completely different from Peshawar yet similar in many ways. The buildings, parks, and roads looked so modern. Snow-covered mountains and lavish villas and mansions were on one side and a very congested city on the other. We stayed at the Hotel Sharzad in the center of Tehran at the famous Azadi Square. The food there was very similar to our food in Peshawar. Their language has many words that we also use. Most of the men and women looked like our people. And just like at home, women covered their hair in public.

The hotel was extremely glamorous. Some walls were covered with either shiny golden plates or mirrors. All the carpets had intricate designs, showing pictures of gardens and possibly heavens with fairies, angels, flowers, and the birds of paradise. We stepped out to the gardens. The outside walls of the hotel and all the walkways were decorated in gorgeous tiles with intricate designs painted in a deep blue on yellow, orange, or pure white backgrounds. Shady trees and flowers filled the grounds. The weather was excellent, not hot at all with just a pleasant breeze. That was one aspect in which Tehran certainly felt like heaven compared to the hot and muggy Peshawar.

As we arrived at the squash club for an informal visit, I watched some excellent matches.

Bilal commented, "Squash is becoming very popular in Iran, especially with women. They have world-class female players here. Remember, this tournament is not as high visibility as the others that you will compete in during the coming weeks. Of course, the prize money is not significant, but playing here and doing your best will give you an experience that will definitely benefit you in the long term."

Matches started, and Bilal was right. I won the earlier rounds readily, but as I approached the final rounds, it became extremely challenging. The semifinal match against Afsie was one of the most dramatic matches I had played in a long while. Other than playing squash, Afsie was also an accomplished mountain climber. She belonged to a women's mountaineering club. Some of the senior members of her club had successfully climbed Mount Everest. She was in excellent physical condition, and her shots were precise. Her most dangerous trait was her control of the pace of the ball. Without giving any indication in advance, she often changed the speed of the ball, throwing my timing off. After coming dangerously close to losing the match, I survived to play in the finals. My final match was less eventful. I won it smoothly. I was treated with utmost respect by the media after winning the tournament.

My next stop was Sharjah, a short flight away. We landed at the airport and were driven into the city. I admired the modernity of the city on our way to the hotel. Dubai is filled with tall new buildings, but the lands surrounding those buildings are all deserts. After putting away our luggage and freshening up, we were all set. We had a few hours to relax before going to the squash club.

"I want to go out to see the rest of the hotel. Do you want to come?" I asked Baba. He didn't resist.

As we opened the door, scorching hot air hit us, making us feel like we had put our faces in the mouth of a tandoor. Since the car and the hotel were both air-conditioned we didn't realize how hot the outside air was. We quickly turned back. The guard at the door said something to us that neither one of us understood. Then another guard came to us. He was Pakistani. He told us in Urdu, "It's too hot outside. You will have to wait until about six in the evening if you want to go out."

We waited around in the lobby. There were shops, restaurants, banks, and even barbershops inside. As we crossed the lobby to get to the other end, we saw the pool. I had never seen a swimming pool in real life. Oh my god, men and women were all in there together. The women were wearing even smaller, much smaller clothes, than the men wore. Most of their bodies were naked. I hoped Baba did not see me looking that way. I quickly turned around, and so did Baba. We returned to the lobby and just spent the rest of the time going from one store to another. A car took us to the squash club. Bilal was waiting for us. We completed the registration formalities, and then there was a round-robin session where players at different levels played friendly matches against one another. After the round-robins, we met up for dinner.

The food was too unusual for our taste. I was told that it was all European cuisine. People were drinking bowls of soups and eating bread and butter. The salads were tasty. I ate some, and so did Baba. But then we were served a plate with a chicken quarter on one side and a lump of white mush that looked like boiled flour dough. Upon asking, we were told it was mashed up potatoes. Neither of those things had any flavor or spices. I tried but couldn't swallow a single bite. I spit it in my hand and put it on my plate, making sure that nobody saw me doing all that. Thank God, there were bread, cheese and nuts. Baba and I ended up filling ourselves with those. There were also bottles and cans of dozens of different wines for everyone to choose from.

"Let's just ask for water. Who knows what those other drinks are?" Baba said to me.

Next day the tournament started officially. I knew who I was playing against. I had watched videos of all the players that I was going to compete against. I knew what they were good at and what their weakness were. Almost effortlessly, I won the earlier rounds. Then I met Sarah. She was number three in the world on the women's squash ladder and was sure to win the tournament.

As I sat on my chair ready to go in, I asked for fresh towels.

"Yes, madam, someone will bring towels for you soon," an assistant said.

"Fresh towels, just as you like them," a familiar voice chimed.

As I looked up, I couldn't believe my eyes. "Khurram, What on earth are you doing here?" I practically screamed.

"You got the expression right this time," he laughed.

"When did you come? Why did you come? How did you come?" I blurted out all my questions, not wanting any of the answers. I was just so happy to see him.

"Is this a pleasant surprise for you?" Knowing very well what my reply would be, he asked anyway just to tease me. "Then reward me with your very best squash today," he said, looking straight into my eyes.

At the beginning of the match, Sarah didn't take me seriously. She played some casual shots, so I quickly capitalized on them and won the first game. Then she became serious. Her pace increased, and she made harder shots in the second game, but I was spot-on with my shots. It got very close, but I caught her off guard and took the second game. In the third game, she returned to the court very aggressive. She played all her best shots, and I was getting tired after two challenging games. I lost the third.

"Now she is going to make a comeback, and you cannot let her do that," Bilal emphasized.

I will have to finish her here. I can't let her get to the fifth game, I planned. I kept my game very tight, and made hardly any unforced errors, but pulling several off her. Fatigue was affecting her timing. She lost her footing and lost the game.

"If she can beat Sarah, then she will destroy the rest of the players," the reporters were all predicting. How right they were. I moved up, defeating high-ranked players one after another.

"Destroyer from Waziristan," they named me. I played in the finals against Ann Ferguson from New Zealand. She ranked in top five players. The previous year, she lost to Sarah in the finals after a long close match.

"This year she has lost five out of seven matches to Sarah. If you took out Sarah so easily, then you should be able to dispose of Ann too," Khurram said supportively.

A sense of calm came over me. I just wanted to maintain my tempo. I won the first game, just like I did against Sarah.

"Keep the pressure on and don't relent," Bilal encouraged me.

"Just stay calm and remember this championship is yours," reassured Khurram. I won the second game. But she won the third.

"You must stop her in this fourth game. Don't let it go to the fifth. You might lose your concentration, and that would be a disaster," Khurram whispered to me during the break.

I went in, and from the first point on, I dominated the game. The crowd was now all on my side. They were roaring at every point. As I played that championship point against Ann, I noticed everyone was standing up at their seats. She fought back, but I didn't show her any mercy. Three smashes in a row gave me the victory.

"Who wanted to give up squash? Please raise your hand," Khurram said, grinning. Everyone looked at me and burst out in laughter.

Cairo was next. There, I faced the same women. The only new player for me to deal with was the Egyptian champion named Fatima. She was also ranked among the top five international players. Known for her strength and consistency, she had made it to number one position more than once in her career. She was the world champion for two years and was defeated only after losing a couple of very unfortunate matches.

Khurram and Bilal discussed different strategies with me while we watched videos of her games. I was in my best form. I repeated my performance of the Sharjah tournament. I won my matches and met Fatima in the semifinals. Her strength and consistency proved too much for me. The match flipped between us several times. We went to the fifth game after each one of us won two. During the deciding game, at first, I was winning, and then she raced forward, and finally, I caught up. Then we played deuce after deuce. It was completely exhausting, but I wouldn't give up. Neither was she in the mood to relent. After playing five deuces, I served an ace.

Now I have my chance, I have to win just one more point and the match is mine, I reassured myself.

She returned my smashing serve very comfortably. I played a very tight drop, which she returned with a close drop. Pretending to prepare for a drive, I played another drop. She tried to drive the ball back but hit the red line. I won the match, and with that, I had reached the finals. My final match was against Sarah again.

"I had just defeated her easily only a couple of weeks ago. I can do that again now. No problem," I confided to Khurram, sounding casual.

Khurram was not amused and warned me, "Don't be complacent. You will have to take this match as the most important one of your life. If you put your guard down, before you know it, you'll lose the match and this tournament. However, if you win this one, you will shoot up into the top five ranking."

I lost the first game for no good reason, but that knocked some sense into my head. Khurram was absolutely right—I couldn't take that match lightly. I was determined not to lose any other game to her. I started the second game with my best effort, but she was not giving me any openings. She was reading into my intentions and strategy easily. Despite winning five points against her at the start of our second game, she came roaring back and took the second game from me. I was terribly disappointed and disheartened. *How could I let her win a second game?* I scolded myself. In the third, I again won four points in succession, but she quickly won back those four points and then went on to win two more. With the score at 6-4 against me, I panicked and made bad shots. I lost two more points. She was now only three points away from defeating me and knocking me out of the tournament.

I was desperate. I took five deep breaths and knocked my head with my racket strings. "Use your court-coverage advantage," I said it ten times while waiting for her serve. I won the next five points, giving her only one. Now I was ahead of her. I used my tricky drop shots, one after another, and with a lot of luck, I won that third game. She looked shocked and crestfallen. She was so close to winning the match and now I was forcing her to playing her fourth game. I pushed myself harder and used all the skills I could possibly muster. We both played our best squash and reached a deuce. We played several deuces, and the match could have easily gone her way at any one of those deuces. Lucky for me, she made an unforced error at a critical point, which won me the fourth game. We each had two games.

The fifth and final game was on, and I was feeling much better. I had survived so far, and now it was my chance to win the match. The fifth game also ended up in a deuce; I saw my chance after winning the advantage, but she equalized it to a deuce again. At the second deuce, I won the advantage. I was desperate to finish the match by winning the match point, but again, she went all over the court and returned all of my most challenging shots. The match could have easily gone to her, but I played a very clever drop, which she didn't anticipate at all. She missed it by far, and I gratefully won. The crowd roared wildly in my favor. It was the hardest fight of my whole career and the greatest comeback from such a deficit ever. Our match was shown live on Pakistan national television, and millions of people watched it, cheering for me. I was later told that as soon as I won the match the crowds in several cities of Pakistan burst into instant celebrations.

Thousands of people showed up at the airport to receive me. My whole club was in the front, surrounded by reporters. Fans were chanting slogans, calling me the daughter of Pakistan. Nobody was more excited to see me than Siama. In front of the whole media, she ran to me and hugged me tightly.

During my absence from Peshawar, Siama had a few successes of her own. She had moved into Bilal's class, which was a huge accomplishment in such a short time. She also won some junior tournaments at the club. Bilal was amazed at her progress. Chacha came to watch her matches. On his way home, he took Siama and Shaaz to the village for a few weeks while their schools were closed for spring break. By then, they had become a part of our family, and their absence was felt by everyone. I missed Siama badly.

My schedule was jam-packed. I was playing about two tournaments per month. Any break that I had in between, Asmat put me through extended training. I was living for my squash. I was eating, drinking, and breathing squash, and I was winning all the tournaments that I was playing.

Khurram told me, "You are in your best form. Please keep this up for the upcoming tournaments in Kuala Lumpur and then in Singapore. Remember, if you win both of them, then you will have the title of the number one female squash player in the world." Just the thought of winning such a title made me giddy with anticipation.

Right before leaving for Kuala Lumpur, I took a couple of days off from my training. I assembled my team that was going to accompany me. Chacha and Siama were going with me for moral support, and Asmat and Khurram came along as my coaches. I was aware that I had some tough competitors lined up in both these events, but I was mentally and physically prepared for that.

Kuala Lumpur went fairly smoothly for me, and after winning it easily, I moved on to play in Singapore. There, I started off quite strongly by winning all the earlier matches. However, the quarterfinals against Xun Dong from Hong Kong became very eventful. All her life, she had trained in England under the world's top coaches. The match was like a seesaw. Even until the last shot, no one knew who the winner was going to be. I was dead tired but was not conceding. My perseverance paid off. She was behind in the fifth game, but started to creep up. That got me worried. I used all my concentration to dislodge her from the center of the court, followed by precise rail smash that turned out to be the winning shot. I moved to the semifinal round. By a sheer stroke of luck, I got a much needed day's break. Without it, I could not have fully recovered to play the semifinals against Maria from Brazil. With that one day of rest, I was totally refreshed, whereas she had played her quarterfinal round the evening before and appeared fairly tired. I took full advantage of the situation and won the match by exploiting her weakness.

Thirty Seven

WORLD'S NUMBER ONE

Just before my match with Ann Ferguson, Asmat advised, "You are now one match away from reaching the world's number one title. Just do what you have been doing in all these matches."

"I know Ann's game, and I am confident that I will win against her. I have never lost to her. Why would I lose this time?" I told Khurram to calm his nerves down.

I won the first few points, and then she played some very strange shots. In all my matches against her and all of those on video, I had never seen her play that way. She had transformed her game completely, and she had kept her arsenal of new shots a well-guarded secret. Her changed style completely distracted me. She won the first and the second games while I could see my goal of reaching the number one position slipping away. During the second break, Khurram and Asmat looked devastated.

"Don't play with Ann in mind. Just play your personal best," advised Siama, who couldn't remain seated in the spectators' rows.

Her advice, beyond all the advice Khurram and Asmat showered at me during the breaks, inspired me the most. I went in playing without once thinking that it was Ann that I was playing against. The strategy worked. I won the third and the fourth games, which put some hope back into me as well as into my coaches. That also sucked the life out of Ann's plans. Her new and improved strategy was beginning to fail. She started panicking and lost her footing. I grabbed the opportunity with both hands and finished her off with a combination of three drops, followed by a lob in the back court. In the flash of those moments, I won the title of number one player in the women's world squash rating. I had achieved my goal. My team jumped and danced with joy. Asmat brought the confirmation printout, showing my name at the top of the list.

"I will frame it for my house," I told him, asking for it.

"No, we will frame it for the club," he declared.

Upon my return to Pakistan, at Peshawar airport, a crowd in the tens of thousands was gathered to welcome me back. "Our daughter of Waziristan," cheered half the crowd. "Our daughter of Pakistan" was the chant coming from the other half.

The governor of the province was at the helm of the crowd. He presented me a Medal of Honor, along with a hefty check, on behalf of the people of Pakistan. Little schoolgirls presented me with bouquets of flowers.

After a two-week break to rest and train, my next stops were Barcelona, followed by Paris. I decided to take Siama with me, but she had to go to the village to visit her mother. Siama proved her worth, not only as moral support but also as technical support. Her advice in Singapore was most likely the advice that saved the day for me. I had to settle for Noor Chacha instead. Khurram was also tied up with something else, so only Asmat and Bilal came with me as my coaches.

Barcelona turned out to be a nightmare for me. Nothing went right. My luggage was lost during the flight, so I had to buy new clothes to wear, including a sweat suit. Thank God that Asmat had my rackets.

The rotation started. I met Sarah in my first match. She was as feisty as ever. After a tough match, I disposed her of in the fourth game. My next opponent was a low-ranking player from Ireland. The match started, and I won the first game without much effort. For the second game, I went in totally relaxed. I lobbed a serve at her, which she returned with a very tight drop. I couldn't do a thing about it. I smiled at her sneaky shot. I promised myself I would get even with her soon. However, anything I tried from that point on, she had an answer to it. None of my smashes, none of my lobs, and, worst of all, none of my drops disturbed her. She won the second and the third games from me easily. Now I was fighting for my life.

What a comeback, I admired her while being furious at myself for letting her get so far ahead of me. In the fourth game, I gave it my best. I was still hopeful of a turnaround, but it never came. I lost to an unranked player. The press was calling it the biggest upset ever. Asmat was blaming the whole loss on my own carelessness.

"Will I lose my number one position because of my loss?" I asked sounding very worried.

When we got back to our hotel Asmat told me the good news with a grin on his face, "Since you had accumulated so many points in your previous victories, you get to keep your number one title, even after losing Barcelona, but that makes Paris absolutely crucial for you. If you lose there, you will fall lower in the world squash ranking. But if you do win there, you will go on to the world cup in Sydney as the number one female squash player, and that is an honor that we should all be rightly proud of."

Over the next three weeks, we toured different cities in Europe. I played several exhibition matches and then headed to Paris. My loss in Barcelona had shaken me. *I might have grown overconfident*, I self-diagnosed.

I was utterly determined to win Paris. My coaches repeatedly reminded me about the cost of losing in Paris and the prize of winning there. Being in that mindset, I went into the tournament. I played each match with full concentration and kept my focus sharp, the way a hawk focuses on its prey. All throughout the tournament, I didn't play a single careless shot. Each match was like the most important match of my life. My efforts paid off. I won match after match, mostly in straight sets. In the final rounds, I met the same players whom I had defeated before. The final match turned out to be somewhat challenging. Otherwise, I completely dominated the tournament. In no other tournament was the term "Destroyer from Waziristan" more often used. In the Paris tournament I only lost three games, three out of some hundred odd games that I played. All the commentators were talking about my signature wrist shot that puts a powerful top spin on the ball, making it nearly impossible for my opponents to return. The older people were comparing my shots to the signature shots of Jahangir Khan and Jahansher Khan. They were guessing that I must have learned that wrist shot at the Peshawar Club where the two Khans were from. Most likely, Asmat had taught it to me without me even being aware of it. They were forecasting that I would dominate the squash world for a decade, just like the Khans did. The general consensus was "No one had an answer to those shots back then, and no one can return them well now."

For a month, I played dozens more exhibition matches in Europe, and everywhere I repeated my Paris performance. I was all set to go to the world cup in Sydney as the number one female squash player in the world. No one doubted that I would win the world cup without much struggle. Even my competitors were conceding openly that they had no chance of defeating me in the near future. In their minds, they had already granted the world cup to me even before a single shot was played in Sydney.

Chacha's family had been blessed with a baby boy. Baba had to accompany Siama and Shaaz on their trip to the village because Chacha couldn't come to get them. I would have liked to go too, but my security had become a growing concern. Mather-Khubi was not well, and she had asked for Baba. I was looking forward to some quiet time with Mamma.

She was very sad those days because she was worried to death about Zameer. We received phone calls from him every now and then, but we had no way of contacting him ourselves; we just had to wait for his phone calls. Every time he called, Mamma appealed to him, crying and begging him to return home. He kept promising to return in a few months, but those few months had turned into years. His conviction for the war had gotten stronger and stronger with every day that he had been on the front. He believed that he was fighting a just war against foreigners who had no business of being in our homeland. Whenever I tried to talk him out of his beliefs, he would give me all those examples of our forefathers who had fought foreign invaders throughout our history. We had grown up hearing the stories of their heroism; now he wanted to walk in their footsteps. It was very difficult to argue with him, but I knew the Taliban was engaging in more than an honorable war.

Baba returned from the village. We were relieved to see him back safe.

"How was it back home?" I asked him at lunch.

"Not only has our beautiful village but our whole region has been ravaged by this war. The mess that the tens of thousands of refugees have created in our society seems not so bad when you see the devastation caused by the war between the Pakistan Army and the Taliban. As if those two calamities weren't bad enough, everyone is living under constant threat of drone attacks. The war between the Pakistan Army and the Taliban on the ground and the drone bombing from the sky are killing hundreds of people each month. I visited more graves than I visited live people," he described with a sigh wiping away the tears behind his sunglasses.

Mamma and I sat there, listening to his narrative with sinking hearts.

My training for Sydney began. Asmat came up with a very strict daily regimen—about six or more hours a day—and showed no mercy. Asmat and I tried again to persuade Khurram to join my team of coaches in Peshawar without much success. To my benefit though, he was closely involved in my training, even without relocating to Peshawar. He visited the club frequently and managed his share of my training. Asmat reduced the number of his students to a bare minimum. He spent most of his time working with me. Since Khurram had very good control of the ball, he trained me on one particular shot for hours. The shot, the placing and the pace of the ball were fine-tuned by repeating the shot thousands of times. Often, I would get annoyed and irritable, but Khurram had his ways of calming my nerves.

The world cup was approaching. We barely had a month left, and we still had a lot of training and planning left. Asmat and Khurram watched the videos of the players that I was going to be competing against. We talked about the strengths and weaknesses of each player and discussed possible ways to handle them. I felt a little nervous that day. Asmat finished the training an hour before the schedule and let me go home to rest.

Thirty Eight

FUNERALS OF INNOCENCE

As I arrived home, Mamma and Baba were waiting for me. Mamma had set dinner on the table. We sat down to eat. Any food at all would have tasted fantastic as I was feeling weak with hunger.

"How is your training coming along? How do you feel about your competition in Sydney?" Baba asked me.

Before I could say anything, the phone rang. Mamma answered. Baba and I kept on talking. A piercing scream came from Mamma. My heart sank. *It must be about Zameer*, I thought, trembling.

Baba ran to the phone, grabbing it from Mamma's hands. It was from the village. Imam Sahib was on the line.

"Is anyone hurt?" Baba yelled into the phone.

I ran and grabbed the extension to hear their conversation.

"A bomb has demolished your whole house. We don't know yet if anyone was in the house when the bomb hit. People are digging in the rubble," Imam Sahib told Baba.

"Do you see my brother around there?" Baba hollered into the phone. "My brother, his family, and my Mather-Khubi were living in my house since I moved to the city. I am leaving this instant, and I will get there in a few hours. Please keep digging and be careful—children, a baby, and my old and sick mother could be in there," Baba begged.

Mamma and I were afraid for Baba to drive so late at night, but he would not listen to reason.

I asked our guard to jump into the car and go with Baba. He didn't hesitate but asked, "Who will watch out for you and your mother?"

"Don't worry about us, you just go with Baba and look after him and his safety."

He had a loaded Kalashnikov gun with him. As Baba drove off, Mamma and I got back into the house. We didn't know what to do.

Should we have gone to the village also? Then what would we have done about my security? We didn't have a guard to accompany us. That time, I really wished that I was like millions of regular people and not a well-known face so that I could come and go anywhere I wanted. We stayed up all night. Baba called us a few times. He didn't know what to tell us. After he arrived, he joined others in their digging. None of our family was found. He was fearful that they were all in the wreckage. Noor Chacha arrived there from Bannu by a taxi. By daybreak, they had moved enough material. We received another call from Baba's phone, but it was not Baba at the other end; it was Imam Sahib again.

"Dear daughter, *Inna-lillah-wa-ina-aleh-e rajeoon*," he uttered.

I knew that these words are only said when someone has died. I knew that the news was going to be terribly bad.

"Your baba has pulled out the dead body of your chacha."

My hands shook; I dropped the phone and put my face in my hands. Mamma also heard the news, and she was sobbing. Baba was in no shape to talk. It was very early in the morning, but I called Khurram in Bannu and told him what had happened.

After a brief pause, he advised, "Stay there at your home. I will make arrangements and take you and your mother to the village."

Within a few hours, Khurram showed up at our door in Peshawar with a car and two armed guards. Mamma and I had already packed up a few of our things. I felt better that Khurram was coming along. We had no way of contacting Zameer. We were hoping that he would hear about the tragedy and join us in the village.

By the time we arrived, Baba, Noor Chacha, and the villagers had pulled out the bodies of Mather-Khubi, Chachee, Siama, and Shaaz. The only one who survived unharmed was the baby. It looked like the whole family was sitting in the *sundalee* after dinner when the bomb hit. They had no advance warning to run away, and the whole house fell upon them. Mather-Khubi's lifeless body was found on the same side of the *sundalee* that she used to always sit. Chacha, Chachee, and their two children were sitting nearby, possibly listening to Mather-Khubi's stories. Chachee had the newborn baby in her lap. By some miracle, the baby didn't get hit by the falling debris. We guessed the mother's body shielded the baby. The bunker that Baba had built for the protection of the family turned out to be their grave.

Baba seemed quiet but well composed. I couldn't understand how he could be so calm when the mutilated bodies of his own mother, his brother along with the dead bodies of his brother's young family were all lined up in front of him. Noor Chacha and Baba ran around, making arrangements for the funeral and for the burial of the bodies. The village elders did what they could to help. Mamma had taken the baby and was trying to feed him some goat's milk. By evening, all five bodies were washed and shrouded. People gathered to offer the funeral prayers. I stared hard at the five bodies of my family, vowing never to forget. Everyone was stopping me, but I pushed my way through and wrapped my arms around Siama's shrouded body. Her face was open and I could still see a peaceful smile on it. The scene when Chacha put her as a newborn in my lap all those years ago ran through my mind. Her hugs, her giggles, her holding my hands—ever since she was a baby—haunted me. I am not sure what I was doing or saying in that final hug, but the feeling of that hug has stuck to my memory.

Most of the men from the whole village as well as from the nearby refugee camps attended the funeral prayers. When the burial was finished, food and water was brought to what was left of our house. Herd of people came in groups to offer their condolences. Everyone was angry, but Baba was not talking. We stayed for the night at the house of one of Baba's cousins. The next morning, more people came trying to console us. They were talking about revenge. They were asking Baba to join the war to avenge his brother's and mother's blood, to avenge the innocent blood of Chacha's family. People were telling Baba that it was his duty and responsibility to avenge the mass murder of his family. Baba was still not talking. They were asking about Zameer and saying that it now was also his responsibility to only live and die for revenge.

"Look how Allah has saved their son. Tell him the story of the murder of his family every day so that the fire of revenge burns in his heart," they insisted.

The baby was crying continuously, inconsolable. Some women were telling us that the baby was too young to digest goat's milk and that he needed a mother's milk. A wet nurse was found, and we took the baby to her. The baby would not take her milk either. We didn't know what to do. The baby had to be fed, or he would die also. The wet nurse tried all night—not until early morning did the baby finally take some milk. Baba, Noor Chacha, and some other men made repairs to our house. They arranged to clean up a few rooms to house us and our guards. People were telling us that it was dangerous for us to live in our house. The drones would return and bomb such houses again. Baba didn't listen.

Khurram arranged for the guards to take turns watching for further drone attacks.

Three days passed. Khurram and the guards had to go back to their families. Without them, there would be no security for us. Khurram asked me what I wanted to do. Baba wanted to stay in the village for a little while longer. Mamma was worried about the baby because he had high fever, and there was no doctor in the village. We had to leave and get to Peshawar quickly to take the baby to a doctor. The baby had made the decision for us.

A doctor in Peshawar gave us some medicine and advised us to put the baby on the baby formula. We tried the formula, but the baby wouldn't drink from the bottle. He kept spitting up and crying. Mamma and I both tried every possible way that we could think of, but the baby wouldn't drink. We tried all day and well into the night with no success. During the night, the baby seemed to be doing worse. We took him to the hospital. The doctor there told us that he was dehydrated, and they wanted to keep him for the night. However, the doctors and the staff were not attending to us properly. We felt so helpless. In desperation, I called the Doctor Sahib at the club and told him the whole story. He immediately came to the hospital. As soon as he showed up, the situation changed. The staff and the doctors started running around, taking care of the baby. They quickly put a glucose drip on him and assured us that everything would be all right. Within minutes of the drip, the baby opened his eyes and gave us a heart-melting smile.

Doctor Sahib said, "The worst is over, and the baby will recover by morning. Fortunately, we intervened just in time. A little longer and the damage of dehydration could have had serious consequences, or even could have been fatal."

Thirty Nine

WHERE IS THE HEALING?

Baba returned after a week of mourning in the village. Then Zameer showed up. He heard about the bombing several days after it happened. It was too late for him to go to the village, so he decided to come home. He had a few weeks off. Baba was still eerily calm, not showing any emotions, even when he saw Zameer. Except for a yes here and a no there, he stayed quiet. As people came to us for condolences, he didn't engage much in conversation with them. He did however repeatedly lament "I lost my father, my chacha, and one eye fighting as American allies against the Russians, and now those same Americans have killed my family. Where is justice in this?"

Some people were saying that he might be in shock and needed to be treated by a doctor. Otherwise, he could lose his mind completely. But no one had the power to take Baba to a doctor.

"We must give him a name," Mamma suggested, holding the baby boy up in front of her. We didn't know if his parents had chosen a name for him. We had asked around the village if Chacha had mentioned a name for the baby.

"Baba, do you remember if Chacha or Chachee called the baby by a name when you went to visit them?" I asked Baba in an attempt to get him involved in a conversation.

"No" was Baba's only word.

"We will call him Faiz, which means blessings of Allah, and who could be more blessed than this child? Look how he has survived," Mamma decided, cradling the baby and kissing his forehead several times.

Weeks and months passed as gloom and depression completely overtook our house. Except for some occasional smiles that the baby brought, our family had stopped living. No one felt like watching TV or playing games. We sat around all day long. People from all over the country came to offer sympathy and condolence. Several politicians, the media, and many of the tribal chiefs called upon us. Pakistani government officials announced that they had launched a strong protest to the Americans against the bombing, but that brought us no relief. We couldn't see what difference such a protest could possibly make to us.

All the big names in squash came to express their sorrow for our loss. Asmat and Bilal came several times by themselves and also many times with other squash celebrities. They both talked a lot about Siama and her squash talent. I wept every time Siama was mentioned.

Asmat and Bilal expressed their regrets, "Had this untimely death not taken her away, she would have reached the highest levels in squash in the very near future." They talked about Siama's squash talent with everyone—even to visitors who had never seen her.

Khurram visited us almost on a daily basis. He was our contact with the outside world. Just looking at his face, one couldn't miss noticing the pain and sorrow that he shared with me. No matter how hard he tried, he wasn't able to cheer us up.

As time passed, he started telling me, "You have been cooped up in the house for months now. Amina, I am sorry, no one else can even begin to appreciate your pain, but you must get out of the house. You need to divert your mind away from this tragedy, even if only for a few moments every now and then. This is necessary for your healing."

Other people would say the same words, but no one would address my questions: "How can we go on living our lives after being through this calamity for which there is no equal? Everyone tells us that time heals all wounds. A lot of time has passed, but where is the healing?" I would ask angrily as they remained speechless.

We had to take the baby to the doctor. Khurram took us there. On the way back, he stopped at the club.

"Just come in and walk around. We can have a glass of tea at the café, and you will get a change of scenery," he insisted.

I didn't want to set foot in the club, but the way he insisted, I couldn't say no. After all, he had been asking me to get out of the house for weeks. I gave in. We walked into the club with Faiz. Everyone knew what we were going through, and they were all very respectful toward us. I stopped outside a court and watched a match. For a few moments, my mind got into the match, and I forgot everything. But then all of my memories about Chacha's and Siama's squash came rushing back. This was the very same court in which I used to train Siama, and now she was buried under a heap of dirt. The scene of her shrouded body started to haunt me again. I wanted to go home.

Occasionally, I returned to the club, but each time, the same episode repeated. Despite a feeling of panic at the end of each visit, my trips to the club did bring me some comfort. Khurram, Asmat, and Bilal would meet me there. We talked about squash a little here and a little there. No matter what we started our conversation with, it always ended at my squash. Khurram liked to play the recordings of my matches at every opportunity.

"Amina, please give us some more of your squash," Asmat begged me every time he saw me.

Months had passed since the tragedy, but I saw no sign of healing. One day as I got to the club, all three of my coaches were with other students, so I just sat outside and watched them teach.

"Amina, I am trying to teach him the lob that you are the master of. I don't think that I am teaching him correctly. Please go in and show him how to do that lob," Khurram requested.

I showed the student how to play the lob correctly. I was about to leave the court, but Khurram asked me to hit a few shots with him. It was always very difficult to say no to him, so I agreed. For a few minutes, I forgot everything else and just concentrated on my next shot, but after several shots, an image of Siama running in the court completely overwhelmed me. I couldn't play a single shot after that. I left the club in a hurry, feeling defeated.

Defeat—how could I accept defeat? First thing in the morning, I returned to the club, changed into my favorite sweat suit, and took my rackets out of my locker. One by one, I held them in my hand, cleaned the grips with a towel, and swung them around. I felt healed. With each swing, my body felt complete, and my mind felt at rest. *I want to play squash again*, my mind demanded of me.

I looked for my coaches, but none were around yet. There were a few early morning players in, warming up to play.

"Do you want a game?" I asked one of them.

"Yes, of course," he replied.

I entered the court, and we started a game. He was no match for me. I won my points and games easily. I felt good about my shots and about my form. Winning points so easily was a boost to my confidence. Suddenly, he hit a perfect rail, just like the ones I taught Siama. That was the last squash shot I trained with her. I vividly heard her giggle. A heart-sinking feeling overwhelmed me: I would never see her play this shot again, ever again.

Then the images of Chacha and Siama in their white shrouds completely possessed me. The sound of Chacha's laughs and Siama's giggles made me deaf to every other sound. I was blinded and numbed by the visions and the flood of memories. Running to the door, I exited the court and smashed my racket on the edge of the court wall. I sat down next to my bag and pulled out a towel from my bag. With the towel came another one of my racket. I held it in my hand and, in a burst of anger, smashed it at the same edge. That racket also broke into two pieces. I snatched three more and broke them in the same manner. Finally, I pulled out my last racket from my bag and swung it up in the air to smash it on the same corner. But this time, my hand froze up in the air. I looked at the racket and remembered; *This one is my favorite. It has won me matches all over the world. Playing with this one—I have won the title of the number one squash player in the world.* I gently laid my last squash racket right beside me. Then I put the broken rackets in a line, covered them with my towel, and cried.

As all five of my rackets lay wrapped in their shroud quiet and eternal just like the five members of my family, I held my only surviving racket in front of my face and wailed to it, "People all over the world are saying that I have defeated the odds. How wrong they are. Look at me. Do you see how the odds have finally defeated me?"

Hugging my racket, I asked, "Will the tulip that dared to bloom in the desert survive this sandstorm?" I repeated my question, but my racket remained silent.